DOLLED UP
FOR
Murder

DOLLED UP
FOR
Murder

A Josie Posey Mystery

ANNA *St.* JOHN

LEVEL
BEST BOOKS

Author Photo Credit: Steve Rasmussen

First edition

ISBN: 978-1-68512-874-6

Cover art by Level Best Designs
Illustration by Lyndsey Mbawuike

This book was professionally typeset on Reedsy.
Find out more at reedsy.com

To my Bruce,
always.

In Loving Memory of
My mother, who taught me to read,
My father, who encouraged me to write,
And my sister, Kim, who believed I could do anything.

Praise for Dolled Up for Murder

"Josie Posey is back and ready to solve another small-town murder! *Dolled Up for Murder* sees Josie investigating the death of Opal, the twin sister of Pearl, an elderly doll collector in English Village, Kansas. When Opal is in town for a visit, she presents Pearl with a valuable doll as a gift. Before the night is over, Opal is killed at the town's annual Christmas market, and Josie plunges into the investigation.

"The case presents unique challenges: was Opal the target, or did the killer mistake her for Pearl? And who are these mysterious figures who keep appearing in the town? And why do they keep putting Josie in harm's way? A fast-paced and quick-witted read, *Dolled Up for Murder* gives readers a front row view of Josie, the Mahjong Mavens, and, of course, Moe the sheepdog as they unravel the mystery and seek justice for Opal. This book is a must read for fans of cozy mysteries and amateur sleuths!"—Travis Tougaw, author of the Marcotte/Collins Investigative Thrillers Series

"I love the interaction between Josie, her Mahjong-playing friends, and Chief Marshall as they work together to solve the mystery, along with the bit of tension between Josie and her potential love interest who wants her to stay clear of the danger her involvement attracts. Josie's English sheepdog, Moe, and her red VW, Piper, come along for the ride as Josie's dogged determination to find the killer supersedes the risk of peril to herself.

"This third book in the Josie Posey cozy mystery series is sure to please lovers of the genre. It's such a delight to immerse oneself in Josie's world! Intrigue, suspense, and a dash of romance—it's all here!"—Ivanka Fear, author of Blue Water Mysteries and Jake and Mallory Thrillers

Chapter One

Wednesday Morning

Some promises are impossible to keep, no matter how hard you try. Believe me, when your expectations are shattered by the unexpected murder of a friend or relative, good intentions fly out the window quicker than rumors race through English Village.

At least, that's what happened with me and my fellow Mahjong Mavens. After a couple of close calls when we helped investigate big crimes in our tiny town, we all vowed to mind our own business and leave the crime-solving to Chief Marshall.

But that was before Nellie's Aunt Pearl arrived for a visit, and a day that started with a snowstorm ended in murder. It began like any other Wednesday, except that Jack Frost swooped into our town. Winter's first snow swirled outside my bedroom window. The chill seeped through Grandma Molly's sweet cottage and touched my nose with icy fingers. I shivered, pulled the covers over my head, and snuggled deeper into them.

When a deep rumble emanated from the foot of my bed, I opened one eye and raised the blanket to peek out at the mound of fluffy white fur as it rose and fell to the rhythmic sound. My 100-pound sheepdog, Moe, snored in his sleep.

"Get up, Josie Posey," I scolded myself for the indulgence. I had a busy day ahead, including my weekly mahjong game and a late afternoon tea with Nellie's Aunt Pearl. The octogenarian doll collector was the scheduled topic of my column for next week's issue of *The Village Gazette*. She had promised to introduce me to a mystery guest, so there was no time to dally.

I sprang from the bed, stepped into fuzzy slippers, and wrapped a thick robe over my nightgown. Moe raised his head as if to ask, "Is it morning?"

I answered him aloud. "Yes, boy, it's time to go outside. Be quick, and I'll have your breakfast ready before you know it."

Moe stretched and rolled over for a belly scratch before he lumbered toward the back door.

"Hurry, Moe. It's freezing outside." I held the door open and urged him forward.

By the time Moe nudged the door to return inside, his food bowl sat on the floor mat, and my mocha coffee steamed on the counter. After breakfast, I lit a fire in the fireplace, then settled into my favorite chair with my laptop and a stack of bills to pay.

A jigsaw puzzle waited half-finished on the long dining room table. Nat King Cole crooned from my surround sound. The snow fell softly outside. Moe rested his head on my feet. It was a peaceful, idyllic moment. How could I possibly know another murder would fall into my lap before midnight?

My cell phone rang, and I recognized the caller. "Good morning, Harvey."

"Hey, it's snowing!"

"I noticed."

Harvey's deep chuckle was one of the things I enjoyed most about him. The lanky hardware store owner had become a good friend. While we weren't what I would call "dating," we were together often enough to be considered "an item" around town. Nothing escaped the gossips in our tiny village—particularly when the Mahjong Mavens were stirring the pot.

"Yeah. So, I'll stop by to shovel your driveway and sidewalk soon. No arguments."

I swear, the man had an independent streak that matched my own. But who could argue with the generous offer?

"Thank you, Harvey. A snow-free driveway would be nice. If you finish by eleven thirty, come inside for stew. I made a pot yesterday."

I could almost see his lopsided grin as he answered, "It's Mahjong

Wednesday; you can't miss it for a few snowflakes."

"True. We're playing at Nellie's today. It's a short drive, but I don't want to be late."

"I'm on my way."

I backed my little red VW, Piper, out of my garage onto a clear driveway at half past noon and drove directly to Nellie's home. The route took me along Main Street, past the bank, the Cozy Cups Café, Miss Betty's School of Dance, and the Pet Stop. Steepled rooftops on the quaint buildings already dripped with melting snow, and icicles formed along the eaves.

My mahjong friends greeted me with hot coffee when I arrived. We played my favorite game every Wednesday afternoon, without fail. I treasured the time with these friends—not just for the sake of the game, but for the companionship we enjoyed as like-minded women. Most of the group had been together for a long time.

Although I learned to play mahjong at my mother's knee as a child, I had only joined this group when I moved to English Village. Every week I learned more about their shared past. Together, they raised their children, hosted neighborhood garage sales, and volunteered in their community. They had weathered storms, survived illnesses, and celebrated each other's accomplishments. Their collective friendship spanned nearly seven decades.

Sharon was the first to call out to me. With her short blond hair and a light sprinkling of freckles, she always reminded me of an energetic little pixie. "Come in, Josie. Tell us what's new." Ever since I'd started my part-time reporting job at *The Village Gazette*, the ladies counted on me to share tidbits of news before they read them in the paper. I willingly obliged.

"The Christmas Market opens on the grounds of The Philbrook Inn tonight."

"We already know that!" Nellie looked up from the Chinese tile game, where she stacked the two-tiered wall in front of her tile rack. Her thick gray bob curled around her face, and she paused to tuck a lock of hair behind her right ear. "What else have you got?"

"They've added a sleigh ride to the schedule. Carolers will wear period

3

costumes from the 1800s. And you can choose from hot wassail or wine, just like they offer at the European markets." The room erupted with excited chatter.

"A sleigh ride would be fun. We should all go together!" Sharon spread her arms out to include everyone. She wore a thick white sweater with round wooden buttons along the flared collar. Her blue eyes sparkled. I grinned at her enthusiasm.

"Costumes for the singers? How nice," Kate said. Her short white hair formed a halo around her face.

"I doubt that I can convince my husband to join us." Nellie stood—hands on hips—as she frowned at us. "That man works too hard." We laughed at her pose. She looked like a pouting teenager.

We all knew she was correct. Nellie and her husband, Tim, owned a furniture store where he still worked long hours, despite the fact that he was several years beyond retirement age.

"Ladies, ladies!" The tallest of the mavens at five-eight, Kate claimed our attention before she spoke. The stately woman had served our country as a US Marine—which didn't surprise me because she's still crazy smart and fearless, even at sixty-nine. She made a sweeping gesture with her hands and motioned toward the game table. "These holiday decisions can wait. Let's play mahjong."

The next two hours, we spent more time playing than talking. As we stored the racks and tiles at the end of the afternoon, we discussed the rest of our week. I was in charge of Story Time for preschool children on Thursday morning at the community library. Nellie and Sharon volunteered at Dress for Success on Friday. Kate had registered to play in a weekend pickleball tournament.

Nellie suggested we bring our holiday gifts to exchange at next week's game, before the Christmas rush. Since it was my turn to host, I offered to prepare a holiday lunch before we played. "I'll make soup if someone brings a salad and dessert."

When we packed the last of the mahjong tiles away, my phone rang. Nellie groaned. "Josie, every time you answer that phone on a Wednesday, someone has been murdered."

"Not this time! See?" I waved the screen to show her the caller ID: Pearl Merriweather. "It's your Aunt Pearl. We're having tea in an hour."

"Good. That should keep you out of trouble for a while."

I gave her a thumbs-up signal. "Agreed."

Nellie hugged me before I headed out the door. "You will love my Aunt Pearl," she said. "And her doll collection is *to die for.*"

I felt a tingle of apprehension at her choice of words, but neither of us could have imagined that her offhand comment would come true.

Chapter Two

Wednesday Afternoon

Before my appointment with Pearl Merriweather, I stopped at the cottage to check on Moe. My sweet dog heard my car pull into the garage and waited at the door with his leash in his mouth.

Instead of rushing to meet me, he cocked his head and sat absolutely still. I laughed at the hopeful expression on his face. "You win, boy," I said.

With plenty of time before tea, I re-buttoned my coat, fastened Moe's leash, and walked outside. Despite the cheery late afternoon sun, the temperature remained below freezing. We easily circled to the park and back in less than twenty minutes, but my nose and cheeks were red by the time we returned. I changed to black wool pants and a cream-colored cashmere sweater, then wrapped a soft cranberry scarf around my neck. I figured Pearl was from a generation of women who considered teatime worthy of holiday attire, and I didn't want to disappoint her.

Traffic on the snow-cleared road was heavier than I expected. I pulled my VW Bug into the Philbrook Inn's parking lot just before five, opting for the valet to find me a spot. Shoppers had already arrived for the opening night of the Christmas Market, and the dining room was filled with ladies gathered for the first holiday tea of the season. Mother Nature had done her best to set the scene, with just enough snow to ring in the holidays and sunshine to allay any fears of a serious winter storm.

I recognized Pearl from Nellie's description the moment I walked inside.

She was a tall woman with lovely gray hair and twinkling green eyes. Her ivory skin looked paper thin, but it was incredibly smooth for her age. A small mole marked her right cheek, just below her eye. If I hadn't already known it was authentic, I might have suspected the elderly woman of placing a beauty mark in that precise spot. It was a dramatic touch to her angular face.

Pearl was absently looking out the window, so I took the opportunity to observe her before she realized I had arrived. She wore a sage green cowl-necked tunic over black palazzo pants. Diamonds dripped from her earlobes, and a dazzling broach sparkled from her shoulder. She looked as regal as a queen—which she was, in the world of doll collecting.

From where I stood in the doorway, I admired her natural poise. Pearl spoke briefly with a server before she studied the menu. As I waved off the hostess and crossed the room toward her, a gentleman with a Sean Connery beard approached Pearl's table. He wore a black woolen cape and a formal top hat. Thinking he might be a personal acquaintance of Pearl's, I stepped back so as not to interrupt their conversation.

I needn't have worried about their privacy: the man had barely spoken to her before Pearl raised her voice. "Go away. I've told you I'm not interested." There was no mistaking her tone. "Leave me alone, or I shall call the police to remove you."

Concerned that Nellie's aunt might need help, I hurried to her side. The man saw me march toward them and dodged out the side exit.

"I'm sorry you saw that, dear," she said, fidgeting with her hands.

"Do you know him?" I asked.

"In a manner of speaking." Pearl's evasive answer puzzled me. During my earlier call to introduce myself, she gave forthright replies to every question. This was the first time I witnessed her hesitate. Without further explanation, she invited me to sit.

"Please join me. My surprise guest will be down soon."

I followed her cue to drop the uncomfortable subject of the rude man. "I can't wait to meet this mystery guest," I said.

Pearl leaned toward me, eyes sparkling. "I may as well tell you," she said.

"It's my sister, Opal! She's here from London, and I've asked her to join us. It won't be long. Her cell phone rang just as we were on our way downstairs to meet you, so she stepped out to take the call."

"Ahh. What a treat. Nellie didn't mention another aunt."

"Probably because Opal lives abroad," Pearl said. "She's quite independent. Always traveling. Opal didn't tell anyone she planned to visit."

"Are the two of you close?"

"Since the day she was born. Opal is a bit younger than I am, but we have always enjoyed each other's company. Most trips, she brings a suitcase and stays in my spare bedroom. This time—with my entire collection of dolls filling that room—she preferred to book her stay at the inn. Not so many eyes looking at her, you know." Pearl winked at me, conspiratorially. "Plus, the Philbrook has room service. I don't provide that luxury."

Already, I felt a warm connection to this delightful woman. I could see why Nellie adored her aunt. Now, I wanted to know more about her younger sister. "Is Opal pleased with her suite?" I asked. "As a world traveler, she must be accustomed to five-star accommodations."

Pearl giggled. "Oh, yes. But she is thrilled with her room. They gave her an upgrade, and you'd think she was the Queen—not just another commoner from America."

Her laughter was infectious; I could see how she had charmed her way into leadership roles with the United Federation of Doll Clubs. The woman was irresistible. We were still chuckling when she glanced over my shoulder and waved at someone behind me.

"Here's Opal now."

I stood and turned to greet Pearl's sister and froze for a moment at the sight. Opal walked gracefully toward us, weaving easily between the tables of seated guests enjoying their tiers of tea sandwiches and sweets. She, too, was tall, with gray hair and bright green eyes like her sister. Her ivory skin was nearly translucent, and she had a small mole just below her eye on her right cheek. She wore a familiar sage green cowl-necked tunic over black pants, dazzling diamond earrings, and a broach. I turned to Pearl, shocked.

"You didn't tell me Opal was your identical twin!"

She clapped her hands, delighted at my astonishment. "I wanted to see your reaction, my dear."

I looked from one to the other and back again.

Opal extended her hand graciously to introduce herself. "I see that my sister failed to mention we are twins. Please allow me to apologize. She has played this trick many times. I am but an innocent bystander in her pranks."

Pearl nearly choked at Opal's words. "Pshaw. Innocent, indeed! You are the one who suggested we dress alike for this little gathering."

I shook my head, enchanted by their banter. "It *is* unusual to see adult twins with identical movements and voices—not to mention your looks! Are you alike in all things? Your favorite foods? Hobbies? Travels? Tell me *everything*." I pulled my notebook from my purse and opened it to a clean page.

We spent the next hour chatting over hot tea and pastries. Though I tried to give them my undivided attention, I was distracted by the sight of the caped mystery man who lurked near the dining room entrance. He leaned against a pillar, pretending to read *The Village Gazette,* but I never saw him turn a page.

Pearl and Opal were oblivious to the man's movements as they prattled on, volleying the conversation from one to the other in a lively exchange. I learned the twins loved the same foods, enjoyed bowling (each still scored well over 150 points per game, on average), and talked to each other daily. They both fell in love with their respective mates in the same year and married in a double-wedding ceremony. The marriages lasted more than fifty years—until both their husbands died within weeks of each other, nearly a decade ago.

"I married a doctor, my dear," Pearl said. "We had a nice, respectable life...unlike my wayward sister."

"Oh, pshaw!" Opal exclaimed. "I wed a movie producer. Pearl never accepted the fact that he was a businessman, not a fickle, publicity-seeking actor."

I laughed at what must have been a familiar debate between the two sisters. "You both led fulfilling lives, it appears."

"We certainly did," the two replied simultaneously.

Pearl took her sister's hands in hers. "We went separate directions, but we were never out of contact with each other."

Opal nodded. Tears filled her eyes. "After we lost our husbands, we became even closer, if that's possible."

I sipped my Earl Gray tea and waited for the sisters to continue their story. Pearl spoke first. "I settled in English Village to be near my son," she said. "We were so proud that he'd chosen a career in medicine—just like his father. He had built a solid practice here in the village." She threw her hands in the air. "Then, one month after I moved here, my precious boy accepted a job in San Francisco. Can you believe it?"

She huffed as she told the story. "He had the nerve to ask me to follow him to California, but I put my foot down. I'm too old to be moving across the country every two years. Besides, I like it here. I can zip up to Kansas City for meetings with the doll collectors. I'm within driving distance to many of the regional doll conventions. And I have friends here."

"Which is precisely why I continue to live in London!" Opal interrupted to tell her own story. "I didn't want to leave the last home my husband and I shared. I also enjoy the theater and still have many friends in the UK. While Pearl is gallivanting across the country, collecting dolls, I am exploring antique stores and attending concerts."

"And you never, ever, initiated any of the childhood mischief Pearl described?" I looked deeply into her green eyes and watched her squirm.

"Perhaps on one or two occasions." She answered primly, rolling her eyes to acknowledge her guilt. "I may have painted a small mole on my right cheek to match Pearl's. It was the best way to confuse our beaus, when we were out dancing and romancing."

Excitement sparked from Opal's green eyes as she reached beneath the table to retrieve a small quilted carryall. She handed the bag to her sister. "Look what I've brought you from London! I carried her all the way on the plane with me and can't wait another minute for you to meet her."

Pearl looked at me and shrugged her shoulders. "My sister always gets her way," she said. Carefully, she unzipped the bag, opened it fully, and peeled away several layers of tissue paper to reveal an antique bisque doll wearing a beautiful white satin gown. Tiny pearls and feathers adorned her white hair.

For a moment, Pearl simply cradled the doll in her arms. Then she raised her eyes to Opal. "Oh my! You have outdone yourself on this one, love. You really shouldn't have—"

"I'm told she was a favorite doll owned by Queen Elisabeth of Romania," Opal interrupted. "It's said to be a replica of the queen herself, at her coronation ceremony. But I think she looks like you, Sissy."

"Or like you, Opal." I winked at her.

Pearl gasped as she studied the delicate antique. "I recognize her from an article I read in *Dolls* magazine. Do you realize what a treasure this is? How ever did you find her?"

Opal could barely contain herself. "I have a new friend. He's an antique dealer with a shop just off of Church Street in London. He negotiated for months to acquire this doll."

Pearl was visibly moved by the gift. She turned to me with tears in her eyes. "Queen Elisabeth—who was later known as the writer Carmen Sylva—had a huge doll collection dating back to 1898. She famously shared the collection on a European tour to benefit a charity."

"People bought tickets to see the display?" I jotted notes to include in my article, but I was baffled to think that a doll collection would be such a popular attraction.

"Yes. Hundreds paid to see the queen's dolls before something mysterious happened," Opal said.

That got my full attention. "Tell me," I prompted her. "Did the money go missing or something?"

"Worse," Pearl said. "The dolls were packed into four train cars for shipment to the next tour location, somewhere in Germany. But when the train arrived, the dolls were gone."

"Gone?"

"Vanished into thin air—railroad cars and all," Opal said. "To this day, no one knows where all the stolen dolls were taken. Only a few have resurfaced."

Pearl's eyes filled with tears as she held the doll close to her heart. "And you have managed to find one."

Opal clapped her hands. "You see! She is the perfect addition to your collection."

Twice more, from the corner of my eye, I saw the mystery man peer around the doorway of the dining room. He disappeared again by the time we finished our tea.

Pearl pushed her chair away from the table and retrieved the bag that held her new doll. "Let's put her into the safe in your room," she said to Opal. "Then we can visit the Christmas Market."

Opal turned to me. "We plan to listen to the carolers and enjoy a carriage ride. Want to join us?"

I thanked them for the invitation before I explained that I only wanted to make a quick stop at Harvey's booth and then head back to my cottage to feed Moe.

We parted outside the Philbrook, where two dozen merchants sold handmade wares from thatch-roofed booths. I strolled across the huge flagstone patio toward the valet parking station. Tiny white lights decorated every tree and draped in graceful scallops between the antique lampposts. By twilight, the area would be bustling with shoppers beneath a twinkling canopy.

I spotted Harvey's display from a distance and slowed my pace to admire it. Intricate wrought iron ornaments hung from a tall, eye-catching metal tree he had created for the occasion. Reindeer and bells, snowmen and Santas, stars, and angels — all handmade — dangled festively from golden cords on its branches.

The booth looked wonderful—even better than the first hastily assembled display our Mahjong Mavens had built for his summer sale.

As I approached, Harvey was deep in conversation with a customer. He looked handsome in a red plaid flannel shirt and blue jeans, his hair glowing in the lamplight. And, although I stood perfectly still at the edge of the booth, he turned his head and gave me a wink to acknowledge my presence.

After he completed his transaction, Harvey strolled over to greet me. I nodded my approval of the thatch-roofed display. "Now, *this* is a booth!"

He leaned his elbows on the counter and grinned at me. "You realize the Philbrook Inn provides these for every merchant?"

"I know. But it's still attractive. And your metal artwork is beautiful." I motioned toward the shelves he had filled with candelabras in various shapes and sizes, all adorned with poinsettias and holly.

"Thank you, Josie. Did you enjoy your tea?"

"Yes! And Pearl introduced me to her twin sister. Those two are delightful. I hope I have as much vitality when I'm their age."

Glancing back toward the plaza, I noticed the ladies deep in conversation. Arm-in-arm, they toured the booths. The mystery man followed close behind. I felt a trickle of unease run up my spine.

"Look there, Harvey. See the two ladies wearing matching gray coats?"

He craned his neck in their direction. "Yes."

"And the man following them? The one in the black cape with the Sean Connery beard?"

"I see him, but I would call that a cloak. See? It has sleeves, and the cape is a separate layer. The top hat is a nice touch."

"Cape. Cloak. Whatever." I kept my eyes glued to the man who trailed the sisters. "He argued with Pearl earlier today. Should we do something?"

Harvey studied the man closely before he shook his head. "He's just a guy walking in a public place, Josie. Dressed like that, he might even be a caroler later tonight. What did you have in mind? You want me to tackle him?"

I sighed. "You're right. I suppose he has a right to be here. He just seems…"

"What?"

"Suspicious."

Harvey walked around the counter to stand beside me. We both watched the mystery man who walked a few paces behind the twins. Finally, Harvey spoke.

"I think your imagination is taking you down the wrong track again. Don't look for trouble where there isn't any. Go home, Josie. I'll check on the ladies in between customers."

Harvey's tone irritated me, but I was too tired to argue. Besides, he was probably right. Still, I kept the man in my sights until I reached the valet

13

stand, releasing him into the surrounding revelry.

Chapter Three

Wednesday Evening

Snowflakes began to fall again as I drove the short distance home. Dusk arrived quickly at this time of year. Holiday lights adorned the rooflines of our local businesses along Main Street and twinkled from a huge tree at the entrance to the historic park.

As I turned onto quiet Persimmon Lane toward my own little cottage, I saw no other cars had disturbed the new-fallen snow. For a few seconds, I had the surreal sensation that my car was floating inside a snow globe. The magical spell ended when I pulled into my warm garage.

Moe greeted me at the door, wagging his entire body in welcome. He dashed outside while I prepared his supper, then returned inside to race into the kitchen on snowy paws that left small pools of water wherever he stepped. I followed behind him with a towel, then watched him gobble every bite of his food.

As for me, I'd devoured so much cake at Pearl's tea party that I immediately sank into my reading chair and propped my feet on the ottoman. An hour later, I woke to the shrill ringtone of my cell. It was Harvey.

"H-hello?" My voice croaked a little as I shook myself awake.

"Josie, something terrible has happened." Harvey's normally calm voice shook with emotion.

"What? When?"

"Minutes ago, at the Christmas Market. A shot was fired. And worse...one of the twins tumbled into the wishing well. I don't know which one. They pulled her out and rushed her to the hospital. But it doesn't look good. I'm so sorry, Josie. I feel responsible. You asked me to look after them, and now..."

"I'm on my way." I ended the call before I realized I wasn't certain where to go—to the inn, or the hospital. I pulled on my boots and grabbed my keys. Before I hit the door, my phone rang again.

"Josie, it's Leslie." I recognized the matter-of-fact voice of our *Village Gazette* editor, Leslie Anderson. She often called at the end of the day with writing assignments for the small newspaper. But I was too rushed to chat with her tonight.

"Sorry, Leslie, I'm headed out right now. Can I call you later?"

"This can't wait," she said. "There's been an accident at the Philbrook Christmas Market. I want you to cover it."

"Oh!" It startled me that she already knew about the incident. This was fast, even for our tiny town grapevine. "That's actually where I'm headed. I'll call you with a story as soon as I have details."

Nellie's incoming call beeped while I was still on the line with Leslie. I quickly switched over. "I thought I told you to stay out of trouble," she said, panic creeping into her voice. "Were you at the inn when the accident happened? I heard a woman fell into the well. Please tell me it wasn't my Aunt Pearl!"

"Yes, you told me to stay out of trouble. And, no, I wasn't there. The whole thing sounds like a big brouhaha. My information is sketchy. Let's not panic until we have all the facts, okay? I'm on my way over now."

"Yeah. Sure. I just want to know she's alright. She's in her eighties, you know."

"True. But she seems much younger. She's smart and steady on her feet. Most likely, the woman who fell was someone else." I crossed my fingers as I told Nellie the little white lie. There was no need to worry her further—not before we knew what had really happened.

"Besides," I continued, "the incident happened only a few minutes ago. How do you know about it, already?"

I could almost hear Nellie roll her eyes on the other end of the line. "Lorene called. She's on her way to the hospital. The chief is headed to the inn now. He's shorthanded again, and he thinks the fall looks suspicious. You might get a call to assist him."

"I'm leaving now."

"Josie?"

"Yes, Nellie?"

"Call if you need us. I know the mavens promised they wouldn't meddle in cases anymore, but we're here for you."

"Thank you, Nellie." I noticed she hadn't mentioned a shooting. Either the chief hadn't included the information when he spoke to his wife, or Lorene had omitted it when she called Nellie. Either way, I kept my tone clear and calm. "Don't worry, my friend. I'm sure this is an accident. It's probably nothing."

"Uh-huh." Nellie's voice dripped with sarcasm.

At the corner of Persimmon and Main, I had to decide: Turn left, toward the Philbrook, or right, toward the hospital? While I hesitated at the stop sign, the chief called.

"Hello, Chief." I knew to keep the conversation direct. The chief had no time to waste.

"Can you meet me at the Philbrook?"

"Be there in five minutes."

He disconnected without another word. My mind reeled after the barrage of phone calls. Had someone been shot? Was it the Sean Connery look-alike? And how would Pearl or Opal have fallen into the wishing well? Which twin was it? I sped to the inn as fast as my little red VW Bug could safely travel over the snowy roads.

Chief Marshall stood near the front of the crowded dining room, a portable bullhorn in his hand. He was a commanding presence, even without the sound amplifier. Just as you would expect from a guy who played fullback on his college football team, the chief was tall and wide. But it was his demeanor that drew everyone's attention. His ebony face was stern as his dark eyes swept the room. He nodded when he saw me at the doorway.

I made my way between the tables toward the back of the distraught crowd. Harvey caught my eye and stepped aside so I could squeeze into the space beside him. I summoned the courage to whisper the one question I was afraid to ask. "Who was it, Harvey? Which twin fell down the well?"

"They say it was Opal," he answered. "The doll collector's sister."

I bowed my head to hide the tears that sprang to my eyes. "This can't be happening. We were together less than two hours ago."

"I'm sorry, Josie." Harvey looked as devastated as I felt. "You told me to keep an eye on the guy who followed them, and I didn't."

"Oh, Harvey! This isn't your fault."

The chief tapped the mic on his bullhorn. The room silenced.

"Thank you for your attention." Chief Marshall had a big voice under normal circumstances. The additional projection reached every corner of the restaurant. "As most of you know, there's been an accident on the plaza by the Christmas Market booths. An elderly woman fell into the wishing well."

The crowded room erupted as people called out with questions. "Who was it?" "What about the gunshot?"

Chief Marshall waited for the clamoring to fade. He searched the room, looking into every face. "We can't release a name, or any details, until the family has been notified. Right now, a woman is fighting for her life in a hospital bed. The question is: How did this happen? We need to speak with anyone who may have witnessed the incident. And we need to do that while the evening is fresh in your minds."

The chief motioned to two officers standing beside him. "Officer Devon and Officer Kelly are here to take your statements." There were easily one hundred and fifty people in the room, but it sounded like double that number when they groaned in response.

"I know it's late, but we need your cooperation. The Philbrook will serve pie and coffee while you wait your turn. Please come to the interview areas we have set up in the tearoom alcove when you are directed to do so. Josie

Posey and Harvey Jacobs, please come forward."

Harvey and I looked at each other, surprised. Then we did as Chief Marshall requested. The staff already circled between the tables, taking orders for coffee and pie. The crowd still grumbled about their confinement, but the free dessert calmed them. As we approached, I noticed the strain at the corner of the chief's eyes.

"How can we help?" I asked.

Chief Marshall lowered his voice. "We can't interview all these people in one night. I'd like you to screen them for us. Take names. Ask everyone what they were doing when the commotion occurred and the woman fell into the well. If they heard a gunshot, or witnessed the fall—or anything unusual—send them to the interview area. If they say they saw nothing, take a name and contact information. We will be in touch with them later."

Harvey nodded. "We can do that."

"We're short-staffed, and I need my officers to conduct interviews with the witnesses who actually saw something. I'm counting on you to keep this room orderly, Harvey." Chief Marshall handed him the bullhorn. "Hold onto this, just in case things get unruly. Work your way through the tables as efficiently as possible."

The chief turned to me. "Josie, I hate to involve you, but I figure you'll be covering this story for the *Gazette,* anyway. Plus, you know how to conduct an interview, and you never miss a detail."

I heard the "but" coming...

"But, don't go tracking down a suspect on your own. Someone who would fire a gun into a crowd, and shove an old lady down a well, is someone you need to stay far away from. Ask bystanders only two questions: Where were you when the incident occurred? Did you witness any part of the event?"

"Don't worry, Chief, I'll let you do the chasing."

Borrowing the bullhorn from Harvey, he silenced the crowd again, to introduce our role as "screeners." I pulled a couple of pens and legal pads out of my oversized handbag. Harvey smiled when he saw them.

"Are you always this prepared?"

I shrugged and grinned up at him. "Not always."

Harvey suggested that we split up to move through the tables more quickly. Everyone from the Christmas Market had been corralled into the dining room immediately after the accident, so they were already complaining about their confinement.

"Good idea." I pulled up a chair and sat at the nearest table. Taking a pen in my hand, I drew matching columns onto the two legal pads. "Let's start with the basics: Name, Address, Phone, Occupation."

"That's more than the chief requested," Harvey said.

"Trust me, Chief Marshall will be happy to have the additional information. If we both complete the same columns, I can easily prepare a spreadsheet for him later."

Harvey rolled his eyes. "You and your spreadsheets."

I raised an eyebrow. "Have a better suggestion?"

"No," he admitted. "I wish you weren't getting involved at all." He set the bullhorn on the table and looked over my shoulder as I scribbled three more questions onto the pads.

Above column five, six, and seven, I added: *Where were you? Did you see it happen? Did you notice anything suspicious?*

Harvey took his pad and headed toward a table near the back of the dining room.

We worked quickly, alternating tables. I started with a show of hands at my first table. "Did anyone at this table see the incident?" A woman in her fifties nodded. I gathered her information, then sent her to meet with the officers. Afterward, I worked the remainder of the table, gathering answers and contact information. With about six guests per table, I spent only ten minutes surveying everyone. Harvey finished his group at the same time.

"That went well," he said. "Only twenty-three more tables to go."

I laughed at his optimism. "At this rate, we will be here two more hours. It's already eight o'clock."

"Let's hope we get faster with practice."

"And that the Philbrook doesn't run out of pie," I said.

The job became easier as we learned to approach two or three tables simultaneously. When the surrounding people overheard our questions, it prepared them for their own answers. Fewer than twenty of them claimed to have seen the incident. Since those witnesses left the room to tell their stories to the officers, Harvey and I never heard the details There was no way for us to know what truly happened at the Christmas Market.

Twice, I asked people to stay for questioning, even though they insisted they had not seen the accident. One was a rotund gentleman with large spectacles that gave him the appearance of an owl. He was an antique dealer. The other was a sweet-faced, middle-aged woman who fidgeted while she spoke. She ducked her head as she answered, and refused to make eye contact.

The woman claimed to have heard two gunshots. "It wasn't one, but two," she insisted. "Pop, pop." The lady listed her occupation as a doll collector. It seemed logical that both she and the antique dealer might know the twins—or at least Pearl—from the doll conventions. Perhaps they could help Chief Marshall fill in some gaps, I thought.

As we approached the final three tables, I realized the mystery man I had seen earlier in the tearoom was missing. We completed our interviews and found a quiet table of our own. One server offered us coffee, and I accepted, grateful to be off my feet and sipping a steaming mocha latte.

"What happened to the Sean Connery guy?" I asked Harvey. "Wasn't he there when this happened?"

He shook his head. "No. I saw him near the carolers before their performance. The next time I looked, he was gone. He disappeared before the police arrived."

"Did you see the shooting?"

"It all happened too fast. I heard a gunshot, and a scream, and people shouting. Then, more screams as Pearl realized Opal had fallen backward into the well."

"You're certain the gunshot came before the scream?"

Harvey shook his head. "I can't swear to it. I just remember the carolers ended a song. The crowd began to applaud, and then, suddenly, there was shouting. I couldn't see anything from my booth."

"And after the shouting?" I pushed him to remember.

21

He stared into his coffee mug before he replied. "I heard the shot, the scream, and more screams. Everyone ran toward the inn to get away from whatever had happened. The manager had the good sense to gather the guests into the dining room for their own safety. He locked us all inside and called the police."

"Who called the ambulance?"

"I did." Harvey looked at me, sadly. "Someone else may have, too. At first, when I heard the shouts, I thought it might have been a purse snatching. But as soon as I heard the gunshot, I called 911. It was chaos. People ran in every direction."

"You didn't see anyone with a gun?"

"No. I was near the back of the crowd, closer to my booth." Harvey scribbled absently on the legal pad, and I took another sip of my coffee.

"Chief Marshall will want to interview you."

"I know."

As we talked, I tried to remember the dimensions of the well. I knew it was a large stone feature in the outdoor plaza—probably ten feet in diameter. The wall surrounding it was wide enough to serve as a bench. People always perched there, bracing small children as they threw coins into the fountain.

"The well isn't actually deep, is it?" I asked Harvey.

"No." He sketched a drawing on the legal pad as he talked. "The wishing well has always been more decorative than functional. It contains water to pump through the fountain during summer. In winter, they drain the water, and decorate the empty fountain with greenery and lights. I'd say the well goes down about four feet—like a shallow pool. Opal fell backward, hitting her head on river rock at the bottom."

"For a woman in her eighties, that's quite a tumble." I sighed.

The grandfather's clock in the entry hall chimed 10:30, and I yawned. Harvey stacked his legal pad on top of mine. "There's nothing more we can do tonight. Let's return our notes to the chief and get your car. I'll follow to make sure you arrive home safe."

But before we reached the door, the chief stopped us. I read the news in his posture and his face.

"I'm sorry, Josie. The hospital called. It isn't good."

The roar in my ears drowned out the rest of his message, and I stared blankly at his mouth as the words escaped his lips in slow motion. Opal. Dead. Pearl. Collapsed.

I deciphered only four disconnected pieces before the lights dimmed, and I dropped to the floor.

Chapter Four

Thursday Morning

My dreams were a jumble of images. The twins, laughing at lunch. Sean Connery in a caped coat. A fragile doll falling in slow motion down, down, down. And then I became the doll, waking with a jerk before I shattered. I opened my eyes to see Moe staring back at me. He whined and licked my face.

I raised my head and reached over to scratch behind his ears. "I'm okay, boy. It was just a bad dream."

But, of course, the reality was worse than my nightmare. As I scrambled out of bed, a fierce, throbbing weight settled behind my eyes and sent shards of pain to my temples. I let Moe into the backyard, poured a mug of coffee, and swallowed a couple of aspirin. For several minutes, I stood watching him from the window. My playful sheepdog raced in crazy circles, making random trails in the snow.

My heart ached at his happiness, and my mind darted in multiple directions, as I tried to make sense of what I knew to be true. The doll collector's sister had died. Nellie's aunt. The sweet, spunky lady who had flown in to visit Pearl—and to surprise Nellie—was gone before she'd had the opportunity to see her niece. I wanted to find out why.

Harvey phoned as I finished breakfast.

"How do you feel?" he asked softly.

"Sad."

"I'm sorry, Josie."

"Why would anyone want to hurt Opal? And what will Pearl do without her?"

"I don't know."

"Harvey?"

"Yes, Josie."

"I have to find out who did this."

Harvey knew better than to argue with me. He attempted a distraction instead. "Why don't you talk to Pearl first? They kept her at the hospital overnight, but she's awake now. Her son is still in California. He won't arrive here until tomorrow. She needs a ride home."

I brushed the tears from my eyes. "You're right. I'll check on her now."

"And, Josie?"

"Yes?"

"Don't worry about helping with the Christmas Market this afternoon. Tim Nester offered to take your shift. Nellie is baking a casserole for Pearl. Maybe the two of you can spend some time with her."

I didn't have the heart to tell Harvey that I'd already forgotten about his booth. The Christmas Market was the last thing on my mind.

By mid-morning, Nellie and I were on our way to get Pearl and deliver the casserole. Nellie drove while I talked. "I never thought we would do this again. I'm tired of losing friends—and now *your aunt*—to untimely deaths. Do you think it was a murder? Who would kill a sweet lady like Opal? Why didn't I stay with them longer?"

Nellie rested her hand on mine to stop my chatter. "Whoa."

"Whoa?"

"Stop, Josie. You're blaming yourself, and we don't even know what happened."

"I. Am. So. Angry." I spit the words out one at a time.

"I understand. But you need to pull yourself together for Aunt Pearl."

It occurred to me that I should be comforting Nellie, not the other way around. But Nellie had a way of calming me when I needed it most. We talked about inconsequential things the rest of the ride. The weather. The holiday lights. Anything to fill the silence and avoid the sadness that weighed heavily on our hearts.

Pearl waited for us at the hospital entrance. Behind the glass doors, she looked frail and forlorn—like a lonely swan in a glass cage. When we pulled into the circle drive, she lifted her head, raised her long neck, and straightened her posture.

We hurried the length of the sidewalk to step inside the entryway. Nellie embraced her aunt, holding her tight. Then Pearl turned toward me, and I wrapped her in another huge hug before we walked her to the car.

"Thank you, dear." She squeezed my hand as I helped her into the front passenger seat.

Nellie waited for us to buckle up before she said anything. With a weak smile, she turned to Pearl. "Where would you like to go, Auntie Pearl? We have a tank full of gas and all the time in the world."

Pearl struggled to answer. She took a deep breath and blinked back her tears. Finally, she spoke. "I'd like to go to the Philbrook first, if you don't mind. I need to remove Opal's things from her room there."

Nellie nodded. "The Philbrook it is." She shifted into gear and pulled the car onto the road.

As chatty as I had been on the way to the hospital, I couldn't speak now. My heart was heavy in my chest, squeezing the words right out of me. Nellie hummed a little tune as she drove. Pearl sat quietly, hands folded in her lap, until we reached Main Street. Then she turned to gaze out the window at the picturesque shops.

"Could we stop at Cozy Cups?" Her voice was barely a whisper.

"Yes, indeed." Nellie slowed the car and pulled into a parking spot near the café entrance. Chief Marshall's wife, Lorene, had turned the popular coffee shop into a bustling business over the past several years. This was the place our Mahjong Mavens came for lunch meetings, birthday celebrations, and all sorts of important conversations.

Pearl sighed as we approached the entrance. "My sister Opal loved this place. And Lorene has been so kind."

26

"Have you tasted their cinnamon rolls?" I finally found the voice to ask an ordinary question.

"Yes!" Pearl smiled at me. "My mouth is watering at the thought. I'm afraid I couldn't eat a bite this morning. But I'm starving now."

"We can take care of that." Nellie opened the door and led us inside.

Except for a few downtown workers on coffee breaks, the café was empty. The breakfast rush had ended, and the lunch crowd wouldn't arrive for another hour. Lorene came from behind the counter to greet us. Without a word, she wrapped a hug firmly around Pearl. Then she held her at arm's length and smiled into her eyes. "It is *so nice* to see you this morning!" For a tiny woman, she knew how to give a big welcome.

"You know the drill," Lorene continued, motioning to the vast number of mismatched cups hanging on the wall. "Choose your own cup. Fill it with the coffee of your choice. Doctor it with flavors or whipped cream. Then, please, take a seat. I'll bring menus to your table."

I followed her instructions. After I poured hazelnut-flavored brew into my favorite blue mug, I turned to see Pearl still selecting a cup.

She saw me watching her and shot me an indignant look. "What? Decisions like this are hard for me!"

I shrugged my shoulders. "It's not a race, Pearl." I squirted two shots of vanilla into my coffee and added a dollop of whipped cream. The steaming brew smelled delicious.

Nellie whispered something into Pearl's ear, and the two of them turned to laugh at me. Nellie pointed to my face. "You have a bit of whipped cream on your nose from sniffing that concoction," she said.

I nabbed a napkin to my face, tossed my head, and marched to our table. Soon, we sat across from each other, deep in conversation. While we talked, Pearl finished a full breakfast and half of my cinnamon roll. She regaled us with stories of Opal. First, we laughed. Then we cried.

After Lorene cleared our plates, she pulled up a chair to join us. Pearl had saved some of her best stories for last—causing us to laugh so hard we cried all over again.

It was Lorene who asked the most important question of the morning.

"What do we do now?"

Pearl reached out both hands to grasp ours. She motioned for us to bring Lorene into the circle. Once we had formed this universal symbol of strength, Pearl answered, "We must find my sister's killer and bring him to justice."

I felt a shiver run up my spine at her words. Her determination was infectious. Pearl turned to lock eyes with each of us, one by one. "Who's with me?"

When her bright green eyes pierced mine, without hesitation, I said, "I'm in."

"Me too." Nellie surprised me. She was generally the voice of reason in our group. But this time, the death was personal. She had lost her aunt.

Lorene shook her head and rolled her eyes. "Sorry, ladies. I will do what I can to help, but from a distance. We need to let my husband handle the dangerous parts. Agreed?"

We answered in unison: "Agreed!"

And just that quickly, we tossed aside our earlier vows to avoid criminal investigations. Together, we formed a pact to track down a murderer. If we had all been fifth graders, we would have taken a blood oath; our intentions were that serious.

Pearl drew us closer to reveal a fact that few people knew. Speaking barely above a whisper, she confided: "They found a bullet in Opal's chest."

"*What?*" The news stunned Nellie and me.

Lorene nodded. "That's why Earl started a full investigation so quickly. He wanted to gather information from bystanders while most assumed the fall was an accident."

"Oh!" Suddenly, I recalled the sweet woman who insisted she heard more than one gunshot. "Who else knows about this?"

Pearl counted on her fingers: "The four of us, the chief, two doctors, one nurse, and the killer."

I knew how fast rumors traveled in English Village. "By this afternoon, everyone will know. Even if *we* keep the secret, the medical staff will tell their own families, and the news will spread like wildfire."

Nellie turned to Pearl. "Where shall we begin?"

"The Philbrook. To retrieve Opal's belongings."

Lorene stayed behind. The Cozy Cups Café wouldn't run itself. She offered to alert the other Mahjong Mavens to our plans. The rest of us climbed back into Nellie's car for the short ride to the inn. I had mixed feelings as we drew closer to the scene of the crime. It was anticipation mingled with fear. I wanted to help Pearl, but I recognized another lurking danger. Pearl and Opal were identical twins. *What if the murderer intended to kill Pearl, instead of her sister?* Or, what if he targeted *both* women, and only eliminated one? How could we protect her from harm?

Since the chief was not likely to welcome our entourage of volunteer deputies, I hoped we could keep a low profile until we gathered helpful evidence. A scolding from Chief Marshall was not my idea of a good time. As luck would have it, the chief's car blocked the entry of the Philbrook, forcing Nellie to drive through a checkpoint.

She rolled her window down and leaned toward the young officer, smiling. He did not return the gesture. "State your business," he said.

"We're here to help my aunt gather her sister's belongings." Nellie nodded her head toward the frail woman in her passenger seat.

"Chief Marshall just completed his survey of her room. You must get his permission first." The officer waved Nellie into a parking spot and waited for her to exit the vehicle.

She stuck her head back through the window. "You two wait here."

Minutes later, Nellie returned to the car. "We're in. Our timing was perfect. They've photographed Opal's room and pulled fingerprints from the dresser and doorknobs. Pearl, they want you to verify nothing is missing."

Pearl frowned, confused. "Why would anything be missing?"

Nellie shot me a look. "You don't know Chief Marshall," I said. "He's super detailed. I'm sure he wants to take a full inventory."

But when we arrived at Opal's room, the place had been ransacked. Someone had broken the lock, tossed the room, and scattered clothes across the floor. Pearl nearly fainted when she saw the mess. She sat on the edge of the bed, surveying the surrounding destruction. I stood with my arm around her. The place still carried the faint fragrance of lavender from

Opal's lingering perfume.

Chief Marshall handed Pearl a glass of water. "I'm sorry, Ms. Merriweather. Someone searched Opal's room ahead of our arrival. We don't know whether it happened before, or after, she tumbled into the well. Can you tell us what they might have been searching for?"

Pearl's voice was faint, but firm. "The safe. Did they break into the safe?"

The chief walked to the closet and opened the door. He motioned to the marred surface. "They tried but failed."

Pearl took a deep breath and pulled me down to whisper a series of numbers in my ear. "Please try this combination," she said.

I followed her instructions, gears clicked, and the door to the safe swung open.

Chapter Five

Thursday Afternoon

Pearl sat frozen in place, barely breathing. I looked into the safe and discovered the quilted bag from our tea party. I unzipped the bag. Inside, the beautiful doll still rested on tissue paper, with two envelopes tucked beside her.

Tears streamed from Pearl's eyes. "*This* is what he wanted! The murderer killed my sister over a doll!"

I handed the bag to her. Pearl removed the doll and cradled her. She smiled into the doll's painted bisque face. "He didn't get you, did he?"

Chief Marshall took several photos of the doll before he asked Pearl about the envelopes. "Do you mind telling me what is inside?"

Pearl handed him both envelopes. "One is a Certificate of Authenticity. The other is a personal note from my sister. I haven't read either of them, yet. We brought the doll directly to her safe after our tea and then went to the plaza for the festivities."

I opened my mouth to speak and then stopped to reconsider. The chief noticed my hesitation.

"What is it, Josie?"

"Nothing." I shook my head and looked at Pearl. "It's just that I saw you walking together on the plaza, and I could have sworn one of you was carrying this quilted tote bag."

"You remembered correctly, dear. Opal gave the doll to me in *this* bag. She had an identical bag of her own. We returned to her room to place the doll, still inside this quilted bag, into the safe. Then Opal took her own quilted tote bag to the market. We planned to use Opal's bag to carry any purchases."

"Where is her bag, now?" I asked.

Pearl's hand flew to her mouth. "I don't know! It hadn't crossed my mind in all the rush to get my sister to the hospital."

Tiny warning bells rang in my head as she spoke. When Pearl completed her explanation, she wrung her hands in anguish. "Oh no! This was *my* fault, wasn't it? When we went upstairs, I carried my doll in a quilted bag. But when we strolled the plaza, Opal carried an identical bag." Pearl moaned and her voice quavered. The killer wanted the doll, and he assumed it was in the bag, so he stole it from her. I should have been the victim!"

Chief Marshall bent down to look deeply into Pearl's eyes. "No. This was not your fault. You are not to blame yourself."

Standing upright again, the chief continued to reassure the elderly woman. "We can't assume anything, Pearl. Either of you might have carried the tote. And the killer may not have targeted the bag. He may have pushed Opal into the well because she was most accessible. It could be he staged a diversion to gain access to her room. We don't even know if the person who shoved her also fired the gun. It's possible we have two suspects working independently of one another."

As the chief spoke, I appreciated—not for the first time—his ability to study every aspect of a crime. If anyone could solve this murder, it was Chief Marshall.

"What do we do next?" Nellie glanced at the chief as she handed Pearl a tissue.

"We have all we need from you, for now. It seems unlikely that the suspect removed anything of value when he was unable to retrieve the doll from the safe. We'll check the hotel cameras to see if they recorded anyone other than Opal entering or exiting the room. You are free to gather Opal's things." The chief moved an empty suitcase from the closet to the foot of the bed.

I suggested that Nellie take Pearl to sit near the fireplace in the lounge. "I'll pack Opal's bag and meet you there soon." With no argument from Pearl, they secured the antique doll and her paperwork in the quilted carrying case and left me to complete the job of gathering Opal's clothing.

Chief Marshall stayed behind. He sat at the desk and jotted notes on his pad while I folded Opal's belongings into her luggage. She had only one suitcase so it didn't take long. I made a last search of the room—checking drawers, closet shelves, and the space beneath the bed. Then I snapped the locks and rolled the suitcase to the door, where it looked so inconsequential that I wondered aloud: "Would Opal have traveled all the way from London with only one suitcase? Surely she had a carry-on bag to transport the doll?"

The chief's head shot up from his notetaking. "That's *it*, Josie. The intruder *did* steal something from Opal's room. He took her smaller case, along with whatever was stowed inside it."

My heart sank in my chest. "Which could have been anything. Money? Jewelry?"

"So far, it's just another theory. Let's keep the missing case to ourselves and continue our search for suspects. We're going to get this guy, Josie. I know you want to help, but please be safe. The best thing you can do right now is spend time with Pearl."

"I know."

"I'll call you if we need you."

"Have you spoken with Harvey yet?"

"He told me about your Sean Connery mystery man." I caught a glimmer of a smile in the chief's eyes.

"And?"

"And we will see what we can learn about him," Chief Marshall said.

"Would you like me to get his name from Pearl?"

The chief sighed heavily. "Yes, Josie. Add him to the list you gathered last night."

I grinned at him. "Don't worry. I'll take good care of Pearl, and I'll share any additional evidence I discover."

As I turned to go, I noticed the blinking red light on the telephone and couldn't resist one more question for the chief. "Did you listen to her messages?"

Chief Marshall looked at me, then down to the phone. He shook his head. "I figured our young officers handled that."

I raised one eyebrow. "The light is still on."

He punched the message button, and we listened together. There were three new messages.

The first was from Pearl. *"I hope you brought your bowling bag, Sissy. We're going to Orchard Lanes this week. See you at tea with the reporter, Josie Posey."*

The next was a man demanding money. *"Opal, you owe me. Those royalties are half mine. Sonny promised. I followed you here, and I won't leave until we talk."*

The third call was from a gentleman whose voice sounded British. *"Opal, darling. It's Edward Gower. Something has happened. I believe you may be in danger. Please call. You have my number. I'll be waiting."*

I stared at the chief. "What does this mean?"

He played the messages again. And a third time. "It means Opal was in trouble before she arrived in English Village," he said. "Finding her killer just became a little more complicated."

The messages baffled me. "Why would anyone want to harm a woman in her eighties?"

Chief Marshall answered my question with one of his own. "How much do we know about Opal?"

"Apparently, not enough," I said. "But I'm sure Pearl can enlighten us."

The chief rubbed his temples. "I have a plan."

Quickly, he outlined next steps for the investigation. I listened and nodded. "I can do that."

"Josie, don't contact anyone without my authorization. Visit with Pearl first, and get back to me. We don't know these men. They may be partners in this mess. Or, they may not be connected to the murder at all."

I draped my handbag over my shoulder and dragged Opal's suitcase into the hallway. "I'll give you a report later."

Pearl's eyelids fluttered as she rested in the rocking chair beside the fireplace, the quilted bag on her lap. Nellie smiled as I approached. "It's time to get

Pearl home," she said.

The old woman sat upright and blinked. "I'm just resting my eyes. But Nellie is right. I'd like to go home now."

We piled the luggage, and Pearl's quilted bag with the doll, into Nellie's trunk beside her casserole and drove to Pearl's two-story home on the east edge of town. If my cottage looked like it belonged in the Cotswolds, Pearl's home resembled a stately manor from the English countryside. We parked in her driveway, unloaded the trunk, and walked to the front door.

Pearl turned her key in the lock and we stepped into a gracious sitting room, where a fire already blazed in the fireplace. A petite young woman with a long dark braid down her back greeted us with a smile. She helped Pearl remove her coat, then opened her arms to take mine and Nellie's. After hanging the coats in the hall closet, she waited for further instructions.

"I prepared your tea, Miss Pearl. Shall I set out a plate of sandwiches for your guests?"

"Yes, Paige. That would be lovely." Pearl motioned to the suitcase and the quilted bag near the door. "Could you also take those bags to my bedroom, please? Handle them with care, dear."

"Consider it done," Paige said.

Pearl turned to Nellie and me. "You will stay, won't you? Paige is a culinary student at the college. She works here three days a week, and today is her birthday!"

Paige tossed her long braid and scolded Pearl. "I thought we agreed my birthday would be our secret."

While she disappeared with the luggage, Nellie and I set our handbags and casserole dish on the hall table and followed our hostess into the cozy living room. With its high ceiling and dazzling chandeliers, the room might have seemed imposing, except for the tasteful furnishings Pearl had chosen. Overstuffed sofas and colorful pillows turned the expansive area into a warm, inviting space.

"Paige helps with light housework and cooking." Pearl's eyes sparkled with tears again. "She shouldn't be here today, but she insisted. When she heard about Opal's accident last night, she rushed to the hospital and stayed until I slept."

The young woman returned with a silver tea tray brimming with fresh-baked croissants. "I made your favorites, Miss Pearl. Would you prefer egg salad, or cucumber and chives?"

"Thank you, dear. I'm famished. The egg salad sounds lovely. Now, please serve my friends while I just pop into the pantry and prepare our dessert."

"But..." Paige started.

"No worries. I'll just be a moment."

Paige poured tea, and we chatted for a few minutes. The girl confessed that she worried about Pearl. "She and her sister have always been close. Even when they argued, they made up quickly. She will be lost without her."

We looked up as Pearl cleared her throat in the doorway. She stood holding a tray of cupcakes, each adorned by a flickering candle. "Surprise! Happy Birthday, Paige."

Paige rushed to help with the tray. "Oh! These are beautiful. Thank you, Pearl. When did you arrange this?"

"I ordered them from Lorene before Opal arrived Tuesday. We planned to deliver them to your apartment, but Lorene brought them here instead. She left them in the pantry early this morning."

As we shared the meal and sweets, Pearl turned the conversation toward her sister's murder. "I can't stop wondering what happened. Opal could be a stubborn woman. I'm sure she made a few enemies over the years. But who would be angry enough to kill her? Or, were they targeting me?"

"Tell me about the man in the tearoom," I said. "Sean Connery wearing a cape."

Pearl waved her arms, dismissing the thought. "Oh, *him*." He's harmless. I don't want to waste a minute on that man."

I decided to let it go...for now.

Nellie suggested we make a list of Opal's friends, identifying those who knew her best.

Pearl huffed at the thought. "No one knew her better than I did!"

Paige caught my eye and signaled for a time-out. I smiled back at her. Then, I turned to Pearl and took her hands in mine. "I don't know about you, but I'm tired. Let's take a break."

Pearl nodded. "Yes."

"Will you be all right if we leave you now?" Nellie was genuinely concerned. Pearl suddenly looked drained and weary.

"I want to have a hot bath and a good cry." Pearl's voice wobbled as she made the declaration.

Paige jumped up and wrapped an arm around the woman. "Let me draw your bath and turn down the bed. I can stay as long as you would like. My schoolwork is in the car."

While she and Pearl climbed the stairs, Nellie set her casserole into Pearl's refrigerator. Then—without a sound—we slipped out the front door.

Chapter Six

Thursday Evening

Nellie sat at my kitchen island, her hands clasped tightly in front of her. "Aunt Pearl knows more than she has shared."

I poured two cups of fresh coffee and set one in front of her. "I agree."

We had driven from Pearl's home to my cottage, where we could review the day's events without interruption. Sweet Moe played with his Lamb Chop toy in the living room while we talked.

"Sean Connery must be involved," I said. "Why won't Pearl tell us more about him?"

"Both of my aunts kept secrets," Nellie said. "You wouldn't believe the stories they could tell when my mom was alive."

I stirred cream into my coffee. "Pearl is fragile right now. We can't push her too hard."

Nellie nodded. "Why don't we reach out to Paige to see what she can tell us?"

"We need to speak to her privately—somewhere she can speak freely."

"I know her family," Nellie said. "I'll track down their phone number and give her a call tomorrow. I'm sure Paige will understand the urgency."

Nellie's forehead creased with worry, and I knew she was right to be concerned. "Until we learn who killed Opal, *and why,* we have to assume Pearl is also in danger," I said. "Meanwhile, Sharon and Tim both volunteered to help Harvey at the market today. Let's head back to the Philbrook and see what the rumor mill has stirred up. "

A weak December sun slanted across the sky as we drove into the Philbrook Inn's parking lot. Nellie and I were frustrated. The chief had asked us to gather basic information—the names of Opal's friends and details about Sean Connery. We failed on both assignments. Pearl had resisted every attempt to steer the conversation in either direction.

The market was nearly as crowded as it had been the day before. People strolled from one display to another, while giving a wide berth to the orange cones and caution tape that marked the crime scene where Opal had fallen. When we arrived at Harvey's booth, Sharon was busy restocking shelves, and Harvey had just completed a sale.

Nellie and I complained to Harvey and Tim about our lack of progress on the case, and they were sympathetic. "At this time yesterday, the twins were shopping, here on the plaza." Harvey gazed across the festive crowd. "I'd say you should give yourselves another twenty-four hours before you declare failure."

Tim agreed. "Pearl needed your attention today. She's still in shock. Give her time to grieve before you push for information. The two sisters were really close. Her son arrives tomorrow. Maybe he can help you talk to her."

We knew they were right, but I still felt important clues were slipping away. I wanted to arrest the mystery man and accuse him of murder. Nellie and I stood in line for hot drinks and found an open bench near the food vendors. Leaving the booth in Sharon's capable hands, Tim and Harvey joined us.

"I think Sean Connery did it," I said.

Harvey raised an eyebrow. "What about the woman who argued with Opal just before the incident?"

"What woman? Pearl didn't mention any argument. And neither did you, when we talked after we screened everyone last night."

Harvey shrugged his shoulders. "Today, the village grapevine says it happened. She was a tall woman—taller and heavier than the twins. She wore a red coat, with a purple hat and scarf."

I shook my head, baffled at the news. "When did this happen?"

"Soon after you left them here at the market. They strolled through several booths, chatting and shopping. As they stood at one booth, the woman approached them and started a conversation."

"Did you see it?"

"No. But the security guard stopped by my booth this afternoon, bragging about how he broke up their argument. He said the three ladies began to yell at each other. When he walked toward them, the tall woman in the purple hat ran from the plaza."

"What did Pearl and Opal do?"

"They brushed it off and went back to their shopping."

"They didn't ask the security guard to go after her?"

"No. They told him it was just a misunderstanding."

I threw my hands in the air. "And the security guard didn't think this was important to share yesterday?"

Harvey shook his head. "It happened way before the shooting incident. His shift was over by then. He didn't recall the quarrel until this morning when he realized one of those ladies had fallen into the well later the same day.

Tim elbowed Harvey in the ribs. "Tell her the rest."

"Two additional witnesses showed up this morning," Harvey reported. "Mildred Wilkerson is another doll collector. She was here on the plaza when Opal fell, but she didn't stick around after the ambulance showed up. Now she's claiming she saw everything."

I felt totally blindsided. Nellie and I had worked hard to gather clues for the chief, with zero results, while Harvey and Tim had stumbled on new leads simply by hanging out at the Christmas Market. "How do you know all of this?" I asked.

"The woman is over at the food court, blabbing to anyone who will listen. She says the chief didn't believe her." He motioned to the small crowd gathered around a heavyset woman. She looked about fifty-five or sixty. Her round face glistened with excitement as she held their attention. She wore a festive top made of a poinsettia-patterned fabric; her hair wound into a tight bun atop her head. I could see her hands waving in the air. Ms. Wilkerson obviously adored being in the spotlight.

Tim answered before I even asked the question. "Yes, we called the chief. A patrolman will be here soon. They will politely tell her to stop talking. She may poison the potential jury pool."

"Who is the other witness?"

"An older man, bald, with a stooped posture and a slight limp. His name is Howard Phillips. He is a retired private detective, here to visit the Christmas Market."

My head was spinning. "All of these people saw Opal fall into the well?"

"Plus the twenty the chief interviewed last night," Harvey said.

Nellie frowned at me. "I'd be surprised if the stories match."

"Me, too. I'd better get started on a giant spreadsheet. The chief will need to sort all the leads."

Nellie took my arm. "Let's get out of here. You have work to do."

We left Tim and Harvey at the market and hurried to Nellie's car. This case grew more complex by the minute. I wasn't sure where to begin. The victim's own sister was hiding information, while strangers appeared from nowhere. Nellie drove in silence.

I turned to her from the passenger seat. "Can we make one more stop?"

"The police station?" Nellie asked the question as she pulled into the parking lot.

"Yes. I have an idea, but the chief may not approve."

Chief Marshall sat across from us in the small conference room where he and I had pondered many conundrums together. The smell of burnt coffee permeated the air; I figured the odor would always be there. The chief rubbed his eyes and leaned back in his chair.

"What have you got for me, Josie?"

I told him about our colossal failure to gain any headway with Pearl. Nellie chimed in with details on the woman's refusal to identify the mystery man or discuss Opal's friends. The chief pulled a pair of reading glasses out of

41

his front pocket and put them on his face, peering at me from behind the silver frames.

"I've never seen you in glasses before!"

"They're new." His gruff answer told me he wasn't pleased about the addition. "I have twenty-seven sworn statements to read, and I find the glasses help with eye strain."

"Twenty-seven?"

"That's correct. Most are from last night's group at the inn. A couple called the station this morning. And we have both Howard Phillips and Mildred Wilkerson who showed up today."

"Does the number include the two extras I sent you last night? The meek little lady who heard gunshots and the round gentlemen with owl eyes?"

The chief shuffled the papers in front of him. "Yes, Josie. The woman is Ruth Stewart, age forty-five. A nervous little woman. Doll collector. In town because our Christmas Market was mentioned in a recent doll collector newsletter as *a quaint place to visit* on the way to area doll shows."

I nodded. "That's the one."

"The man's name is Michael Fuller. Age fifty. A small-town banker from Lindsborg, just up the road. Said it was his civic duty to tell me everything he knew."

"Twenty-seven?"

"Give or take a few."

"Who are we missing?"

"I haven't tracked down the two who left messages on Opal's phone at the hotel—Edward Gower and the unnamed guy who claimed Opal owes him money."

"But they weren't in town when it happened."

"We can't assume that."

I stared at him, realizing he was right. There was no way to tell where they were when they recorded the calls. "What shall we do next?"

Chief Marshall shook his head and set both his hands on the old metal table. "*We* do nothing."

"Nothing?" I hated when the chief told me to 'stand down.'

"Keep your eyes open. Let me know if Pearl talks. We have plenty of leads to follow for the next few days. Our officers will go through the statements and review a few photos from witnesses."

"There are photos?"

"Yes. Your nervous doll collector even made a video of the carolers on her cell phone. Pearl and Opal are clearly in the background."

"Can we see it?"

"I'm having it enhanced at the lab in Wichita right now. We want to magnify it and get a slow-motion version."

Nellie and I looked at each other, disappointed.

"Our department will reconstruct the event to the best of our abilities. By this time tomorrow, I should have a pretty good idea of the chain of events."

"Do you still want the spreadsheet?"

"Sure. Send it over as a live file. Devon can add notes about key observations from each witness."

"Chief?"

"Yes, Josie."

"I had one more thought that might be helpful."

Chief Marshall looked at me without commenting. It should have been a signal for me to do the same, but I couldn't.

"I think there's a connection between the doll collectors, the antique dealer, and the twins. I'd like to check it out."

"How do you intend to do that, Josie?"

"I can make a few calls and pretend I am asking questions for the story I'm writing about Pearl. The doll collectors will talk to me, as a reporter. You never know. I could stumble across something that would explain why Opal argued with the woman in the purple hat."

The chief rubbed his chin in that thoughtful way of his. "I'd prefer that you stay away from anyone who might be a suspect, Josie."

"Do we have a suspect?"

"Not yet. No one except your mystery man, Sean Connery."

"Then I shouldn't have any problem. We don't know who he is."

He glared at me before he gave in. "Treat this like one of your stories for

The Gazette. Make calls to learn more about these doll collectors. But if you discover anything that might relate to this murder—a feud, an argument, a tiff—bring it to me immediately. Do not explore it on your own."

How could a few calls to doll collectors cause trouble? I hoped to discover how others in the industry felt about Pearl. Was she respected as a leader, or hated as a competitor? I imagined most doll collectors were sweet little old ladies. How would any of them commit murder?

"I wouldn't think of it," I assured the chief.

And I meant it when I said it. I really did.

Chapter Seven

Friday Morning

Morning brought fresh snow. I shivered in my bathrobe while Moe romped in the backyard like an overgrown bunny. He pounced on the new drifts and buried his head deep under the bushes, emerging with his favorite bone. When he returned with snow caked around his nose and paws, I welcomed him at the door, wrapped him in a beach towel, and rubbed him dry. This happy sheepdog never failed to lift my spirits.

While Moe devoured his breakfast, I cradled my steaming coffee mug in both hands and studied the blizzard of note cards scattered across Grandma Molly's long antique table—messy evidence from my late-night efforts.

I studied the aftermath of my research with satisfaction. After several hours, I had accomplished three important goals. First, I completed the spreadsheet for Chief Marshall. Now, he could easily sort the list of witnesses by age, occupation, location, and three other pivot points. He could compare statements between witnesses who heard a gunshot, those who observed the argument, and those who saw Opal fall into the wishing well. With the click of a button, my spreadsheet would plot the precise times when the people saw, or heard, the event they described.

A second pile of notes documented the world of dolls. I had surfed the internet for information about dolls and their collectors. Then, I assembled a list of doll shows taking place in our area and studied recent news feeds for stories about doll auctions. The resulting printouts contained dozens of interesting facts—including some about the Coronation Doll Opal gave Pearl during our tea.

After midnight, I had researched organizations that served doll collectors. One stood above the others. The United Federation of Doll Clubs offered an abundance of news, educational resources, and support for serious doll collectors. Even better, they were located just a few hours away, in Kansas City. It surprised me to learn their offices were a short drive from my old stomping grounds when I was a crime reporter for the *Kansas City Star*. The federation also ran a doll museum with a permanent collection and special exhibits. I had probably driven past the place many times without noticing it.

My eyes were blurry from staring at my computer monitor, but I was eager to meet the mavens for coffee at Cozy Cups. I had asked Nellie to rally the other mavens for a morning brainstorming session. We had work to do. And the tasks now called for undercover work that included some travel. Quickly, I showered and dressed in warm woolen slacks and a bulky red sweater. There were still a few tasks to accomplish before I drove to the little café.

First, I called Pearl to see whether she needed anything. Paige answered. "Pearl Merriweather's, this is Paige."

"Good morning, Paige. This is Josie. I'm calling to check on Pearl. How is she?"

Paige spoke in a hushed tone. "She's still sleeping, Ms. Posey. The doctor gave her some medication to help her rest. She took a pill after her bath. That's why I stayed overnight. Her son arrives today, but I didn't want her to wake up to an empty house."

"Thank you for doing that. I'm sure Pearl appreciates your concern."

"I'll make her a hot breakfast. Then I need to go to class. She should be awake soon."

"Paige, did Nellie contact you?"

"Yes. I have an entire list of questions to ask if I get the opportunity. Mrs. Merriweather is usually at her best in the mornings. She loves to tell me stories about her childhood and about her dolls. You must visit the dolls the next time you're here. They fill two upstairs bedrooms!"

"I'd love to see her collection. *The Gazette* scheduled a photographer to take a few pictures of the dolls on Saturday. We will most likely postpone that appointment."

"She calls them her girls."

I chuckled. "I'm sure she's quite attached to each of them."

"Most of the dolls are in glass cases. She keeps a few of them locked in a safe, so I know they must be valuable."

"I can't wait to interview her, when she feels up to it. Please let her know I called."

Bundling the notes into two separate piles, I stuffed them into envelopes. One set was for the chief, the other for the mavens. Nellie called as I pulled several photos off my printer. "The snow is a little deeper today. Do you need a ride?"

I glanced out the window and saw that Harvey had cleared my drive again this morning. Owning a VW Bug convertible was clearly more advantageous in the summer, but I hated to make Nellie chauffeur me two days in a row. "I think Piper will make it as long as the major roads are cleared."

"Call me if you get stuck somewhere," Nellie said. She drove a four-wheel-drive SUV, and she wasn't afraid to take it off-road if necessary.

"You know I will."

"See you at Cozy Cups at ten o'clock. Everyone will be there."

I glanced at my watch. In order to stop by the police station, I needed to pull out of my driveway in ten minutes. As I changed from my house slippers to a warm pair of UGG boots, I ran through a final checklist in my head. *Lights off. Doors locked. Paperwork ready.*

Slinging my bag over my shoulder, I glanced back at Moe. He dozed on the rug in front of the fireplace and barely raised his head to watch me go. "Be good, boy. I will see you this afternoon."

The chief was not available when I arrived. Officer Devon offered to give him my research, but I declined. The young patrolman was likely to pile my notes in the middle of Chief Marshall's already overflowing desk. I preferred to hand-deliver the information to him myself.

It was too early to meet the mavens, so I visited the Pet Stop instead. Barbara Chamberlin greeted me from behind her glass bakery display. "I have something new for Moe!" Barbara's smile was so wide it covered her face. She wore her traditional black pants and red apron, but she had added a festive Santa hat to her uniform.

"That's why I'm here," I said.

Barbara opened her case with a flourish. "These are fresh out of the oven!" She brought a tray of goodies from the shelves and set them on the counter. "We have Gingerbread Men, Apple Cranberry Biscuits, and Peppermint Pinwheels."

I admired the colorful cookies. "They look good enough to eat."

"They're only for dogs," Barbara reminded me. "Moe will love them. Guaranteed. That sheepdog of yours is still my best customer."

"He is definitely a fan," I said. "Give me three of each. We'll share a few with Kate's dog."

Barbara bagged my order and tucked a flier into the sack before she lowered her voice so a customer who browsed near the window couldn't hear her comment. "I heard about Nellie's Aunt Opal," she said. "Are you working on the case with Chief Marshall?"

I leaned closer to her. "Not officially," I answered. "But I'm supposed to keep my ears open for any leads that might pop up."

"Got it." Barbara winked. "You'd be surprised at the conversations I overhear when shoppers think they are alone in a pet store," she said. "Just between us, there's already speculation about whether Opal was the intended victim. Pearl is her identical twin, you know?"

"Yes, I'm aware of that," I said. "Rumors are often based on a nugget of truth, so I'd appreciate any tidbits you hear."

"Sure. I'll let you know if I learn anything that might help."

I marveled at Barb's energy. She arrived at the shop early each morning to bake most of her own treats. The woman retired from a corporate job two years earlier and opened the dog bakery soon after. Now, the shop drew customers from a sixty-mile radius. One of them might easily unveil a potential lead to the engaging store owner.

"Thank you, Barb." I paid my bill, and she raised her voice to call out to me as I made my way toward the exit.

"Don't forget to bring Moe in next Saturday for a picture with Santa," she said. "I'll have free Canine Candy Canes."

I grabbed a few extra fliers for the mavens and promised to return with Moe for the Santa event.

The mavens had already helped themselves to coffee when I walked into Cozy Cups. We gathered around the conversation area near the front windows, and Lorene set a platter of cinnamon rolls on the table in front of us. "These are on the house. People complained about the enormous size of our cinnamon rolls, so I made a batch of minis. See what you think of them."

Kate groaned. "I can't resist the regular cinnamon rolls. When they are bite-size, I'll probably devour twenty of them." She sat with her pen poised over a legal pad. "Let's get started, ladies. I have a hair appointment at eleven thirty." I smiled at my friend's impatience. She was always our most punctual maven—probably a habit she developed in her military service. But her comment had the desired effect: the group turned to me, expectantly.

I pulled a stack of papers out of my tote bag and handed one to each of the mavens. "This is a list of people and places we need to investigate," I said.

"Has the chief approved it?" Sharon's question caught me off guard. I expected it to come from Kate—the one with the greatest respect for rules.

"Not exactly."

"Maybe you should explain what that means?" Nellie prompted me to continue.

I nodded. "What I meant to say was that I'm sure the chief will approve. I just haven't shared details with him, yet."

"But he knows you're looking into the doll collecting aspect?" Sharon studied the list in front of her as she asked the question.

"Yes. He said I could pursue any research related to the story I'm writing on Nellie's aunt, Pearl Merriweather. She's a doll collector. All

49

of this information fits those parameters. When you review the list, you'll understand why I need your help: everything happens this weekend."

Kate gazed up at me through her oval tortoiseshell frames. "This looks interesting. I'd like to talk to the banker, Michael Fuller. And I can call a few local auctioneers to learn more about the values of doll collections."

"Done." I checked two items off my list.

Sharon raised her hand. "I'll do the road trip to Kansas City. I've always wanted to tour the doll museum, and I can easily talk to the United Federation of Doll Clubs. I'll ask about their membership and see what collections they have on display."

"Sounds good," I said. "Those are located near each other, Sharon. You can easily visit the UFDC museum in the morning, have lunch on the Plaza, and be home by mid-afternoon."

Nellie's eyes sparkled at the thought of adventure. "I want to visit the Wichita Doll Show. It's minutes away, and I can see what other collectors say about Pearl and her competitors."

Kate glanced through the list again. "My conversations with the banker and auctioneer won't take long. How about if I also take the Tulsa Doll Convention on Sunday? Maybe Lorene can go along. If not, I'm happy to explore on my own."

I made a few notes on the sheet in front of me. "Thank you, ladies. I will talk to Ruth Stewart and Mildred Wilkerson this weekend. Both are doll collectors who were at the Christmas Market the day Opal fell. They should be able to tell me something about why they were there, and what they saw."

Kate picked up her car keys and draped her handbag over her shoulder. "Before I go, is there anything specific you want us to find?"

I realized I'd forgotten the most important instructions. "Yes! Watch for a large woman in a red coat and purple hat and scarf. She argued with Opal at the market. Several people witnessed it, but no one knows her name. If you see her, let me know, and I'll contact the chief."

"Anything else?" Sharon spoke out for the group.

"Jot down your observations as you go. And be careful. There's a killer out there who wanted something badly enough to murder a lovely old woman.

Our job is to figure out *who* killed Opal, and *why*. Get names and phone numbers of helpful contacts, but don't put yourself at risk."

I left Cozy Cups filled with optimism. My mind raced so fast I almost didn't see the car that followed on my tail. If he hadn't kept creeping closer to my bumper and begun flashing his lights at me, I might not have noticed the guy at all.

Chapter Eight

Friday Midday

I t was broad daylight on a Friday. I drove two blocks down the center of the village with an idiot tailing me so close I could almost smell his breath. Was he crazy? When the flashing headlights weren't enough to get my undivided attention, he began to repeatedly beep his horn.

I peered into my rearview mirror and tried to rationalize his behavior. Maybe a Good Samaritan desperately wanted to tell me my trunk was open, or that I'd lost my handbag. I didn't recognize the vehicle. It was a big black thing with tinted windows—just like the mafia cars in the late-night movies. Maybe doll collectors had their own organized crime ring, and I was their target. Who knew?

In an abundance of caution, I did the first thing that came into my head: I dialed Chief Marshall. Ever since we had worked together on another case, I had saved his cell number on my speed dial. I tried not to use it often. While it rang, I circled the block. The kingpin followed, lights and horn still blaring. The chief answered, his deep voice already soothing my nerves.

"What is it, Josie?"

"A guy is following me. A strange guy, in a big black vehicle."

"Where are you?"

"About two minutes from the police station."

"Pull around back. I'll meet you at the door."

Now I worried about what the crazy man might do to the chief, but he was more qualified to deal with the situation. The car stayed on my tail, honking its way down Main Street and around the corner. When I pulled into the police station's rear parking lot, he followed, blocking me into the parking space. I jumped from my car and dashed for the door, where Chief Marshall stood on the threshold. I leaped behind him for protection.

The headlights and horn continued to blast away until, finally, the mafia man turned off the ignition and opened his door.

"Stop where you are!" The chief walked toward the car, aiming his gun at the driver.

"Hands up, where I can see them."

I watched from a distance. To my surprise, a bald, old man climbed out of the vehicle. He didn't look the least bit dangerous. He walked with a limp, stooped over, hands held high in the air.

The chief holstered his weapon and called him by name. "Mr. Phillips. Put your hands down. What are you doing, disturbing the peace of our fine community?"

"I apologize, sir. I saw Ms. Posey leave the café, and I wanted to get her attention."

"You succeeded," the chief said.

The old man turned to me. There was something familiar about him, but I couldn't place it. His eyes? His voice? I watched him cautiously.

"Sorry, ma'am. That darned switch on my headlights went haywire, and before I knew it, the horn was beeping, too. I'm driving a rental, so I can't really say what happened. I didn't mean to startle you."

Finally, I found my voice to respond. "Why did you want to speak to me?"

"Well, that's the interesting thing." He spoke with an exaggerated southern drawl.

I waited, puzzled by his country-boy mannerisms. The man wore a bow tie but talked like a cowboy.

"As the chief knows, I used to be a private detective. I'm in town to visit the Christmas Market, and I met your young fella at his booth. The artist. Harvey."

"Harvey suggested you chase me down?"

Mr. Phillips laughed a hearty farmer-style belly laugh. I couldn't help feeling there was something incongruous about him: such a big laugh coming from a weak old man's body. "Nope. You see, I'm on the hunt for a chandelier. He told me about one you have hanging over your dining room table. Harvey offered to get me a photograph. But I saw you driving right in front of me, and I figured maybe I could just follow you home and see it for myself."

"I'm sorry, Mr. Phillips, but that's impossible. I have a huge, vicious dog at home. He would never let you inside. I'd suggest you work with Harvey. If he wants to show it to you, I'll take the dog out of the house while Harvey shows you the chandelier."

Chief Marshall chimed in beside me. "That's a fact, Mr. Phillips. I've witnessed Ms. Posey's watchdog in action. You don't want to go near her place without an invitation."

The old man stood there, nodding his head. "Well, alrighty then. I'll talk to Mr. Jacobs."

We watched as he climbed into his vehicle and drove away.

"Thank you, Chief."

"You're welcome, Josie. Lock your car and come inside, if you have the time."

"I'll bring your spreadsheet."

We sat at the chief's old metal table. I hesitated before I handed him the printed spreadsheet and a bright red thumb drive that held the live version.

"Chief? Where did that man come from? Should I add him to your spreadsheet?"

"Mr. Phillips?"

"Yes. I've never seen him around here."

The chief leaned back in his chair and crossed his arms. "He's a retired private detective from Missouri. He showed up yesterday as a visitor at the Christmas Market. When he heard about the incident with the doll collector's sister, he was quick to offer his services."

"Did you accept?"

"No. I thanked him for the offer. Then I suggested he enjoy his holiday."

"Would you agree that he's a strange character?"

Chief Marshall laughed at my description. "I'd call him a lookie-loo."

"What?"

"He's harmless, Josie. He misses being part of the action. As a retired investigator, he's itching to help with our case. That's all."

"That's probably what I'm sensing. But how did he know who I am, or what kind of car I drive?"

The chief shook his head. "An experienced investigator could find you in a heartbeat. Everyone in town knows you—and that little red Bug you drive. Most of 'em know you named your car *Piper*."

I shivered to think how easily a stranger could locate me—or anyone— with a little effort. All the more reason to find Opal's murderer and get him, or her, off the streets. The chief and I put our heads together for the next hour, reviewing the long list of witnesses and the information they had provided.

Midway through our discussion, patrolman Devon knocked on the door and poked his head inside. "Lorene brought lunch." He set two boxes on the table, along with containers of hot coffee. I smiled when I saw the writing on the side of my cup: *For Josie—Vanilla Hazelnut + Mocha.* My friend knew I would never drink the burnt coffee from the chief's old glass pot.

"Your wife is a saint," I said.

"Hey, give me some credit," the chief said. "*I* ordered our lunch."

I smiled at his claim. We both knew Lorene had a habit of sending lunch when the chief didn't show up at the café by 12:30. I had no doubt she called the station first. When the staff confirmed I was meeting with the chief, she sent two lunches.

We ate in silence for a few minutes, savoring the hot pastrami sandwiches. Then I waved at the pile of paperwork on the table.

"I thought it would be easy to identify the murderer, with so many people on the plaza when it happened." I looked at the chief over the lengthy spreadsheet spread between us. "Instead, the crowded Christmas Market worked in the killer's favor. The place was packed with merchants and shoppers, strollers and carolers, food trucks and sleigh wagons. Everyone was distracted by the festive bustle around them."

"Nothing about this case is easy." Chief Marshall waved his ballpoint pen at the mound of paperwork.

I looked at him over the rim of my coffee cup. "What do the witnesses say? Do any of their stories match?"

The chief handed me a single sheet of paper. "This is the sum of our knowledge, based on eyewitness accounts. We made meticulous notes of every observation. Then we deleted any uncorroborated items."

"So, if only one person mentioned it, the information was removed? What if that person saw the murderer?"

"No one did. At least, no one who has come forward so far. The people we interviewed only agreed upon the list you see in front of you."

I read the list while he waited.

1. The plaza was crowded and dark. The holiday lights were bright but didn't fill in shadowy areas.
2. It was cold. Everyone wore coats, hats, scarves. They were bundled up; it was hard to see faces.
3. It was noisy. The carolers had gathered to sing. People jostled for the best spot to watch the performance.
4. The rock ledge around the wishing well was crowded.
5. One woman heard a "pop." Two others heard a "crack" and looked toward the sky, thinking there might be fireworks.
6. One person saw someone in a red coat running from the scene.
7. One person saw Opal fall backward into the well. Two others heard screams and then saw that she had fallen into the well.
8. Some people ran toward the benches, including the ones at the wishing well.

The chief watched as I waved the paper in front of him. "That's it? No one saw a gun, or a shove?"

"No one. All the other witnesses made statements that contradicted each other. One man saw a drone flying above the wishing well. A woman claimed it was a toy airplane some kid threw to his sister. For every person who saw someone wearing a red coat, someone else reported a green coat, or a black jacket."

"How is that possible?"

"These people are trying to help, Josie. If our killer wore a pink tutu and carried a rifle, someone might have noticed. But he didn't. He looked like everyone else on the plaza that night. He approached the wishing well in a non-threatening way. He either shot Opal—knocking her over—or shot her and shoved her. She toppled into the well."

"What about the gun?"

"No one saw a gun."

"But Opal was shot!"

"Yes. The bullet most likely came from a small pocket pistol. It was a .22 caliber. The trauma surgeon pulled it out of Opal's lung. He said the bullet would have given her a jolt at close range, but it didn't kill her. She hit her head on the river rocks at the bottom of the well. The blow to her head caused her death."

"Can't you match the bullet to a gun?"

"If we have a gun, yes."

"What about other evidence? Fingerprints?"

The chief sighed. "With few exceptions, everyone at the scene wore winter gloves."

"We know Opal's blue quilted bag is missing, but no one mentioned it?"

"No."

I told the chief the Mahjong Mavens were traveling to three area doll shows this weekend. "We will have ladies in Kansas City, Wichita, and Tulsa."

He smiled. "Nice job, Josie. You never know what you might learn at a doll show."

"Are you making fun of me?"

"Not at all. I appreciate your dedication to the story you're writing."

I grinned at him. "I'm also calling Ruth Stewart and Mildred Wilkerson. They are on the witness list, but both are doll collectors."

"Be careful, Josie."

"I will. Someone out there killed an innocent woman. If his only purpose was to steal the valuable doll, he must have been dismayed to discover he had taken an empty bag."

The chief frowned. "Trouble is, he hasn't given up his search. He broke into Opal's room in an attempt to find the doll, but she had locked it in the safe."

"He will likely keep trying until he succeeds," I said.

Chief Marshall clenched his fist on the table. "We have to find him before he harms anyone else."

I studied the chief's tired eyes. "How can I help?"

"The Wichita crime lab should have the videos ready by tomorrow. I'll need you to look at them to see if you recognize anyone. Maybe they will point us to the murderer." The chief stood and opened the door, signaling that it was time for me to leave.

He walked me to my car and gave me a wink. "Now go home and give that ferocious dog of yours a treat."

Chapter Nine

Friday Evening

Harvey called as I drove home from the police station. I pulled into the post office parking lot and turned off my radio. "Hey."

"Where are you, Josie? I've been trying to reach you."

"At the post office. Did you need something? I'm on my way home, but I could swing by the Philbrook if you are shorthanded at your booth."

"No, I wanted you to be on the lookout for a pushy guy who stopped by my booth."

"If it's the private detective, we already met." I looked over my shoulder to make certain the black vehicle wasn't tailing me.

Harvey practically jumped through my cell phone. "What? I never gave him your name or address. He wanted to see pictures of my iron chandelier work. I left him at the Christmas Market while I drove to the hardware store for the photos. By the time I returned, he was gone."

"How would he get my name?"

"Someone at the market must have told him."

"It's odd that he would see me walk out of the café and attempt to follow me home."

"You didn't let him into your house, did you?"

"Nope. I led him to the police station, and Chief Marshall sent him away."

I could hear the relief in Harvey's voice. "Josie, you are unbelievably smart."

"I wasn't smart. I was frightened." Harvey listened as I told him about my

59

race to the police station, the honking stranger close on my tail. He asked questions about the color of the car and the route I drove. When I repeated the conversation about my ferocious watchdog, he laughed.

"That should keep him away from your door!"

The story was amusing now, but I couldn't dispel the shadow of fear that hovered over me. "Mr. Phillips was persistent. The chief thinks he wants access to our investigation. Could the chandelier be an excuse to get closer to me, because I'm helping with the case?"

Harvey was silent.

"Harvey?"

"I'm still here. Just replaying the encounter with Mr. Phillips in my mind. The entire conversation was odd, now that I think of it. I didn't have any chandeliers on display, but he asked to see them. The whole town knows about the one I made for you last summer. It's possible he contrived the interest in my work as a way to get introduced to you. Once you met, he could ask you about the case."

I considered Harvey's conclusion, but it seemed like a convoluted way for the detective to get access to the murder investigation. "That's possible," I said. "But it's more likely that he really wants a handmade chandelier. He probably asked someone at the market where he might find one, and they sent him your way. Regardless, I felt uncomfortable around him. It's a good thing I have Moe for protection."

"And *I'm uncomfortable* with your involvement in another murder case," Harvey said. "Be careful, Josie. Lock your doors."

I checked my rearview mirror all the way home, where I pulled safely into my garage with a sigh of relief. Despite Harvey's not-so-subtle hint that I back away from the case, the incident with Mr. Phillips only made me more determined to find Opal's killer. I began by contacting the sweet-faced doll collector I met the night Opal died. Ruth Stewart sounded surprised to hear my voice.

"Ms. Posey! I remember you, but I already told the police everything I know."

I smiled into the phone, hoping she would sense the friendly vibrations.

"Yes. Thank you for that. But I'm not calling today about murder. I want to know more about dolls."

"Dolls?"

"I'm writing a story for *The Village Gazette,* and I am hopelessly lost."

The woman's voice fell into a relaxed tone. Her tinkling laughter startled me with its eagerness. "How can I help you?"

"I'm not sure where to begin. Could you provide some basic information about doll collecting? What attracts people to become collectors? Are they all women? How do they decide which dolls to collect? Do they see each other as friends with a common interest—or as competitors? Is it a hobby or a business?"

I stopped, slightly out of breath. In my experience, people were happy to share information about the subjects they enjoyed most. I hoped Ruth Stewart was one of them.

"How much time do you have?" Ruth asked. "I'm free for the next thirty minutes, if you'd like to talk now." Her voice was all business, and I was happy to seize the opportunity.

"Let's attempt an overview right now," I said. "Then, we can talk again in a few days, if I'm still fuzzy on details once I begin to write the article."

"Agreed," Ruth said.

I grabbed my pen as Ruth jumped immediately into her topic.

"Here's what you need to know," she began. "Every story is unique. Some collectors begin as little girls. They fall in love with their first baby doll and continue to acquire more through a passion that lasts a lifetime. Others don't become collectors until they are widowed or divorced. The dolls fill an empty space in their hearts. They are mostly women—but a few men collect dolls, too. In my opinion, the women are emotionally connected to their dolls; the men are looking for a return on their investment. Although, both can result in valuable collections."

I was interested to learn that doll collecting might begin at any age and for diverse reasons. "Are there different categories of collections? I know most model train collectors choose between HO or N sizes, for example. Do doll collectors specialize, as well?"

"Oh, yes," Ruth said. "That's why there are so many types of doll shows. Some conventions are limited only to baby dolls. Others include only bisque or porcelain dolls. The variety is remarkable."

I jotted notes on my ever-present cards as she spoke. Sometimes, the smallest comments led to important breakthroughs. My goal was to discover one of those unexpected clues.

"Have you ever heard of a doll collection owned by Queen Elisabeth of Romania?"

Ruth didn't hesitate with her reply. "Absolutely. Every serious collector knows the story of Carmen Sylva. She gathered a huge collection of stunning quality. Then, she shared it in a traveling charity exhibit. Every doll survived the tour. Then, mysteriously, the collection disappeared. It was more than a century ago. No one knows when they will surface—but we dream of seeing them."

Ruth told the story as though it were a fairy tale. She seemed like a different person from the nervous woman I had seen the evening of Opal's death. I knew I shouldn't keep her on the phone much longer, but I had several more questions to ask. Referring to my notes, I shifted the conversation in a new direction.

"What about the interactions between collectors? Are they generally friendly toward each other?"

"People are people, Ms. Posey. Some collectors are polite and helpful. Others are rude and hateful. I think the friendly ones outnumber the others by at least twenty-to-one."

"What about Pearl? Is she considered a friendly collector?"

"She's one of the best. My first doll show, Pearl introduced herself and made me feel welcome. Everyone respects her. During her tenure on the UFDC board, membership grew significantly. Pearl has always been an ambassador for doll collectors worldwide."

"That reminds me: I saw a man at the Philbrook. I think he is a doll collector, but I didn't get his name. He was tall, wearing a black coat with a cape. He had a Sean Connery beard. Do you know him?"

"Oh my! What a perfect description!" Ruth chuckled as she recalled the mystery man. "I noticed him in the lobby of the hotel; but, unfortunately, I've never seen him before. He spoke with a British accent."

"Interesting," I said. "I didn't notice his accent; I just saw him argue with Pearl. She raised her voice to him."

"There you go! It should be easy to find out who he is. Just ask Pearl for his name."

Ruth made an excellent point—one I wanted to avoid. "I will, eventually. She is still reeling from her sister's death."

"I understand. It was a tragic accident. She must be devastated. Is there anything else?"

"There was a woman on the plaza that day. She wore a red coat with a purple hat and scarf. Did you see her?"

"No, I'm sorry. I don't recall anyone fitting that description."

I fought the urge to question Mrs. Stewart about the gunshot she reported to the police. Instead, I ended the call with a promise to phone again. "I'm sure I will have additional questions."

"And I will try to answer them!" She seemed pleased that I considered her an expert.

We ended the call and I shuffled through my notecards, selecting two of them from the stack. On one I had written "British accent?" I underlined the note and placed it under a yellow glass paperweight; this was the stack designated for additional research.

The second card held two questions: "Bisque? Year?" I jotted Pearl's name on the card and slid it into the paperweight stack. It would be interesting to learn what types of dolls our local collector preferred.

Throughout the afternoon, my earlier encounter with the private investigator from Missouri nagged at the corners of my mind. Finally, I opened my laptop. It was time to investigate the investigator. Turning to Google for assistance, I typed his name into the browser: Howard Phillips. In less than a second, I had 142 million results—from politicians to video game producers. I laughed aloud, and Moe came to look over my shoulder.

"Let's narrow the search, Moe." This time, I typed his name but added an occupation and a location: Private Investigator. Missouri. There were hundreds of results, but no exact match. If Mr. Phillips had practiced in the state of Missouri, he had successfully maintained a low profile.

Still curious, I checked the professional registration board in the state and found no one named Howard Phillips. I wondered how long he had been retired. It made sense that he would allow his license to lapse. Maybe I misunderstood the chief when he said Phillips lived in Missouri. I repeated my search, using filters for Texas, Oklahoma, Colorado, and Nebraska. Nothing. The screen was blank.

For the next two hours, I scoured the internet for any information about Howard Phillips. I browsed through LinkedIn and studied licensing reports from neighboring states. Baffled at the lack of information on this man, I resorted to Facebook. Still no results. Either Howard Phillips was licensed under a different name—perhaps his initials or his middle name—or he had wiped his online history clean.

I called the chief.

"Hello, Josie. What have you discovered?"

I delivered the news in a single sentence: "Mr. Phillips is an imposter."

Quickly, I described my attempt to learn more about the investigator, and the void of information available. The chief wasn't surprised at my report. Instead, he said it verified his own suspicions.

"I've seen his type before. Doubt he ever had his own detective agency, Josie. *If he was a detective at all*, he probably freelanced for the bigger firms. He may not have been licensed. My guess is that Mr. Phillips never succeeded as an investigator—except in his own mind. He is still looking for a way to be in the limelight. He acts like a big shot because that's what he wants to be."

As the chief talked, I remembered some of the private investigators from my days as a crime reporter. A few were excellent. But many were down-on-their-luck guys hanging onto the fringes of law enforcement, just to stay close to the action. Mr. Phillips appeared to be one of those.

"Do you think he is dangerous?" I asked.

"No," Chief Marshall replied. "He is a sad old man, looking for a way to make a name for himself. He probably travels between small towns, offering his services to understaffed police departments like ours."

"Okay. I'll cross him off my list."

And I would have happily deleted Howard Phillips from my spreadsheets. Except the man popped up on my doorstep that very night.

Chapter Ten

Friday Night

He didn't know it, but when Aaron Neville crooned "The Christmas Song," he filled my cottage with a holiday spirit that simultaneously made me both happy and lonely. I loved the bustle of the season, but it also opened the floodgates to years of beautiful memories.

This was the time when I missed my old life so much it hurt to breathe. I longed for those years when our sons were small enough to leave treats for Santa Claus...the Christmas Eve's when my husband and I stayed up until dawn, filling stockings and placing gifts under the tree. Both of my boys lived too far away to come home this year, so we planned to do a video call, instead. Better than not seeing them at all, I supposed.

Fortunately, I knew how to dispel the nostalgic waves of melancholy: I baked cookies. In defiance of my sadness, I added logs to the fire, lit a pine-scented candle, and cranked up the music. I didn't have a tree yet, but the mantle held fresh greenery and my grandmother's nativity set graced the hearth.

Harvey and I had agreed to visit our local tree farm on Sunday. Three generations of one family still lived and worked on the farm. Every year, people flocked to their gates for hayrides into the wooded fields. I looked forward to selecting the perfect tree. Harvey promised to cut it down and haul it back here to the cottage. We would set the fresh pine tree in the center of the bay window, so it could be seen from Persimmon Road. My neighbors had already decorated for the holidays—with reindeer and a sleigh on the lawn to my east, and a family of snowmen to the west.

I had mixed my dough earlier, using the simple recipe my mother taught me when I was old enough to stand on a step stool and reach the kitchen counter. There was nothing fancy about the ingredients: flour and baking powder, one egg, butter, sugar, vanilla, and a pinch of salt. The trick was in the chilling. I always rolled the sticky dough into a disk, wrapped it in plastic cling, and set it in the refrigerator for two to three hours. In this case, the neglected dough had chilled for three days, but I was confident it would still result in perfect cookies.

I set the dough on the kitchen counter to let it rest while I poured a glass of white wine and preheated the oven. Just as I raised my rolling pin to spread the dough, my cell phone rang. It was Paige.

"I spoke to Pearl," she whispered into the phone. "We need to talk."

"Now?"

"No. She's at the dinner table with her son right now. He has been with her all day, but he has a business call tomorrow morning. He wants to be certain his mother is in good hands during that time."

"What did you have in mind?"

"Could I drive by on my way to work and give you a ride? We can visit in the car before you spend time with Mrs. Merriweather."

"When would she like to meet?"

Paige hesitated. "Actually, she would like you to go bowling with her."

"Bowling! I can't remember the last time I was in a bowling alley!"

"So, you'll go?"

I pictured myself in rented shoes, with my hair pulled into a ponytail, rolling a fifteen-pound ball into the gutter. Then I smiled at the thought of Pearl, barreling her own ball down the lane. "Sure. That sounds like fun."

"I'll be at your house by ten o'clock. Pearl has a lane reserved at eleven."

I set my phone on the kitchen counter and chuckled at the bowling alley image my mind had conjured. I was still laughing when Harvey called.

"Hey, Josie. What are you doing?"

"Baking cookies with Aaron Neville."

Harvey's laugh always made me smile. "What? You aren't buried in notecards and tracking a murderer?"

"Not tonight. I had enough excitement earlier today."

"Good. I hoped you would say that. Would it be okay if I stopped there on my way home? I have something to show you."

"Only if you'll help ice the cookies."

Fifteen minutes later, a car pulled into my driveway. And because I knew Harvey was on his way, I didn't think to look through the keyhole before I unlocked the front door. Mr. Phillips stood at the glass, holding a huge basket filled with wrapped packages.

I glared at him, then opened it a few inches to ask, "Why are you here?"

"Don't worry, little lady. I'm on my way out of town." He motioned to the basket. "This is a peace offering."

"That isn't necessary." Moe hovered behind me, and I heard a growl begin deep in his throat.

"May I come in?"

"No."

I attempted to close the glass door, but he had already shoved one shoe over the threshold. My heart raced as I calculated whether I could hurl the heavy wood front door into his face before he forced his way inside. From the corner of my eye, I saw headlights turn into my drive. Harvey slammed the door of his truck and appeared on the porch behind Mr. Phillips, who had withdrawn his foot from the doorway.

"Can I help you with something?" Harvey demanded.

The old man handed Harvey the basket. "Merry Christmas, buddy. I wanted to pay my respects before I hit the road."

"I'm not your buddy. And you are not welcome here."

"Yes, sir. I understand." Without another word, the old man ambled to his car and drove away.

Harvey set the basket on the porch, stepped inside, and shook the snow from his parka. I poured him a glass of wine and sat beside him at the kitchen island. Somehow, I couldn't stop chattering. It was all nonsense—rapid-fire conversation about Aaron Neville and sugar cookies. Finally, Harvey held his hands up in front of my face.

"Josie, stop."

I looked at him, tears welling in my eyes.

"He's gone. You're safe now."

After a deep breath, I looked at the calm man beside me. "Thank you, Harvey. I'm not frightened, I'm angry. I know the guy is harmless, but he gives me the creeps."

"It appears you have an admirer," Harvey said, trying to lighten the mood. "But you've probably seen the last of him."

"What shall we do with the gift basket?"

"I'll put it in my truck and deliver it to Chief Marshall tomorrow."

For the next hour, we worked side by side to ice the freshly baked cookies. He decorated candy canes and Santas; I frosted the snowflakes and stars. Harvey was clearly the better artist. For the last batch, we adorned tree-shaped cookies with green frosting and added small candy beads as ornaments. When I told him about my bowling invitation, Harvey shook his head. "That would be a sight to see."

It wasn't until after he left that I realized Harvey had never shared whatever he had planned to show me. By then, I felt a little silly for overreacting to the old man with his gift basket. Still, he was an uninvited visitor who got under my skin. I locked my doors and turned off the lights.

In the wee hours of the morning, I woke with a start and blinked my eyes to clear the remnants of a terrible dream. The bedside clock read 3:15. In my nightmare, I had accepted the old man's gift, and the basket exploded in my hands. Sooty flakes floated from the sky, covering me in dust. The old cowboy reared back on a horse and laughed. I screamed for help, but no sound emerged from my throat.

Moe must have sensed my distress, because he sat at the side of the bed, watching me. When I raised my head, he whined and nudged my pillow. Since neither of us could sleep, I slipped into a robe and let the dog out my back door. While I waited for him to return, my phone beeped with a text message. It was from Harvey. His timing was unusual, but the message was a familiar one: "I'm okay. Are you?"

I tapped the thumbs-up emoji and pressed "send."

I was surprised Harvey was awake, too. Maybe our encounter with the old man had also given him nightmares. My dream had felt so real, I wasn't even surprised when a patrol car pulled into my driveway, blue lights flashing. I opened the front door to Chief Marshall, who entered, scanning the room behind me.

"Good morning, Josie." He acted as though we were meeting at Cozy Cups for a ten o'clock coffee break, instead of standing in my living room in the dead of the night.

I turned on the coffee maker. "Coffee?"

The chief's dark eyes were weary. "Thanks. I could use a cup."

He stalled for a few minutes, pulled his spiral notepad out of his pocket, and set it on the counter. "Harvey's okay."

And in that moment I realized something unthinkable had happened. "What? Why wouldn't he be?"

"That gift basket of yours exploded in the back of his truck less than an hour ago."

My hands flew to my mouth. Just like in my dream, I screamed, but the sound wouldn't come. Chief Marshall locked his eyes on mine and placed his hands on my shoulders, forcing me to sit at the kitchen island.

A roar filled my ears. I saw the chief's lips moving but couldn't comprehend the words. Finally, I heard his voice. He repeated the same thing Harvey told me, earlier. "You're safe now."

I swallowed hard before I spoke. "I don't feel safe."

"We believe Mr. Phillips—whoever he is—left the village tonight. He checked out of his room at the Philbrook earlier today. Law enforcement agencies across the state are on the lookout for his car. There's no sign of him, so far."

"What about Harvey?" I believed his text but needed to hear the words again, from the chief.

"Harvey is fine. He will call you tomorrow."

"What happened?"

Chief Marshall pulled up a bar stool and took a seat before he answered. "Harvey's snowplow was in his driveway, so he parked his pickup on the street last night. The package was in the bed of the truck. About an hour ago, an explosion knocked the tailgate off the pickup. There were no other damages, and no injuries."

The word "explosion" ricocheted in my head. "He could have been killed, because of me!" I clenched my hands on the counter to keep them from shaking.

"No, Josie, the blast was a small one," the chief said. "The guy meant to scare you, not injure you."

"It worked." I swallowed hard before I asked, "What now?"

"Our team is with Harvey, gathering evidence. I came here to check on you."

"Thank you, Chief." I poured his coffee—two sugars, no cream—and set it in front of him.

"You and Harvey did the right thing," he said. "Imagine how much worse it would have been, if you had accepted the package into your home."

I shivered at the thought. "Did he kill Opal?"

The chief rubbed his temples. I saw the doubt in his eyes. "We have to assume that he is a suspect. But, I don't think he fits our profile. He's old and moves slowly. As far as we can tell, he had no connection to the twins. He is not a doll collector. He didn't surface until the day after the incident. He inserted himself into the investigation on purpose. That seems contrary to the actions of a murderer."

I agreed with the chief's logic, but I couldn't accept his rational conclusion. "The man tried to plant an explosive in my home," I said. "Why would he target me?"

"Could be, he's angry that I trusted you to help with a case he hoped to crack."

Now that the danger had passed, my mind moved into crime-solving mode. I pictured the frail, bow-tied cowboy with his pushy attitude. "What do you think, Chief? Is he just an unstable old man?"

We went through our standard "means-motive-opportunity" checklist together and ultimately agreed on two important points. First, Mr. Phillips had no clear motive to kill Opal. And second, he did not check into his room at The Philbrook Inn until *the day after* the incident, so presumably, he had no opportunity. Without the motive or the opportunity, the man could not have murdered Opal.

Then Chief Marshall stated the biggest dilemma of all: "The problem is, we don't know what we don't know. The man hid behind a good old boy act that fooled us both. What else was he hiding?"

I felt helpless to answer the question. "We don't even know if Phillips is his real name."

"It doesn't matter," the chief said. "He loves attention, so he won't hide for long. When he's located, we will arrest him as a person of interest in the case."

I refilled my coffee and added cream before I looked across the counter at Chief Marshall. "I should have tried to talk to him."

"No, Josie. Your instincts were correct. I owe you an apology for dismissing your earlier concerns."

I smiled and handed the chief a platter of sugar cookies. "No apology needed. Have a cookie. We can catch bad guys tomorrow."

Chapter Eleven

Saturday Morning

It was barely dawn when I woke again, this time to the ring of my cell phone. Harvey was on the line.

"You still okay?" he asked.

"Yes. And you?"

"Nothing exciting here," he said.

My voice cracked as I began to apologize. "Harvey, I'm sorry I put you in danger. Please forgive me."

"You didn't plant the explosive, Josie, but..."

For a moment, I thought I'd lost my signal. "But?" I prompted.

"We should talk about it in person," he said.

"No. Tell me now." I sat on the edge of my bed and waited for him to continue.

"That basket might have caused far more damage if it had been inside your home," he said. "Your cottage could have erupted in flames. You and Moe caught inside..."

"But it didn't," I said. "We're all fine."

"For now," Harvey said. "But if you continue to investigate this case, the next attempt may succeed. And I don't want to be the one picking up the pieces."

"But..."

"Don't give me any excuses," Harvey interrupted. "I've heard enough."

I shoved down an angry retort and forced myself to answer him in a civil tone. "You're right," I said. "We should talk about this in person."

Harvey's voice was cold as ice on the other end of the line. "I want you to walk away from this, okay?"

"Chief Marshall said the danger is over," I countered. "Today, I will go to the bowling alley with Pearl, make a few phone calls, and finish my article for *The Gazette.* You worry too much."

"Rrriiiight," Harvey stretched the word so I would know he hadn't finished with the subject. "We will talk more on our trip to the tree farm tomorrow."

I forced a cheery smile into my voice. "Sounds good. Have a great day!"

Before I could spend too much time stewing over Harvey's attitude, my cell rang again. Sharon was on the speaker phone in her car, on her way to the doll museum in Kansas City.

"Good morning!" She sang the words into my ear.

I groaned.

Sharon was insistent. "Wake up, sleepyhead. I have coffee-to-go and my GPS is loaded with instructions to the United Federation of Doll Clubs. I'll arrive by the time they open at ten."

I pictured my friend merrily driving on the highway through the Flint Hills, simply to help me gather information. "Have fun today. But be careful."

"I'm going to a *doll museum,* Josie. I think I'm safe." Sharon's voice held a trace of sarcasm.

"I understand," I said. "Still, keep an eye out for a big black car. If anyone follows you, drive straight to a police station."

Sharon realized I was serious. "What happened, Josie? Are you okay?"

I explained my encounter with the bald private investigator and the exploding Christmas basket. "The man—Howard Phillips—has disappeared. It's unlikely that he would go to a doll museum. But, be cautious, anyway."

Sharon pulled her car off the highway and insisted that I repeat every detail. "Are you sure Harvey is okay? What about you? Are you traumatized? How could you sleep, after all the commotion?"

I assured my friend the danger was over. "Chief Marshall says this man only wanted our attention. He hoped to help solve the case. When we excluded him, he went out with a bang."

"I'll say! Poor Harvey. He loves that old truck."

"No worries," I said. "Knowing Harvey, he will have a new tailgate before Christmas."

Sharon repeated her earlier question, and I heard the concern in her voice: "Seriously, are you okay?"

"I'm fine. Thank you for making the road trip today. I hope you enjoy the doll museum."

"I confess, I can't wait to get there," Sharon said. "Did you know I still have my first baby doll? She's riding in the back seat!"

I laughed at her enthusiasm. "I'm sure she will make a wonderful companion."

"Don't be silly, Josie. I'm taking her to see if she qualifies as an antique."

As I turned on the coffee pot for the second time that morning, I reminded Sharon to ask questions about our Sean Connery mystery collector and the woman in the red coat and purple hat. Surely, someone in the organization could identify such colorful personalities.

"Keep your phone nearby," she said. "I'll text if I see anyone suspicious."

"Send pictures," I added. "Meanwhile, I'll alert you if I get any important new leads."

As soon as Sharon ended our call, I dressed, ate a light breakfast, and gathered my notes to phone Mildred Wilkerson. Just after eight-thirty, I placed the call.

"Mrs. Wilkerson, this is Josie Posey."

If she was surprised at my early morning call, she didn't show it. In fact, she seemed happy to hear from me. "Hello, Josie. Please call me Millie." She sounded exactly as others had described her, like a woman in her late fifties with a loud voice.

"Thank you, Millie. I know we haven't met, but I'm—"

"Oh, I *know* who you are," the woman interrupted. "You are the woman investigating Pearl's sister's murder."

"Not today."

"No?"

"Today, I'm writing an article about dolls, and I'm told you are a collector."

"Oh! Yes. I am. What would you like to know?"

"Are you a member of the United Federation of Doll Clubs?"

"Every *serious* collector is a UFDC member." Mildred's voice oozed arrogance.

"How often do you attend the annual convention?"

"Why, every year, of course."

"Does it include a doll show and sale?"

"Certainly! I once saw a woman pay $5,000 *in cash* for a doll at the annual convention. She pulled out a wad of one-hundred-dollar bills and counted fifty of them into the seller's hand."

If she had hoped to impress me, she had succeeded. "Whoa. That seems like a lot to pay for a doll, Mildred," I said.

"It's Millie," she repeated. "And buyers often spend thousands of dollars for a doll, when it fits into their collection."

I jotted notes onto the legal pad in front of me, resorting to shorthand to capture her comments word for word. Millie seemed delighted to share her knowledge. "May I ask, what kind of dolls do you collect?"

Mildred launched into a description of her collection—largely composition dolls from the 1920s–1940s. "I prefer dolls made in America," she said. "But I'm particularly interested in specific character dolls."

"Character dolls?" Clearly, Millie was far more familiar with the world of dolls than I, after my brief foray into Google.

"Yes. For example, I collect the Campbell Kids dolls from the twenties, but not the Tiny Tears dolls from more recent years."

I was beginning to understand that this industry was far more complex than I had imagined. "How do you decide which ones to buy—and how to determine their value?" I asked.

Mildred sighed to signal my ignorance before she replied. When she spoke, she slowed her words as though addressing a child. "Surely you can understand, Josie? I look for only the best quality. If I can find one still in the original packaging, I'll pay more for it. But sometimes I find a rare doll that I absolutely must have, regardless of a few small imperfections."

"That makes sense," I said. "What can you tell me about Pearl Merriweather's collection?"

For the first time in our conversation, Mildred hesitated. "Pearl Merriweather is known for her *antique* dolls. Most were made in Germany or France. They are quite valuable, of course. But I find them less interesting than my own collection."

I sensed the competition between the two collectors. "Would you say Pearl is a respected doll collector?"

She hedged in her answer. "She is well known. She served on the UFDC board of directors. People listen to her. But I dare say she isn't as well-respected as a few others. I mean, I don't like to brag, but *my following* is certainly larger than hers."

"Mrs. Wilkerson, you appear to know everyone in the doll business. I wonder if you could help me identify some people?"

She laughed loudly at my assumption. *"Pa-lease* call me Millie," she reminded me for the third time. "I do know *almost* everyone. May I introduce you to someone?"

"Do you know a tall man with a British accent and a Sean Connery beard? I saw him at the Philbrook; he was wearing a coat with a cape."

Millie answered immediately. "No. I can't say that I do. Are you certain he is a collector?"

"Unfortunately, no."

"Is there anyone else?" She was eager to demonstrate her expansive knowledge.

"I wonder whether you noticed another doll collector at the Christmas Market? She was tall, wearing a red coat with a purple hat and scarf."

"Aha!" Millie seized on the description. "I saw that woman. She was rude—shoving through the crowd in a big hurry. The lady nearly knocked one of the carolers to the ground!"

Millie rambled on, describing the woman in greater detail. "She wore black boots, and her stride was long. Honestly, she moved across the plaza in about five giant steps. I noticed because she carried one of those lovely quilted Vera Bradley bags. It is new this season: pale blue with gold stitching."

The mention of the quilted bag startled me. Opal carried a similar bag that went missing when she fell into the well! "Do you know the woman's name?" I asked.

"No. But if *she's* a doll collector, I'll *eat* that purple hat she was wearing."

"Why do you say that?"

"She was a large, loud, overbearing woman. Noticeable, but not in a good way. If she had attended a doll show, I would have remembered her."

I thanked Millie and ended the call. The conversation had provided additional insights into the world of dolls, but nothing new about Sean Connery or Ms. Purple Hat. I wondered whether the mystery woman had stolen Opal's quilted bag, or coincidentally had one of her own. I didn't believe in coincidences when it came to investigating a murder case. But, without her name, the lead was useless. I hoped the Mahjong Mavens would have more success during today's road trips than I did with the call to Millie.

It was barely nine in the morning and I already felt frustrated. I placed the phone on top of my notes and turned to see Moe at the door. He sat patiently, his leash draped from his mouth to the floor. The sight was comical but effective. I pulled on my boots and parka to take him outside. We walked to the corner and back, then shook the snow off our feet as we stomped back into the house.

Paige arrived promptly at ten, in a silver SUV with four-wheel drive. I slipped into the passenger seat. "Thank you for driving!"

She grinned at me. "I was afraid your Bug might not make it through the snow drifts. Mrs. Merriweather insisted that we carpool to the bowling lanes."

I rolled my eyes. "You realize I haven't bowled in at least twenty years?"

Paige tossed her long braid over her shoulder. "Don't worry. Mrs. Merriweather will give us some pointers."

My young chauffeur turned carefully onto the snow-packed road. "I had an opportunity to question Pearl about your Sean Connery mystery man," she said.

"What did she tell you?"

"She said he was a pain in the tuchus."

"The tuchus?"

"Yes, Mrs. Merriweather said it means *the rear end.*"

"I know what it means, Paige. I hoped for something more specific—like a name or an occupation."

"According to Pearl, Mr. Connery arrived, unannounced, at her home. He wanted to see her doll collection. He claimed an antique dealer referred him. Pearl told him to wait until after the holidays. She wanted to spend time with her sister."

"Naturally. Family comes first."

"Yes. But the guy persisted. When he found out where Opal was staying, he showed up at the Philbrook and followed Pearl to her sister's third-floor room. He hammered on Opal's door and asked her to reason with Pearl."

The image of Sean Connery at the door of the eighty-year-old woman made me smile. "He underestimated the sisters," I said. "They stick together."

Paige kept both hands on the wheel as she answered. "That's exactly what happened. The two ladies peeked at him through the keyhole but refused to answer. Later, he approached Pearl in the restaurant. She ordered him to leave. That was the last they saw of him."

"Did Opal know him?" It was a long shot, but Opal lived in London and the mystery man spoke with a British accent.

Paige stopped at the light and turned to face me. "That's the interesting part. According to Pearl, neither of the sisters had ever met the man. Pearl figured he was just a wealthy collector accustomed to getting his way. Not the type to wait around for a glimpse at her dolls. She was happy to see him go."

The explanation made sense. Now I understood why Pearl brushed my questions aside: to her, the man was insignificant. Still, the mystery man was at the Philbrook the day Opal was killed. He should be considered a person of interest, or at least a potential witness to the events that occurred that day.

He might have observed something—or someone—related to the crime.

As we entered the avenue to Pearl's home, Paige lowered her voice and spoke quickly. "One more thing: Pearl and Opal argued on the phone that day of the tea. I thought you should know."

"What are you saying? You think *Pearl* killed her sister?"

"No, of course not! But she raised her voice. I've never heard her so angry"

"What did you overhear?"

"She said: 'No, Opal. Don't pay that conniving man. You don't owe him a penny of Sonny's royalties. You must report him to the authorities immediately.'"

The phone message from Opal's hotel room flashed into my mind. "Do you know who the man might have been?"

Paige shook her head. "No. I only heard that part because I walked past Mrs. Merriweather's office on my way upstairs to tidy her bedroom."

I couldn't believe Pearl hadn't mentioned the call. Instead, she insisted Opal had no enemies. This might be an important lead. "Thank you, Paige. I'll see if the chief wants more information. He plans to visit with Pearl on Monday."

"She won't talk about it. She thinks this is *family* business, and *one should never air dirty laundry in public.*"

I laughed at her accurate imitation of Pearl's voice. Then I reminded her, "Chief Marshall can be persuasive."

Paige tossed her long braid behind her back. "So can Mrs. Merriweather."

Chapter Twelve

Saturday Midday

For a frail old lady, Pearl Merriweather reigned supreme at the bowling alley. She walked through the double glass doors like a queen. The staff called out to her by name and rushed to help carry her monogrammed bowling bag. Without a doubt, she was the equivalent of royalty here. Paige and I checked in at the counter, while Pearl went straight to our lane.

While we waited, I swept my gaze across the massive building. Christmas music blared from surround-sound speakers, barely masking the ever-present rumble of falling pins. Holiday garland festooned the walls and draped from the rafters. Pool tables and video games filled a center section—between the registration counter and the lanes. Guests gathered at an old-fashioned soda fountain opposite the front desk. A pizza-by-the-slice café anchored one corner, and a Starbucks the other.

The place was a full-service entertainment center with the bowling lanes as the star attraction. A ten-year-old boy celebrated his birthday with friends in party hats at one end of the building. A couple of families occupied the next several lanes.

A stocky woman in an Orchard Lanes bowling shirt greeted us—"Ava" embroidered above her pocket. She spoke with a Jamaican accent, and her dark eyes sparkled with amusement. "I see you are in the Merriweather Challenge Lane today."

Based on her confident air and wide smile, I guessed her age to be in the early forties. But she might have been much younger, with a beautiful complexion the color of melted caramel and thick dark hair braided into cornrows tightly against her scalp.

Paige and I grinned back at her. "I'm afraid we won't be giving her much competition," I said. "Paige is new to the game, and I haven't played since Jimmy Carter was in the White House."

"Things have changed since then." Ava motioned proudly at the modern facility, pointing out the electronic scorekeeping on huge plasma screens. She pointed to the locker rooms at the end of the hallway. "For those who arrive straight from work, we have dressing rooms where they can store their valuables. League bowlers appreciate the locker rooms most. After bowling several games, they often shower and change again before they drive home."

I nodded my approval. "Impressive," I said. "The old bowling alley in my hometown had indoor plumbing, but it wasn't as sophisticated as this place."

"We have lane-side food and beverage service, too. Just give us a buzz, and we will deliver your order to your table."

Paige nudged me with her elbow. "Look, Josie. We have our own private lane near the Starbucks coffee shop. At least no one else will be watching us bowl."

Ava handed each of us a pair of rented bowling shoes. She arched one eyebrow. "Care for some advice?"

Paige grasped at the opportunity. "Yes, please!"

The woman leaned closer and lowered her voice. "Don't try to beat her. Pearl is practically a pro. Remember, this is a game. Get out there and have fun."

Ava flipped a switch, and the pins dropped into place. Pearl waved to us from the bench where she sat, tying her shoes.

Paige and I marched toward our assigned lane. "There's no turning back, now," I told her. "Grab a ball, and let's play."

I had to admit, Pearl was a patient teacher. Soon, we referred to her as

"Coach" Merriweather. She spent several minutes explaining the difference between pin bowling and spot bowling. "Forget about the pins. Don't look at them. They are sixty feet away. It is impossible to focus that far. You'll never hit them."

Paige wrinkled her forehead. "Isn't that the point of the game?"

Pearl laughed at her confusion. "Yes! You want to knock them down, but there's an easier way to get the ball to the right place." She demonstrated by rolling her own ball straight down the lane, hitting a strike on her first ball.

"You made that look easy." I clapped my hands, and Pearl rewarded me with a modest curtsy.

"I always aim for the arrows, not the pins," She pointed to the small target arrows spread across the lane about fifteen feet down from the foul line. I was embarrassed to admit that in my younger days, I'd assumed the marks were decorative, not functional.

Paige and I listened attentively as the old woman shared her bowling secrets. "If you aim your ball according to these seven arrows, you will have a better chance of consistently hitting your target. If you can roll the ball over the correct arrow, it will most likely continue down that path and hit the corresponding pin."

She watched as Paige and I barreled several balls down the lane. All three of mine landed in the left gutter. Then she gave each of us three tips. I appreciated her rationale. "You will never remember more than three things. Besides, if you do these three, you will knock down a few pins and enjoy the game."

Coach Merriweather's instructions for me were easy: Smooth roll (not too hard). Stand on spot two. Aim for arrow seven. Pearl didn't attempt to change my grip or stance. Instead, she adjusted my aim to fit my natural curve ball. By the end of the first game, I understood the strategy involved—and it worked. Paige and I both rolled respectable scores. She achieved 145, and I bowled 119. Pearl beat us both, with a whopping 199.

In between the lessons, the three of us talked like old friends. It struck me that we represented three generations of women, yet we chatted easily about familiar topics—like family, education, and life lessons. At one point,

Pearl grasped my hand and thanked me for my efforts to locate her sister's killer.

"Opal would have loved bowling with us. She is the reason I wanted to come today. I feel closer to her, doing the things she enjoyed. I still can't believe she is gone. My mind knows it is true, but not my heart."

"Your heart will never let her go." I spoke from experience.

Pearl's eyes glistened with tears. "Do you have any leads on the murderer?"

I placed one hand over hers. "Not yet," I said. "We have a couple of suspicious characters, but no solid connections. I hope to cross a few of them off my list soon. Can you tell me anything about the mystery man you argued with?"

Her sharp green eyes peered intently into mine. "Josie, that man intruded on my time with Opal. First, he appeared at my home without an introduction. He said he wanted to see my dolls. I explained he could make an appointment after the holidays. Next, he hammered on the door of Opal's room at the inn. Finally, he pushed his way to my table at the restaurant, and he tried to bully me into showing him my collection. I told him to go away. End of story."

"I saw him hovering in the restaurant after Opal gave you the doll."

Pearl patted my hand. "Trust me, dear. I've been around long enough to tangle with all kinds of rude people. That man was an avid collector. He probably hoped to get a glimpse of the doll. But he had no reason to harm Opal, or me."

"Do you remember his name?"

She sighed. "Unfortunately, no. He had slipped his business card under my door when I refused to let him inside, but I was so distraught that I threw it away."

I pushed harder. "*Think*, Pearl. Do you remember anything that would help identify him?"

She shrugged. "He was British. He might be wealthy. He wore a ruby ring on his right hand."

"Anything else?"

"Oh! Yes. He said he was referred to me by an antique dealer." She clapped her hands and smiled in delight.

"And the dealer's name?" I asked.

Pearl's happy expression disappeared. "I'm sorry, Josie, I've forgotten that, as well."

Later, we slipped into Starbucks for a coffee. Pearl reveled in her triumph. Paige congratulated her on the victory. The young girl raised her paper cup to toast her elderly employer and gazed at Pearl from the corner of her eyes. "You knew you would win before we arrived, didn't you?"

Pearl giggled before she replied. "Yes, dear. However, at my age, every success should be savored."

While Pearl sipped her coffee, relaxed and happy, I took the opportunity to ask more questions. "Ladies, I still need to eliminate three suspects. I could use your help."

Paige leaned forward. "Who are they? I want to help."

"I have names for two of them, and a description for the third," I said. "Mildred Wilkerson. Edward Gower. And an unnamed woman who wore a red coat and purple hat to the Christmas Market."

Paige shrugged her shoulders. "Sorry, Josie. I don't know *any* of those."

Pearl sat with her hands clasped primly on the table. "You're on the wrong track with Millie Wilkerson," she said. "Millie is an impossible woman. She is arrogant and conniving. I don't like her, and she doesn't like me. But she is not a killer."

I wasn't surprised by her assessment. In my experience as a reporter, I discovered that most people are reluctant to imagine their friends or acquaintances as murderers. Instead of arguing with her, I changed the subject. "What about the other two?" I asked.

Pearl shook her head. "I don't know Edward Gower. The name sounds familiar, but I can't say why."

"You can't say, or you don't know?"

My friend threw her hands in the air. "I don't know, Josie."

At her frustration, I ducked my head in shame. "I'm truly sorry, Pearl," I said. "You've just lost your sister, and I've treated you like a suspect. I didn't intend to upset you. Please forgive me."

Pearl's voice trembled. "It's okay, Josie. I understand that you're trying to help. I just don't remember where I heard the man's name. Is he important?"

"He left a voice message on Opal's phone in the hotel. He warned she might be in danger."

"Oh no!" Pearl's hands flew to cover her mouth. She shook her head. "I'm positive Opal never mentioned anyone named Edward."

"And the woman on the plaza? Someone said you argued with her?"

"She was a crazy woman," Pearl declared, "wearing that long red coat and ridiculous purple feathered hat. She ran up to Opal and gushed about recognizing her from somewhere. When Opal insisted they had never met, the woman waved her arms in the air and screamed at us. Her scarf wrapped around her face, and feathers flew from her hat."

"What did she say?"

"She said: 'You know me. I'm Felipa.' The woman was confused, Josie."

"Did she threaten Opal?" I asked.

"No. She rushed away. We had a good laugh about it. Opal joked that if the woman recognized *her*, she should have known *me*, as well."

Her comment gave me the opening I needed. "You two were as close as two peas in a pod. Did you ever disagree or argue?"

Pearl cocked her head. "We were sisters. Not saints."

"What did you argue about?"

Those vivid green eyes melted into tears. "Nothing important."

"Can you tell me about your last quarrel?"

"Oh, yes. It wasn't that long ago, and now I feel terrible about making such a fuss." Pearl paused to sip her coffee before she told the story. "We fought about a screenwriter, of all things. Opal received monthly royalty checks for the reruns of a show her late husband, Sonny, produced. The writer claimed Sonny cut him out of the royalties contract. He wanted money."

"What did Opal do?"

"Opal felt sorry for him. She agreed to split the checks."

"And you disagreed with her decision?"

"I thought the guy was a con man. I wanted her to consult an attorney. It turned into a big argument."

"Opal won?"

"She always won. No one was more stubborn than Opal." Pearl smiled through her tears.

"Would he have reason to harm her?"

"No way. With Opal gone, the royalty checks would stop."

I sighed. "Can you think of anyone who would benefit from her death?"

Pearl shrugged. "She had no children. I'm her only family, and I don't need her money. The last time we talked, she planned to leave everything to charity."

After the emotional conversation with Pearl, I wondered whether I would ever get a solid lead on Opal's killer. It seemed hopeless. I was ready to quit trying. And then I remembered my Grandma Molly's advice from when I was a little girl, struggling to accomplish a task. She always encouraged me with a sunny smile.

"Where there is a will, there is a way, Josie. The moment you want to give up, is the moment you must try harder."

But just as I decided I needed to follow her advice, Leslie Anderson called. I answered even though I already knew what she wanted.

"Good afternoon, Leslie."

"Tell me the story about the *murder* will make today's deadline," she said.

"Still working on it." I matched my tone to hers. "I can send you a quick blurb with the facts if that will help."

Leslie wasn't impressed. "We need more, Josie. Nobody believes this was an accident any longer. Word is out Opal died of a gunshot wound. I want the names of any suspects and details on the investigation. If you can't get that for me, I'll have to send Hannah to badger Chief Marshall for the scoop."

"The intern?" My voice went up an octave. "You have no idea how complicated this case is, Leslie. We have dozens of witnesses, and none of them can identify a suspect."

"Then write a story about that. And while you're at it, include the fact that Opal was shot. Surely the police are ready to announce *something?*"

"Not yet. But I'll try harder. I promise." I quoted my grandmother's words, even though I knew they were not enough to satisfy my impatient editor.

Leslie's exaggerated sigh carried loud and clear over the phone. "Just get it done, Josie."

"I'm on it," I said. But she had already ended the call—and neither of us believed I would meet the deadline.

Chapter Thirteen

Saturday Afternoon

Inside the cozy warmth of my kitchen, I was determined to focus on the news article.

I poured a fresh mug of coffee and took a seat at the marble-topped island. Moe played with his tennis ball near my feet. The fireplace crackled, and Tony Bennett crooned "Winter Wonderland" in the background.

I set a stack of handwritten note cards on the counter in front of me. Shuffling them like a deck of playing cards, I flipped them over one by one. My mahjong friends referred to this method as Josie's Tarot Cards. They claimed my note cards promoted inner wisdom and guidance—like a magic trick for crime-solving.

Actually, there was nothing supernatural about the process. It was a brainstorming exercise I learned long ago in a creative writing class, called the Random Combination Technique (RCT for short). My professor insisted the system helped to generate new ideas or view old information in a fresh way. Some days, the results sparked an idea. When it didn't work on the first try, I simply shuffled the cards and tried again.

Since the system worked best when I engaged all of my senses, I pulled out all the stops. I dimmed the lights, turned up the music, and lit a fragrant candle, for maximum effect. Today, I was desperate for answers. At least, that is how I justified eating another sugar cookie. Taste is one of our senses, right?

Hopeful that the process would produce results, I dealt the cards face up, in a random pattern. Then, I spread them into small groupings across the expanse of the island. The kitchen now looked as messy as my dining room—both had piles of paper haphazardly strewn on every surface. Just as I selected my first card to read aloud, Kate called.

"What's new, Nancy Drew?"

I chuckled in spite of myself. "Very funny, Kate. At the moment, I'm a disgrace to crime solvers everywhere, including the fictional Miss Drew. I have no leads. Even Moe has lost faith in me."

Kate pooh-poohed my anxiety. "It can't be that bad," she said. "I bring you greetings from a banker and two doll appraisers."

I grabbed my pen and switched Kate to speaker mode on my phone. "I'm listening," I said. "What did you discover?"

My Harvard-educated friend was quick to share her news. "First, the banker is more than a banker. Michael Fuller knows literally everyone in the doll collector world. He served as a UFDC board member for three years, as part of his bank's commitment to support nonprofits. During that time, he gained a reputation as a trusted advisor for doll investors nationwide."

"What did you think of him?"

"He was impressive. I met him at his office, so I had his full attention. He's short and round, with huge glasses that make him look more like a scholar than a financial wizard. Mr. Fuller never reveals the names of his clients, which is an indication of his professionalism."

Kate's enthusiasm was contagious. "Did you tell him we are investigating Opal's death?" I asked.

"No. But he's a smart man; he probably figured it out on his own. I asked a lot of questions about doll collectors. When I mentioned Pearl, he offered his condolences on the loss of her sister."

"Did he identify our purple hat lady?"

"No. He said she sounds like a fraud."

"Why would he say that, if he didn't know her?" I asked.

"According to the banker, doll collectors are all part of a tight community. They are easy to track through their relationships with other collectors. The reputable ones are dues-paying members of the UFDC. Everyone knows everyone. A purple hatted woman would stand out in the crowd."

I scribbled her comment on a notecard. "Sounds a lot like our little village," I said. "What about the Sean Connery collector?"

Kate's excitement carried over the phone. "We hit the jackpot on this one! Earlier this week, Mr. Fuller spoke with a collector who matches our description. The man introduced himself as a collector from Europe and said he planned to acquire a rare antique doll before the holidays. He asked the banker to provide an authentication of the doll—and its value—once he has the item in his possession."

"Is he certain it is the same guy?"

"He didn't actually see the man, but his caller spoke with a British accent."

"Did he provide a name or contact information?"

"Unfortunately, no."

"No?"

"Mr. Fuller said it isn't unusual for collectors to withhold their name and contact information. Often, they buy through a third-party broker, to maintain confidentiality. If the item is part of an auction, the transaction becomes a matter of public record."

"And if it is a private sale?"

"A private sale may never disclose the parties involved or the purchase price."

I drew dollar signs on a notecard in front of me and tried to make sense of Kate's information. "This guy sounds like he's in a big hurry for an appraisal," I said. "Why would he need one, anyway? Wouldn't the seller provide a Certificate of Authenticity?"

"Great question," Kate said. "Mr. Fuller had the same concerns. The mystery collector claimed the doll's owner wanted a quick sale and offered a low price, with the paperwork to be sent by certified mail after the sale."

"The whole thing sounds fishy to me," I said. "It makes me believe Mr. Fuller's collector is our Sean Connery character. How can we find out?"

Kate chuckled. "That's the good news. Mr. Fuller offered to alert us when the man calls to set an appointment. Chief Marshall can record the meeting or intercept the doll collector afterward!"

I took notes as she provided details. Our elusive mystery man was within reach, after all. I couldn't wait to tell the chief.

"Thank you, Kate. This is a huge breakthrough."

My friend sensed that I was ending our call and interrupted my thank-you speech. "Wait, Josie. There's more!"

I laughed at her exaggerated declaration. "Tell me!"

"Mr. Fuller encouraged Sean Connery to get another appraisal on the doll before he brought her to the bank. He provided the names of two professional appraisers. It's likely our suspicious doll collector will approach one of them to certify the doll's value."

I shared my friend's excitement. "If he does, we have another opportunity to capture him!"

Kate was jubilant. "Yes!"

"Who are the appraisers?"

"One is Marshall Martin, a popular appraiser on *Antiques Roadshow*. I looked him up. He is a long-standing member of the United Federation of Doll Clubs and the National Antique Doll Dealers Association. Mr. Martin once valued a Jumeau Automaton doll—made in France in the early 1900s—at up to thirty-five thousand dollars. He does private appraisals by appointment. And he will be at the Tulsa doll show tomorrow!"

Immediately, my mind raced to the road trips on the mavens' task list. "Perfect! You and Lorene can visit with Mr. Martin when you're there. Maybe he can help us connect with the mystery man."

Kate agreed. "It seems logical for our suspect to approach Mr. Martin at the show because it's an easy drive, and he wouldn't need to make an appointment. However, if the guy prefers a private consultation, he might choose the second appraiser. Her name is Connie Harrell. She is a well-respected, certified appraiser. She owns The Doll Cradle—a retail store and doll hospital in Kansas City."

"A doll hospital?"

"Yes. They restore and repair damaged dolls."

"Are the appraisals done in their store?"

"Their website offers *personal service and full confidentiality*. The mystery man could schedule an appointment to meet the appraiser at her shop, or at a private residence. Mrs. Harrell accommodates her customers by meeting wherever it is most convenient for them."

Kate made a good point. "One appraiser is high-profile, in a public setting. The other is low-profile, in a private setting. He could choose either of them. We will have to contact both, to ask for their cooperation," I said.

"The interesting thing is that all these people seem to know each other. Everyone in the industry belongs to the same association. Most of them have served on committees together or exhibited at the same doll shows."

Kate's comment made perfect sense. I had been busy tracking information about each of the people on our list. I hadn't stopped to think about the tight circle binding them together. "You're right! It's a small world. The collectors know the appraisers. The retailers know the exhibitors. The auctioneers know the bankers. And all attend the same conferences."

I offered to text Sharon the location of The Doll Cradle. If she had time, she might stop there on the way back this afternoon.

"This is perfect, Josie," Kate said. "Lorene and I leave for the Tulsa Doll Show first thing tomorrow. We already planned to keep our eyes open for the crazy purple hat woman and the mystery man. Now, we will also seek out Mr. Martin to enlist his assistance. A guy like that should be easy to find. He is probably signing autographs at a booth."

I envisioned Kate and Lorene approaching the well-known appraiser. They would make an interesting pair. Kate, tall and imposing at five-eight, and Lorene, barely four-ten, with her boots on. I had never known more determined women. Once they set their minds to something, they stayed on it till the end. The thought made me smile. Two smart women, requesting help from one man. The poor guy didn't have a chance.

Feeling more confident, I made new note cards from Kate's information, gathered them into a deck, and began my Random Combination process all over again. Shuffling the cards, I dealt them into straight rows, side by side, face down. Then, I began to flip them over. As I read them aloud—in a crazy quilt of mismatched phrases—a few logical patterns surfaced.

93

Purple hat. Argument. Distraction.
Connery. Collector. Con Artist.
Phillips. Hiding. Explosion.
Merriweather. Valuable. Theft.
Banker. Appraiser. Screenwriter.

I shook my head and stared at the phrases in confusion. They were interesting combinations, but none of them jumped off the table to claim my attention. I wrote the lines onto my legal pad and set them aside.

Sharon called as I cleared the snowstorm of paperwork from my tables. Her message was brief: "I'm headed to the doll hospital. It's an extra stop, but it's right on the way. Can you meet after church tomorrow?"

"Tomorrow morning is good. Harvey and I are shopping for a Christmas tree in the afternoon."

"Is that a date?" Sharon had prodded me to spend more time with Harvey when we first met. Now, she watched for signs that her matchmaking efforts had succeeded.

"It's more of a mutual outing."

"Well, it sounds like a date to me."

"No. Just two friends, shopping for a holiday tree," I hedged. "To be honest, we've had a bit of a rough patch in our relationship."

"What? When?" Sharon pressed for more information, but I wasn't ready to share the details of what I still hoped was a simple misunderstanding.

"It's probably nothing," I said. "Harvey's trying to look after me, and I think he's hovering. But we're going to the tree farm together and to the ice rink afterwards. Is that considered a date?"

"Josie Posey, you are impossibly independent. Give that man a chance." Sharon's voice bubbled with laughter. "Gotta go. I'm pulling into the hospital now."

After Sharon's call, I finished cleaning up the debris from my research and pulled a well-worn recipe from my grandmother's cookbook. It was time for a break from the murder investigation. Maybe the aroma of a steaming pot of chili would clear my mind...and my thinking.

Chapter Fourteen

Saturday Night

By the time Harvey arrived, chili simmered on the stove and cornbread was baking in the oven. He came through the front door just like he always did, without any hint of our previous tension. A blast of frigid air and a swirl of snowflakes swooshed inside as Moe rushed to greet him. I watched the familiar routine with a smile.

First, Harvey knelt down to Moe's level. He ruffled the fluffy mass of fur and brushed the hair from the dog's eyes. "Well, look here! It's my buddy, Moe."

My happy sheepdog wriggled in front of him until Harvey reached into his coat pocket and pulled out a dog biscuit. "Here you go, boy. This is for you." Moe took the biscuit and rolled onto his back, all four legs in the air. Harvey accommodated the dog with an enthusiastic belly scratch.

I had known Harvey for several months before I learned that he always carried three things in his pocket: keys to his truck, dog biscuits, and Juicy Fruit gum. The keys were a practical matter—he drove his old blue pickup truck between the hardware store and the blacksmith shop every day. Keys to all three were on that ring in his pocket. The dog treats and gum were purely for the joy of giving. Harvey never met a dog—or a child—who refused the treat. (Though he only offered the treats after parental approval.)

He draped his coat on the peg that hung in the front alcove and shoved his snowy boots under the bench. "Something smells good."

"Chili and cornbread. I know you enjoy fine dining."

He rewarded me with a big, happy laugh. No wonder Moe adored this man. I hadn't seen him in person since the explosion late last night. I knew— from the chief and from Harvey—that he wasn't injured. Still, I felt a lump forming in my throat as I realized it had been a close call for him. No wonder he had overreacted about my role in the investigation. I hoped we had set aside our earlier conversation permanently.

"How is your truck?" I felt a twinge of guilt that my encounter with Mr. Phillips caused the explosion.

Harvey knew me better than most. He looked directly into my eyes. "It wasn't your fault, Josie."

"I know. But I still believe I should pay for the damages."

"That's crazy. My insurance covers it. Besides, you won't believe what happened. I called around, and I found an exact tailgate to replace mine."

"But it is at least twenty years old! Who carries antique tailgates, as spare parts?"

He grinned a lopsided smile. "First, it's twenty-*two* years old, and it doesn't qualify as an antique."

"I stand corrected," I said.

Harvey pulled a barstool up to the kitchen counter. "Nutter's Repair Shop had one. Some guy totaled his pickup last week. He sold it to Lee Nutter for spare parts. The tailgate was about the only piece without a dent in it. They have to paint it, but I'll have it by Wednesday."

"You are the luckiest man alive."

He nodded. "I'm beginning to think that's true. Wait until I tell you what happened at the Christmas Market today."

We sat at the kitchen island, eating chili as we talked. Harvey asked about any progress on the murder investigation, and I described what the mavens were doing to gather more information. He listened for a full ten minutes before he asked a question.

"Let me get this straight. Kate has formed an alliance with a banker who will alert you if he sees Sean Connery. Sharon is on a road trip to Kansas City, exploring a museum and a doll hospital. Kate and Lorene will gang up on a famous TV star appraiser tomorrow in Tulsa. And your tarot card system failed you."

I laughed at his description of my report. "That's correct. We still haven't determined any motive for killing sweet Opal. Everyone loved that woman. It almost certainly involves the doll she gave Pearl, but the doll isn't missing."

"Your team is working hard. Surely you have made some progress?"

"Not enough. I haven't found any suspects for the murder—even with more than twenty witnesses. And I can't even locate the guy who nearly killed you. The mysterious Sean Connery and the explosive Mr. Phillips are still at large. I haven't talked to the chief because I have nothing to tell him until the banker connects with Connery again. Now tell me about the Christmas Market. Did you sell out?"

Harvey ran his family's hardware store by day and created beautiful iron artworks at the blacksmith shop at night. He sold them only a few times each year. The Christmas Market always generated more revenue than the Summer's End Festival. Harvey shared the blacksmith shop with two other artists. They counted on the holiday profits to pay for next year's raw materials. While Harvey specialized in iron, another artist focused on glass blowing, and the third worked with silver.

"That's what I wanted to show you before we were distracted by the gift basket episode last night. I made a chart of our sales figures." He thumbed to a screen on his phone and handed it to me.

I studied the numbers before I returned the phone to him. "It's a great chart, Harvey. Congratulations."

Harvey beamed at the praise. "Christmas-themed items are running low. Everyone wants the holly candle holders. The sleigh bells are popular as front door decorations. And the art signs are going fast. But the year-round items are selling, too. I'm almost out of the decorative mirrors and bookends."

"It sounds as though you had a good day."

He leaned back in his chair and grinned at me.

"What? Did something happen?" I asked.

"I had an idea about your murder case."

"And you waited until now to tell me? What is it?"

Harvey held his hands up in the universal motion for "slow down." "Wait a minute, Josie. I'm still not sure it is helpful."

I waited for this exasperating man to continue his story. He took his sweet time doing it. "Remember the exploding gift basket?"

"Of course, I remember. It happened last night!"

"No, I mean, do you remember the basket? Could you describe it?"

I thought about his question. I remembered the old man with his bald head and his limp. I remembered seeing him on my front porch, holding the basket. I closed my eyes to picture him more clearly.

"He wore a black coat. He held a huge basket, filled with gift-wrapped packages. Some were red with green bows, and others were gold boxes with red bows. I was surprised he had gone to the trouble of wrapping packages."

Harvey nodded his head. "Good. Anything else?"

"The basket had leather handles on both sides. It was one of those handwoven wicker designs with red and green accents...like an Amish basket!"

Harvey grinned, again. His head bobbed faster now. "Exactly like ones at the booth across from mine at the Christmas Market. Three families sell handmade gift baskets there."

"Mr. Phillips bought the basket at the market! Did they remember selling it to him? Do they have his credit card information, or an address?" I fired questions at Harvey faster than he could answer them.

"No. They had something *better*. When I walked by their booth today, I realized one of the baskets looked exactly like your exploding gift. They stock some large baskets with surprise gift packages included. Those wrapped packages contain other Amish treats—like cheeses and muffins."

"And?"

"And every time they sold a basket, their teenaged son carried it to the car for the customer. His sister went along to snap a photo of the happy customer with his gift basket."

"You're kidding!"

"Nope. The daughter is in charge of social media. She posts the photos online to promote more sales."

"The Amish families are on social media?"

"Yes. And they are good at it."

"You mean, the investigator is pictured on the internet, holding the exploding basket?"

Harvey's grin was so wide, I could barely see his eyes scrunched behind his dimpled cheeks. "Better. The license tag of the rental car is captured in the photo. I gave a copy to the chief. He is tracing it now."

"I can't wait to see what he finds," I said.

"I'm pretty sure the chief would prefer that you keep your distance from both of those mystery men. You promised to stay focused on your doll-collecting story, anyway."

"That's true. It's just that I know they are connected in some way. Kate suggested the people I'm interviewing most likely know each other. Someone has information about Opal's murder. I used to be a crime reporter. I should be able to get someone to talk."

"The chief will find them." There was an edge to Harvey's voice, but I ignored it.

"I know. I just want to help."

"As I recall, he asked you to help by keeping an eye on Pearl. How's that working out for you?" He raised one eyebrow in a comical expression that made me smile.

I picked up my phone and swiped to a photo Paige had taken at the bowling alley. "Look at this. I almost forgot to tell you about our bowling adventure."

Harvey studied the photo. "What a trio. I'm impressed the three of you were able to accomplish a selfie where everyone is smiling. It looks like you had fun."

"We did! Paige took the picture. I bowled the best score of my life. Pearl had just beaten us soundly for the third game in a row. She was quite pleased with herself."

"I can see that." He chuckled and handed the phone back to me. "Aside from getting trounced at bowling, were you able to learn anything new from Pearl?"

"Did you know those little pointer and dot thingies on the lanes can help you bowl better?"

"I believe they are called arrows, not pointers—and spots, not dots. You might be interested to know I once bowled on a league team: The Jacobs Hardware Wrecking Balls. We hit the lanes every Monday night for three years. I still have my own shoes and ball in the hall closet."

"I can't interest you in lessons, based on the training Pearl gave me?"

"Sure. Pearl has been bowling for years. I'm happy to try any tips she shared."

"Maybe you should go with us next time."

"There's a next time?"

"Coach Pearl thinks we need an opportunity to redeem ourselves. She reserved the lane again next Saturday."

Harvey laughed. "I was really asking whether she shared information about Opal…a lead you could give to Chief Marshall?" He paused before he added, "Since you will no longer be on the case, I mean."

I skipped over his final comment and told Harvey about Pearl's description of the Sean Connery look-alike. "He tried three times to get a peek at her doll collection. She thinks he is annoying, but not dangerous."

"Did Pearl name anyone who might want to hurt Opal?"

"No. There was a screenwriter who claimed Opal's husband owed him money. Opal agreed to pay the man. Pearl wasn't sure of the details. There was no reason for the screenwriter to kill her; with Opal dead, his payments would cease."

I rubbed my eyes and looked up at Harvey. "Do you think we will ever find her murderer?"

Harvey's brow wrinkled, and he shot me a serious look. "*We?* I thought you decided to let the chief solve this crime on his own."

"No, *you* decided that." I folded my arms across my chest.

His jaw clenched, and *bam*! Suddenly, we were knee-deep in the conversation I had hoped to avoid.

"You have to stop, Josie." Harvey's kind eyes had turned to steel.

"Stop what?" I dared him to answer.

He met my stare. "All of it. The investigation. The article. Everything that

100

puts you in danger."

I glared back at him. "This is *my* life, Harvey. You don't get to make those decisions for me."

He stood and set his chili dish into the sink. In silence, I watched him walk to the door and let himself out. Then I sat, stunned by his abrupt departure. I refused to follow after him.

Several minutes later, Moe came to nudge my knee, reminding me I hadn't moved from the kitchen since Harvey left. I let him out the back door and cleared the remainder of the dishes. Then I carried a plate of sugar cookies into the living room, flipped open my laptop, and hammered out the article Leslie Anderson wanted—minus the names of suspects:

"Ms. Opal Crawford, sister of English Village resident Pearl Merri-weather, was pronounced dead at Mercy hospital after an untimely fall into the wishing well during the Philbrook Inn's annual Christmas Market earlier this week. The victim experienced severe trauma to her head and brain. Doctors also found a single bullet lodged in her lung,

"In search of the perpetrator, the police have interviewed more than two dozen witnesses, but have not yet identified any suspects. No weapon has been found. No motive for the shooting has been determined. No suspects have been named.

"Authorities have asked for assistance in identifying three persons of interest who may have additional information regarding the case. One is a tall woman wearing a red coat and purple hat. Another is a man in his sixties, of average height with a well-groomed beard and a British accent. The third is an older man who walks with a slight limp and goes by the name of Howard Phillips.

"If you have any information regarding this crime, please contact the English Village Crimestoppers Hotline with details. All leads will remain confidential A reward is offered if the information leads to the arrest and conviction of a suspect or suspects in the case."

I dashed off a quick email to Leslie, in time to meet her deadline for this week's newspaper. Then, for the next ninety minutes, I forgot about murders and exploding packages. Instead, Moe and I watched the classic movie *Miracle on 34th Street*. The 1947 film still brought me to happy tears. Somehow, they weren't as happy tonight.

Chapter Fifteen

Late Saturday Night

When my phone pinged with a text just as the movie ended, I was sure it would be Harvey. I was wrong.

I swiped to read a message from the chief: "Too late to call?"

I pressed the button to call him and placed the phone on speaker so I could take notes, if needed. The chief's deep voice rumbled into my living room, and Moe raised his head to see if we had another visitor. I scratched behind his ears and handed him a dog biscuit from my pocket.

"Be quiet, boy."

"I hope I'm not disturbing you. It's nearly eleven," the chief said.

"It's not a problem," I assured him. "Moe and I watched a movie."

"I wanted to share news about our efforts to locate Mr. Phillips."

"Have you tracked the car?" I asked.

"Yes. And no." The chief had a flair for storytelling.

"Maybe you should explain from the beginning." I pulled a legal pad from my bag.

Chief Marshall continued. "After Mr. Phillips delivered his exploding basket last night, I assigned patrolman Devon to locate the man's vehicle. Our officer has been on the phone to every car rental place in a three-state area."

"That's a big list," I said.

"Uh-huh," the chief grunted in agreement. "He started by asking the top rental companies in the country to check their databases for Howard Phillips. No one could match the name. Then, he called smaller companies—regional and local agencies. There were no rentals listed under Mr. Phillips' name."

"Sounds like a dead end. Maybe he didn't rent a car, after all?"

The chief nearly shouted his approval. "My thoughts, exactly! There was no evidence—except his own claim—that the car was a rental. Until Harvey sent me a photo. Did he show it to you?"

"Yes. Earlier this evening. Was it helpful?"

"It was, indeed. Using the license tag number, we tracked the car to a rental agency."

"And you finally found Mr. Phillips?"

"Nope. But we discovered the car was owned by a small local company in Bolivar, Missouri– a one-man shop that closed at noon."

I tapped my pen impatiently on the legal pad, waiting for the chief to get to the point.

"Fortunately, Bolivar is a small town. The police chief there is the car rental guy's brother-in-law. He provided a home number."

"Did you reach the rental agent? What did he say?" I rushed to squeeze both questions into the space in the hope that Chief Marshall would speed up his story.

"He remembered the vehicle. Said he rented it to a woman. He went to his office to get the details. We have a name, driver's license number, address, and phone."

"A woman? Have you tried the phone number?"

Chief Marshal sighed heavily over the phone. "Yes, Josie, we tried the number."

"Let me guess: it was fake."

"Either the number was bogus, or the rental agent wrote it down incorrectly. He doesn't own a computer. Every transaction is on paper; he still has *carbon paper* copies. Can you believe it?"

As the chief ended his story, I thanked him for sharing it with me. "Chief, I'm taking notes. Do you have the woman's name?"

"Yes. It's Felipa. Felipa Garcia." He spelled the name for me, and I jotted it onto the pad.

"Wait," I said. "Wasn't Felipa the name of the woman who argued with the twins at the Christmas Market?"

"There was an argument?" Chief Marshall's voice reflected his surprise. "No one reported an argument."

"Er, ah, sorry, Chief. Harvey heard about it from the security guard. He mentioned it to me. I questioned Pearl, and she brushed it off as a misunderstanding. But I'm pretty sure the woman's name was Felipa."

"Riiight. Well, I have it on my radar, now. Thank you."

The chief hesitated so long that I wondered whether he would continue. Finally, he spoke. "One more thing."

"Yes?"

"Remember the photos and videos? The ones I mentioned to you and Nellie?"

"You sent them to the lab in Wichita."

"Yes. I have the edited version on a thumb drive at the station now. Would you and Nellie both look at them? If your Sean Connery mystery man is in the video, you can identify him."

"We could stop by after church tomorrow. The mavens are meeting at Cozy Cups at eleven."

"Come to my office at ten forty-five. You can pick up a copy of the video. Take your time watching it. If you notice something important, call me. Otherwise, we can talk again Monday."

I knew the chief wanted our input but hated to request a Sunday meeting. I felt the same way about protecting his time. That's why I promised to borrow the video on Sunday and get back to him on Monday. And it's why I really hated to bother him in the wee hours of the morning.

But I did. Because at three, I awoke to the sound of a growling bear. In seconds, I realized the low-pitched rumbles weren't from a wild animal. They were warning snarls coming from deep within Moe's throat. My docile Old English Sheepdog was huge—weighing in at 105 pounds—but he rarely raised his voice.

I could count on one hand the number of times I had heard Moe bark.

Once, a raccoon snuck up to the back porch and attempted to eat from Moe's dog dish. He barked at the intruder and chased the coon up a tree. Another time, a frisky squirrel had Moe running in circles as the trapeze artist soared from tree to tree above him. The dog barked frantically, trying to convince Mr. Squirrel to come down to the ground to play. And last spring, when Moe sniffed a little too near a skunk, the animal raised his tail and sprayed my dog in his face. Even then, Moe didn't actually bark; he yelped, then whimpered and ran to the cottage, where I reluctantly brought the stinky dog inside for a shower.

This was different. Moe stood, poised to attack, near the back door. A sheepdog is a herder, not a hunter. But Moe quivered at attention, his front paw raised and his nose pointed toward the door. A deep rumble emerged from the depth of his throat. Something—or someone—was outside the house. I hoped it—or he—heard Moe's growl. Harvey had installed security lights last summer, after we discovered an intruder's footprints in the soft earth beside the house. I hoped the light bulbs still worked.

My heart raced. Could someone see me, cowered behind the bedroom blinds? I peered through the slats, trying to catch any movement in the shadows. Normally, I loved the thick trees and foliage in my wooded backyard. Tonight, I longed for a wide-open space, without natural hiding places. I heard my own ragged breathing. I saw nothing in the darkness, but Moe continued to growl.

Cautiously, I leaned closer into the window and pressed my face to the glass, I studied the edges of the bushes. The security lights blinked on, startling me with their bright beams. There! The spotlight shone on a dark figure, crouched at the edge of the back deck. He was so near the house that I jumped backward, nearly tripping over Moe in my haste to get out of view. The man must have been as surprised as I was. He tossed something toward the back door, then he ran away. He raced for the rear of my property and slipped near the corner of the gardener's cottage. I saw him fall, scramble up again, jump over the fence, and take off down the tree line.

Moe dashed to the back door where he pranced on his feet and whined for me to open the door. I stroked his back, as much to calm myself as to soothe him. We stood together like that, both of us shaking, for several minutes. At last, my breathing slowed to a normal rhythm. I felt certain the man would not return. But what object had he tossed onto my deck?

I sighed. There was no getting around it. I dialed Chief Marshall's number. For the second night in a row, I woke him with an urgent call. Technically, Harvey had called the chief Friday night, but *my* exploding basket prompted that call. I hated to bother him again, now that the offender had run away. When the chief didn't answer immediately, I was tempted to hang up. Surely it could wait until daylight? Just as I started to press "end," I heard his familiar voice.

"What is it, Josie?" Chief Marshall sounded gruff but concerned.

"I'm sorry, Chief."

"Are you safe?"

"Yes. I shouldn't have called."

"What happened?"

"Moe woke me, growling. The security lights flashed on. We saw a man run through the backyard. He tossed something onto my deck. It can probably wait until morning."

"No, Josie. You did the right thing. Where are you now?"

"Standing in my pajamas at the back door; Moe is beside me."

"Do not open the door. Understand?"

"I won't."

"Dress quickly. I'm on my way."

With Moe trailing behind me, I hurried into jeans and a sweatshirt. By the time the chief arrived, I met him at the door with a steaming mug of coffee. The cottage was lit up like an airport runway; the chief could have found me with his eyes closed.

"I see you left the light on for me." Chief Marshall had a dry sense of humor I had come to appreciate.

"Too much?" I grinned up at him. Somehow, seeing his ebony face split wide open with a bright smile made me feel better. The chief was my friend. He cared about my safety, even when I caused extra work for his department.

We talked about tonight's intruder while the bomb squad investigated the package found on my back deck. The chief suggested we sit in his patrol car, parked in my driveway. "I will leave the engine running. We can stay warm and safe at the same time."

"What about Moe?" Tears formed in the corners of my eyes. The chief knew I couldn't leave my sweet watchdog alone in the house.

"There's room in the back seat. He can bring Lamb Chop." I glanced down at Moe. He hadn't left my side since the stranger woke both of us from a sound sleep. Now, he held his favorite toy in his mouth and looked up at me.

"Guess what, Moe? You get to ride in a police car!" I grabbed his leash and slipped a couple of dog biscuits into my pocket.

In the end, we only spent twenty minutes in the car. That's how long it took for me to repeat my story to the chief three times—and for the bomb squad to confirm the contents of the mystery package. There was no bomb. The stranger had tossed a gift-wrapped message onto my porch.

The chief read a text from his officers, notifying him of the contents. He shrugged when he shared the information with me. "This is your garden-variety intimidation, Josie. The guy assembled a threatening note by cutting letters from a magazine and pasting them onto an ordinary sheet of typing paper. I'm sorry to say, it isn't very original. He rolled the note, wrapped it with holiday paper, and tied a ribbon around it."

"What did it say?"

"It's a Christmas poem. Would you care to read it?" He handed me his phone.

You better watch out
You better not cry
You better not pout
I'm telling you why
The doll man is coming to town

I'm making a list,
And checking it twice,
I'm gonna find out who's naughty or nice

The doll man is coming to town

I see you when you're sleeping
I know when you're awake
I know if you've been bad or good
So be good for goodness sake

Those mavens need to watch out.
I'm gonna make you cry.
It's time for you to get out
Or someone else might die.
The doll man is coming to town.

I looked up into the chief's kind eyes. "You're right. It isn't original. But it does convey a clear message."

"Are you sure you didn't recognize this guy? Could it have been Mr. Phillips?"

"No. This was a younger man. He ran fast, without a limp."

Chief Marshall scribbled a note on his spiral pad. "One thing is certain."

"What's that, Chief?"

"We are closer to identifying Opal's murderer."

"We need to do it quickly," I said. "The doll man is watching."

Chapter Sixteen

Sunday Morning

I t was a good thing I set my alarm when the chief left my cottage. After the early morning interruption, Moe and I both snored through our normal wake-up time. I dragged myself out of bed and dressed for church. Kate always saved a place for me. If I didn't show, she worried.

Before the Sunday service, I usually had an early breakfast of scrambled eggs and bacon that I shared with Moe. Today, he would have to settle for plain dog food, as the mavens planned to meet for brunch at Cozy Cups Café at eleven.

I had barely bundled into my coat when Harvey texted. The message was brief: "Still want to get a tree this afternoon?"

I replied with a "thumbs up" emoji.

It wasn't a long discussion, but far better than the stormy exit last night. He would not be happy to hear about my three a.m. visitor—or the threat contained within his Christmas poem—but *that news* could wait, I decided.

The sun shone brightly on the snow; sharp sparkles of light glistened, like glitter, over the frosted fields. The English Village Chapel was lovely in the summertime, but it became truly magical at Christmas. The church sat in the center of a garden, now covered in white. Christmas carols played over the clarion, sending sweet notes from the bell tower that could be heard all the way to Crystal Lake.

As I walked the length of the sidewalk, I admired the life-sized nativity scene Tim Nester and other volunteers from the congregation had built for the holidays. There was a manger, complete with the Holy Family, the Magi, and an angel. Shepherds gathered with their flocks off to the side of the cozy scene. On Christmas Eve, members of the choir brought the nativity to life—stepping into the character's positions. A host of angels, from ages five to twelve, sang hymns in fifteen-minute programs for visitors brave enough to bundle into coats for the performance.

This little church, with Pastor Pinkerton's gentle leadership, had become a favorite attraction for visitors year-round. Kate waited for me in our pew, one row behind Nellie and Tim. The sanctuary smelled of pine wreaths and candles; sunlight sent beams of colored light through the stained-glass windows, bathing the worshipers in red and gold.

I'm sorry to admit that I didn't hear a word Reverend Pinkerton said. I only intended to rest my eyes for a moment, but I nodded off during the service. When Kate nudged me with her elbow, I stood by her side for the closing benediction. Then she punched me again—this time, it was so hard that I yelped.

My friend grabbed my arm and whispered urgently in my ear. "Hush. Don't say a word. But I'm sure the woman in the purple hat is standing at the end of the third row, up front, on the left. Can you see her?"

I craned my neck, but Kate is a good four inches taller than I am. There was no way I could catch a glimpse of anyone, over the heads of half the congregation. Not unless I climbed onto the pew for a better vantage point. I shook my head and whispered back. "No. Let's get out of here and try to catch her as she leaves the sanctuary."

"Are you crazy? What would we do with her?"

"You tackle her, and I will call Chief Marshall."

Kate couldn't help it. She giggled. Making me snicker. And then we both choked with laughter as Pastor Pinkerton solemnly gave his final blessing. Kate's shoulders shook so hard I couldn't look at her. She hiccuped, and I held my breath until tears streamed down my face.

Nellie turned around in her pew to glare at us. I hadn't felt so thoroughly admonished since the second grade, when Mrs. Crenshaw scolded me for squealing in a school play. Was it *my fault* that Danny Scott poked me in the ribs when we were supposed to be quiet?

Anyway, by the time we recovered from our laughing fit, the woman in the purple hat got away—if she was even in the church. Kate was the only one who saw her.

We separated after church, to meet again shortly for brunch. On my way, I stopped by the police station for my ten forty-five appointment with the chief. He handed me the thumb drive with one simple instruction. "Watch it from beginning to end. If you spot anything important, make a note of the time code so I can easily view it."

"Got it," I said. "I'll have it back to you tomorrow morning."

I had blamed my giggling in church on my lack of sleep, but it started all over again when I caught Kate's eye across the Cozy Cups Café dining room.

"Stop that," she said. And I tried. After a few mild chuckles, the episode was over.

All four of us gathered round our favorite table to enjoy the brunch and compare notes. Lorene pulled another chair to the table to join us. First, I told everyone about my early-morning intruder and his "doll man is coming to town" poem. Lorene—as the chief's wife—already knew the details. The others commended me for my bravery.

"Moe was the brave one," I said. "I hid in my bedroom; he was ready to chase the man out of the neighborhood."

Nellie frowned. "I don't like to see you in danger, Josie. Maybe we need to back away from this case."

My mind flashed back to Harvey's angry words the previous evening, but I shoved them away and tried to reassure Nellie. "The chief says these threats are meant to scare me, not to kill me. Anyway, I'm not confronting a murder suspect. I'm interviewing people for a story about dolls."

Sharon agreed. "We aren't pointing guns at anyone. We are just touring museums and visiting doll shows. I don't see how that can be dangerous."

Kate raised her eyebrows and gave me a sidelong glance. "Well, you *did* suggest tackling a woman in a purple hat at the church today!"

"Wait. Wasn't that your idea?" I tried to look innocent.

"I think not."

As Kate described the woman we "almost" accosted at the church, Nellie shook her head. "I'm glad you came to your senses without further interrupting Pastor Pinkerton's sermon," she said.

The mavens were eager to hear about Kate's calls, as well as Sharon's road trip to Kansas City, so we settled into our seats for their reports.

Kate went first. "I talked to Michael Fuller, the banker. He was approached by a British man who wanted a doll appraisal. We don't know whether the man is our Sean Connery, but Mr. Fuller promised to alert us when the guy confirms an appointment. The banker also provided the names of two other appraisers—Sharon talked to one of those yesterday in Kansas City. I will see the other one in Tulsa this afternoon. No matter who the British doll collector contacts, we will be informed."

"Great work, Kate." Nellie raised her coffee mug in a mock toast to our friend's accomplishments.

Sharon reported next. She handed each of us a brochure from the UFDC Doll Museum, and another from the Doll Cradle. "I had a great trip. I met with the regional director of the UFDC—she was a lovely woman—and learned more about doll collections than you can imagine."

She read from a notebook as she shared the highlights of her research. "There are literally thousands of doll collectors in the United States. The hobby began centuries ago. Many collectors are generalists—they buy a mixture of styles. Others specialize in dolls from certain years or countries. There are collectors who only buy baby dolls or Barbie dolls. Some focus on bisque dolls; others prefer composition dolls. You get the picture."

Sharon pointed to the museum brochure. "The UFDC museum is small, but the doll collection is excellent. Nearly every style and year is represented. People travel from around the world to see them. In addition to all the dolls in their glass cases, they have a research library, videos, and catalogs. Their biggest resource is their staff. I have never seen such helpful, knowledgeable people. They valued my doll at fifteen hundred dollars!"

"What did they say about Pearl Merriweather?" I had my pen in hand.

"She served on their board for many years. Everyone respects and admires her—as a person and a collector." Kate pulled a photograph from her purse. "The regional director gave me this photo for Pearl. It's a snapshot from the convention they organized together twenty years ago."

I studied the picture closely. Three women smiled up at me: Pearl and Opal, on either side of the director. The twins were younger versions of the dynamic duo I knew. They stood in front of an exhibit featuring European dolls.

"Pearl will love to see this," I said. "I wonder how often Opal traveled to the doll conventions with her sister?"

"That's what makes the photo a special one," Sharon said. "As far as the regional director knows, this is the only convention Opal attended. She knew her sister Pearl had worked hard to plan the event, so Opal arrived to surprise her."

Sharon set her coffee cup on the table. "Unfortunately, that's all we learned at the museum. No one knows our Sean Connery look-alike, or a woman in a purple hat. I'm sorry to disappoint you, Josie."

"You still learned something," I said. "If the UFDC can't identify them, our mystery people must not be reputable collectors. At least we know that much. What about the doll hospital? Any news there?"

Sharon was enthusiastic. "The Doll Cradle was fascinating. They repair simple things, like a broken arm or a torn leg. But they also restore antique dolls. The owner is an appraiser—one of the two Kate mentioned. I asked her to be on the lookout for our Sean Connery. She agreed to call if he contacts her for an appointment."

I turned to Nellie. "That leaves you, Nellie. How was the Wichita doll show?"

"It was fun, but very small," Nellie said. "I bought a Tiny Tears that reminded me of my first baby doll. Organizers told me that participation had declined in recent years. Collectors shop online now because they can buy dolls from anywhere, without leaving home. People still attend specialty shows—or when they want to visit with an appraiser—but they go less often."

Nellie handed me a package wrapped in brown kraft paper. "I brought you a book on the history of doll collecting. It includes a story about the famous Carmen Sylva collection. I'm afraid I don't have anything else to contribute. The show organizers all remembered Pearl. A few of them knew Mildred Wilkerson. No one recalled Sean Connery or a purple hat woman."

Kate looked at Lorene from across the table. "What do you think? Should we still go to Tulsa this afternoon? Or are we wasting our time?"

"It's never a waste of time to see something new," Lorene said. "I could use a road trip."

Kate dangled her car keys in front of Lorene. "I will drive if you'll bring coffee in to-go cups. Maybe we will have better luck than the others."

As we gathered our things to leave, I asked Nellie to stay behind. "Do you have time to view the video the chief prepared? The lab made a copy for us. He says they were able to piece together several angles from the cell phone footage and security cameras. There's footage of the carolers, the market booths, and the decorations."

"Has the chief seen it?"

"Yes. But he thinks we may notice something he missed. He wants our independent observations by tomorrow morning."

"Did they capture the face of her killer?"

"I don't know, Nellie. I hope so."

A shadow of sadness crossed Nellie's face. "Could we watch it together after you're home from the tree farm? I don't think I can do it alone."

Inside my cottage, the events of the night before descended on me in a wave of exhaustion. During the past twenty-four hours, Harvey had walked out on me in anger, I'd been stalked by the "doll man," and Kate had spotted the purple hat woman in our church service. I was too tired to sift through all the emotions that raced through my mind.

And so, as desperately as I wanted to watch the video, I set the thumb drive on the table beside my laptop to view later with Nellie. Right now, I needed a nap.

Chapter Seventeen

Sunday Afternoon

Whary arrived mid-afternoon, I was happy to climb into his restored truck for the ride to Crystal Pines Tree Farm. I'd read their history online and recited part of it to Harvey in an attempt to fill the silence between us.

"Did you know a Dutch immigrant named Finn Jansen planted the first pine trees at the edge of English Village, when the town was so small it was barely a dot on the map?" I forced a bright smile onto my face.

"Yup."

Determined to break him, I rambled onward. "The farm back then occupied eighty acres, and Finn's idea was to turn part of his ground into a forest of pines. He selected a half dozen varieties compatible with the Kansas seasons, planted seedlings, and tended them with love."

Harvey kept his eyes on the road.

"Then his son, Finn Junior, took over the business." I considered Harvey's silence as a challenge. "Junior added a nursery and several greenhouses. He made Crystal Pines one of the largest garden and landscaping businesses in the country."

"Humph," Harvey said.

I accepted the one-syllable grunt as permission to continue.

"Now, Finn *the Third*—affectionately known as Trey—runs the farm. He's the one who built the cavernous red barn for a retail shop…"

Harvey pulled to a stop beside the road. "You can stop talking now," he said. "We're almost there."

"Is this how it's going to be, between us?" My voice trembled.

"I don't know what you expect from me, Josie."

I looked steadily into his kind face. "Could we push everything else aside and simply enjoy the afternoon? Is that too much to ask? It's almost Christmas."

Harvey's rigid jaw softened, and he gave a nearly imperceptible nod. "You're right. This is a time to enjoy the holidays. I'll try to remember that."

"Thank you," I whispered, as he pulled the truck back onto the asphalt.

When we rounded the curve and drove through the front gate, fourteen-year-old Pieter Jansen greeted us. He wore a red flannel shirt with denim overalls and a Santa hat with the Crystal Pines logo embroidered on the white fur trim. I knew Pieter from the library where I volunteered some weekdays; he was an avid reader.

"Welcome to Crystal Pines." The young man leaned into the truck and handed me a flier. "Follow the drive and take a right at the arrow. We opened a new parking lot. There's plenty of room."

Three minutes later, we checked in at the warming hut. A teenage girl with a long blond ponytail handed Harvey a tree saw. We climbed aboard a horse-drawn hay wagon and rode toward the tree fields. As we approached each stop, the driver called out the variety of trees: "Looking for an Austrian Pine? This is your stop."

Harvey and I jumped off at the Scotch Pine field. I adored the sturdy branches of this variety—plus the fact that it rarely shed its needles, even when I forgot to water it. For several minutes, we walked together in the snowy field, surrounded by trees and silence, with no awkwardness between us. The scene was so magical that I couldn't bear to speak...if I disturbed the solitude, it might break the spell. We hiked through the drifts, with only the scrunch of snow beneath our boots to accompany our journey.

It might have been a lifetime or a ten-minute walk—I was too lost in the moment to keep track. I only know that a sunbeam directed my eye to the trees huddled together on the right side of our path. There, I spotted it: my perfect tree. It stood six feet tall, and I couldn't wait to get it home and decorated, to stand proudly in the front bay window.

"This is the one!" I hopped from one foot to the other in front of the beautiful tree.

Harvey smiled at my delight. "I guess we'd better grab it, then."

He set his backpack on the snow and pulled a folded tarp from the zippered pouch. Quickly, he spread the tarp at the base of the tree, stretched his lanky frame beneath the branches, and began to cut the base of the trunk. I held on near the treetop to keep the severed tree from falling on him. Soon, the beautiful Scotch Pine gave way. We tagged the tree with my name and waited for the wagon master to pick us up on his next trip around the fields.

Harvey had already purchased a Fraser Fir from a youth group that sold them in the Jacobs Hardware Store parking lot. He had shown me a photo the previous weekend. "It isn't as much fun as the tree farm, but the money goes to a great cause," he had said.

By the time the wagon dropped us off at the retail shop, my fingertips and nose were bright red from the cold. We rushed to the warmth inside, where we sat on a bench near the roaring fireplace. While we rested, I admired the colorful holiday displays that decorated the Crystal Pines Barn. The place was filled to the rafters with wreaths and trees, holiday ornaments, and décor. I spotted tree stands, skirts, toppers, and more. Against the wall opposite the huge barn doors, the local high school glee club sold sugar cookies and hot cocoa while several of their members sang Christmas carols to entertain customers. The crisp scent of pine filled the air.

On our way across the barn to purchase cocoa, I noticed a huge furry animal asleep on the floor in one corner. Harvey saw me study the beast. "That's Lola, the Jansens' current *Newfie*," he said. "She's a gentle giant. Newfoundland dogs have protected this farm for generations."

For the first time since we had argued, Harvey seemed almost back to normal. But just as I was certain the afternoon would slide by without interruption, my cell phone pinged with a text from the chief. I raised it to show Harvey the message: *"Can we talk?"*

"Chief Marshall never contacts me on a Sunday," I said. "And I already saw him once today when he gave me a thumb drive of the video. It must be important."

Harvey clenched his jaw and signaled me to take the call. Instead of texting the chief, I pressed the speed dial.

He wasted no time in small talk. "We have a breakthrough in the case," he said.

"Is it Mr. Phillips?"

"No."

"Who then?"

"We received a call from the Philbrook Inn. A new guest registered there this evening. His name is Gower. Edward Gower, Esquire."

"The man who left the message on Opal's machine!"

"Yes. He arrived this evening. When he checked into the inn, he mentioned that Opal Crawford had referred him."

"Uh-oh."

"Let me guess. The desk clerk handed him today's edition of the *Village Gazette.*"

"He saw my story about Opal's untimely death?"

"The man became agitated. He stood in the lobby, read the article, and moaned that it couldn't be true. Then, he raced outside to his vehicle. He was in such a hurry that he left his overcoat and luggage behind."

"Where is he now?"

"I put an officer on his tail. Gower drove a black rental car with tinted windows. He parked in front of Pearl Merriweather's home for more than an hour, but he didn't go to the door."

"Did you question him?"

"Not at that time. We had no evidence that he was involved, Josie. It isn't a crime to mention a woman's name."

"Why did the hotel call you?"

"Because Mr. Gower fits the description of our person of interest."

"He looked like Mr. Phillips?" I still didn't understand where the chief was headed with this information.

Chief Marshall chuckled over the phone. Then he spoke more slowly, and with the patient tone he might use when he explained something elementary to his young daughter, Suzy. "No, Josie," he said. "The man had a mustache and beard, and he spoke with a British accent."

"Sean Connery!"

"That's it. I knew you could figure it out," the chief said dryly. "Our detective intercepted Mr. Gower when he returned to the hotel. He requested an interview."

"Did Mr. Gower agree?"

"Yes. He followed our officer to the station. He was cooperative. He insisted he would never hurt Opal. In fact, he said he was quite fond of her."

"Did you arrest him?"

"No. We verified his identification and his travel schedule. He offered to come back tomorrow afternoon with receipts from his stay in Kansas City."

"Does he look like Sean Connery?"

The chief sighed. "Not to me, but the hotel clerk thought so."

"What's next?"

"I will interview Mr. Gower again tomorrow afternoon. Could you stop by to confirm his identity as *your Sean Connery*? We need to place him at the scene on the day of the murder. You and Pearl may be the only witnesses able to do that."

"Pearl's son flies back to California in the morning. I'll bring her to the station with me after lunch."

The chief hesitated on the other end of the call.

"Is there something else?"

"Just your notes on the video. Will you and Nellie still have time to watch it before tomorrow?"

"Yes. She's coming to my house later tonight. I think she needed a couple of hours to prepare herself for what we might see."

"Understandable. Thank you, Josie."

I ended the call and glanced over at Harvey. "The chief has a person of interest at the station. He thinks it may be Sean Connery."

"Do you want to cancel our plans for tonight?" The glint of steel had returned to Harvey's eyes. He had arranged to take time off from his booth, to spend it with me at the community tree-lighting ceremony. This might be my only opportunity to repair our relationship.

I shook my head. "No. Let's decorate the tree and go to the skating rink for the sleigh rides and lighting event. They light the tree at six-thirty. We'll be home by eight. Nellie and I can watch the video after that. I'll make popcorn."

Harvey loaded my tree into his truck and drove to my cottage, where we would spend the remainder of the afternoon decorating it. Whatever was happening in the murder case could wait a few hours. I had already devoted the last two nights to worrying about intruders. Today, I wanted to enjoy the holiday spirit with Harvey.

Things between us almost felt normal while I pulled ornaments from storage boxes, and Harvey wrapped the tree in strands of lights. Moe sniffed the branches with mild interest. When he understood they contained nothing edible, he meandered back to his favorite napping spot, next to the couch.

We had nearly completed the tree when Kate called. I stood atop the stepladder with an angel in my hands, but I recognized her ringtone and pulled my phone from the pocket of my jeans to answer. She raced to give me the news. "We saw her! The purple hat woman was here, in Tulsa." Kate spoke so fast it took me three times to understand what she was saying.

"Where?"

Harvey sensed my urgency and gave me a hand to step down the ladder. I set the phone on one of the rungs and put the call on speaker so we could both listen to Kate's conversation.

"She was here. In Tulsa. Lorene and I spotted her the minute we arrived. She stood at a booth in the exhibit area. The place was packed, but she's tall. And with that feathered purple hat, we couldn't miss her."

I heard Lorene in the background, prompting Kate with details.

"The woman is taller than Chief Marshall. She has blond hair, but we think it's a wig. No one has real hair *that* perfect. She was alone."

"Did you talk to her?"

"Yes. She had a light blue quilted tote bag over her shoulder, so I introduced myself and told her my friend Pearl Merriweather carried a bag like hers."

"How did she react?"

"She said she didn't know Pearl, but figured she must have good taste. According to Felipa, her own bag was a gift from her cousin Howard."

"She mentioned *her cousin?*" I couldn't believe Kate had smooth-talked her way into a genuine conversation with the purple hat lady.

"Oh, yes. The woman was quite cordial. Although she seemed confused when we first approached her. She asked if Howard had sent us to meet her. Apparently, he asked her to wear her purple hat and meet him at the Tulsa doll show, but he stood her up at their designated meeting point."

"Whaaat?" My pulse quickened as I realized my friends had spoken to one of the chief's primary suspects.

"We told her we were from English Village, and had come to Tulsa for the doll show."

"How did she react to that?" I asked.

"Felipa commented that she'd heard someone had been murdered in the village and that there was a killer on the loose,"

"And...?" I prompted Kate to continue.

"Naturally, we assured her that our police chief and our reporter friend were close to solving the case, so there was no need for alarm."

Harvey shot me a disapproving look over the ladder, but I plowed forward with another question. "Did you ask her more about her cousin?"

"We did better than that," Kate scoffed. "We took her to coffee. Her name is Felipa Garcia, and her cousin is apparently a prankster who often drags her into his wild schemes."

"Schemes?" I felt little prickles of goosebumps on my arms, listening to Kate's tale.

"Yep. According to Felipa, Howard has been a masterful impersonator and actor since his high school drama days. She said he was always good at imitating accents, and he perfected his makeup and hairstyling tricks during his career as a screenwriter and stuntman."

"Did you say *screenwriter?*" My voice squeaked as I grasped the significance of the details Kate and Lorene had uncovered.

"A screenwriter *and* stuntman," she repeated. "So I told her I knew a reporter who would love to do a story about him—"

"You *didn't!*" I interrupted.

"I *did*. And I asked for her number—so you could get in touch for the story." Kate spoke with pride.

I congratulated my friends on their success. "Good job. Text me her information. Tell her I will try to reach her tomorrow."

"Sorry," Kate said. "I can't deliver any messages. She rushed out of here after our conversation almost an hour ago. We tried to call you earlier, but our cell connection is terrible in this convention hall."

"Are you headed back soon?"

"Lorene is in line to meet the illustrious *Antiques Roadshow* appraiser. We hope he can point us to Sean Connery."

Static interrupted Kate's call. "I'm losing you," she said. "Talk more later..."

I didn't have the heart to tell her the chief had found Mr. Gower, who might be the Sean Connery look-alike. Besides, I really wanted a comment from the antique appraiser to include in my article. Suddenly, the investigation—and my story—were both making progress. I texted the chief with a cryptic note that I had new information on Felipa Garcia, and her cousin Howard, that I would share when we met.

My only problem now was Harvey.

After Kate's call, Harvey's face returned to stone. He gathered his things and left the cottage to "run a few errands" before the city tree-lighting event. Suddenly, I felt that I was walking on eggshells whenever he and I were together. I had no idea where he had gone, but it couldn't be good, or he would have shared it with me.

Chapter Eighteen

Sunday Evening

By the time Harvey returned from his errands, his mood had lifted again. He gave me a hand as I climbed into his truck for the short ride. The snow came softly again as dusk fell over the village. The scene reminded me of carriage rides in Kansas City in years gone by. Lights on The Country Club Plaza were always spectacular there. Here, in English Village, the holiday celebrations had a small-town coziness.

The tree stood proudly in the center of the park, next to the ice rink. Horse-drawn carriages circled the lake, dropping riders at three vantage points, so they could choose to stop near the refreshments, the announcement podium, or the children's area. Promptly at 6 p.m., our local volunteer firefighters drove Santa to Crystal Lake, lights and sirens blaring. The jolly man himself had agreed to flip the switch that would transform the twenty-foot tree into a blinking mass of light.

Harvey and I arrived in time to hear the good-natured banter between Santa and Mayor Minter and to see the traditional tree lighting. The mayor wore her infamous holiday coat—made of green velvet and festooned with twinkling red and green lights. She looked like a walking Christmas tree. Despite his immersion in a murder case, Chief Marshall showed up, too. The chief was determined to help maintain a sense of normalcy for our little town during the holiday festivities. He interrupted Mayor Minter's announcements to address the crowd.

"Listen up, everyone. I need your help." The crowd silenced as the chief called for their attention. "We received a report of a stranger lurking nearby." Then he waved his arms dramatically and bent toward the microphone with a playful look on his face. "It seems the stranger is quite short and totally green. Yes, GREEN!" At which all the children gasped and giggled.

"And…" The chief held his hands in the air until the crowd grew silent

Then, he whispered into the microphone. "I'm told he intends to *steal* Christmas!"

Now, the crowd roared.

Behind Chief Marshall, a life-sized Grinch ducked and swayed, hiding in the crowd. The children saw him first. They began to point and shout: "The Grinch! The Grinch!"

The chief pretended not to understand their words. "What's that? You see something? If you know where this creature is hiding, let me know. We will not tolerate the disruption of our holidays in English Village."

The children continued to call out, pointing at the Grinch as he bobbed and ducked behind the trees. Finally, the chief turned and saw the villain in the crowd. Santa and the mayor grabbed the Grinch while the chief handcuffed him. We all cheered to see the grumpy green creature tossed into a waiting patrol car.

When the kerfuffle subsided, Santa proclaimed, "Let the Christmas activities begin!"

Children formed a ragged line for a turn to sit in Santa's sleigh and whisper their wish list into his ear.

I turned to Harvey. "This never happened in the city!"

"No?"

"Absolutely not. We were far too sophisticated." I adjusted the woolen scarf around my neck in a mock gesture of sophistication.

"Well, that's a shame. Fun stuff like this happens all the time in English Village." Harvey carried our skates over his shoulder as we walked to the carriages.

"I wish the chief could find Opal's murderer as easily as the children discovered the Grinch."

Harvey nodded. "Me, too. I'm uncomfortable knowing there's a killer among us. Especially when he seems to be focused on you."

"I don't understand why I have become a target."

"You ask too many questions. He thinks you will expose him."

"But I don't know who it is."

"It doesn't matter, Josie. The whole town knows your reputation for digging into these crimes. They assume you're a threat…which is why I want you to back away." His voice was calm, but I knew we were on dangerous ground.

"Look, here's our carriage," I said, and Harvey dropped the subject.

The gravel road circled the frozen Crystal Lake and the expansive meadow where people gathered near several scattered fire pits for warmth. We rode to the halfway point before we climbed out of the carriage. Hay bales rimmed the snow around the rink. We chose one and sat to lace our skates while we watched friends and neighbors glide across the ice.

"Look, there's Pieter from the tree farm." I pointed to the young man who raced around the outer edge of the pond.

Many of the skaters were couples, moving gracefully across the ice. A few soloists twirled in pirouettes—spinning through the air like professionals. One section of the rink was designated for beginners. Families with small children held hands as they shuffled in halting steps near the railing.

The temperature dropped quickly as night fell. I was relieved that we'd bundled up. My fingers and toes were warm, but my nose and cheeks were stiff with the cold. I already longed for my cozy fireplace and a hot mocha latte.

A concession stand at the edge of the rink offered sandwiches and hot drinks. Volunteers made s'mores, selling the sticky treats to the hungry children. "I'll get us hot chocolate and meet you on the ice," Harvey said.

"Sounds good," I agreed. We had planned to spend a half-hour skating, then I would return to my cottage to watch the chief's video.

Harvey headed toward the concessions, the blades of his skates gliding smoothly over the ice. I stood in the snow, wobbly on my blades, and walked awkwardly to the ice. Within a few minutes, I found my stride and skated steadily into the flow of the traffic.

I'd almost completed my first trip around the rink when I saw Harvey, again. He skated toward me, with cups of hot chocolate in each hand. I nodded to him and motioned to meet me at the hay bales. Then, from the corner of my eye, I noticed a flash of red. It zoomed toward me so fast I had no time to change directions. I stopped, mid-stride, to stare. It was the crazy purple hat woman!

Beyond her, in the background, I saw Harvey do a double take. He dropped the hot chocolate on the ice and raced toward the woman, but he was too far away. She charged, head down, and rammed me just below the hips. I did a head-over-heels slow-motion flip, twisting my ankle as my full weight landed in a heap at the snow fence. The woman didn't stop; she raced to the opposite end of the rink and slipped into the crowd.

Harvey rushed to my side, lifted my head gently from the snowdrift. "Josie, can you hear me?"

"She clipped me!" I still couldn't believe I'd been tackled on the ice with hundreds of skaters nearby.

"Can you move your legs?" Harvey tried again to get my attention.

I looked down at my tangled limbs and then up at Harvey. "Ouch."

"Stay where you are. I'll get help."

He stood and whistled, getting Pieter's attention. The young man skidded to a stop beside us. "Whoa. What happened here?"

"Josie had an accident. Stay with her while I get the medics."

That was the last I remembered until I opened my eyes in the ambulance. Harvey rode at my feet, and an EMS nurse peered into my face. "Hello there!"

I tried to sit up, but the nurse gently pinned my shoulders to the cot. "You had a nasty fall. We're taking you to the ER."

Chief Marshall showed up at the hospital as the doctor wrapped my ankle with a compression bandage. He stayed to interview me while I waited for a prescription and a medical release. At the chief's request, Harvey stepped into the hall.

"What can you tell me about this woman, Josie?" Chief Marshall asked. "Harvey reported the attack to our patrolman, but the woman disappeared into thin air."

"She hits like a man. And she doesn't play fair. If I were a ref, I would have given her a flag on the play." The chief did not smile at my attempt to make light of the incident.

"I'm serious, Josie." Chief Marshall glared at me, his pen poised over his notepad. "Did you notice any distinguishing marks?"

I stared at him. "No, Chief. My head was buried in the snow."

"But, what about as she was running toward you?"

I thought for a moment. "She was on skates. She could have been a hockey star. The woman literally raced toward me and knocked me down. The only thing I noticed was a blur of red with purple feathers on her head."

The chief wrinkled his brow. "Everyone describes this woman in the same way. Doesn't she have another hat or coat?"

A faint bell rang in my aching head, and I remembered Kate's call. "She has blond hair!"

"Aha. New information."

I explained the two encounters the Mahjong Mavens reported from earlier today. "Kate saw her in church this morning. Then, Kate and Lorene talked to her at the Tulsa Doll Show."

"My Lorene?"

"Er, yes. She and Kate drove to Tulsa for the afternoon."

"She didn't mention a conversation with the purple hat woman."

I stammered, trying to cover for the chief's wife. "Well, I don't know if she actually talked to the woman. Kate did. Lorene was in line to see a doll appraiser for the story I'm writing."

"Uh-huh." He scribbled more notes, but the chief didn't look happy.

"Anyway, Kate said she carried a bag like Pearl's. And she seemed friendly. She claimed she had never been to English Village, and was in Tulsa to meet her *screenwriter* cousin. Although, she *did* ask a couple of questions about the murder case." I halted, abruptly.

128

"And?"

"And...Kate told her we were about to solve the case."

"I see."

Judging from his tone, I was afraid the chief understood more about my role in the investigation than I wanted him to. "Do you think that's why she returned to English Village?" I asked. "To put me out of commission?"

The chief's worried eyes met mine. "I don't know, Josie. There is something odd about this woman. No one really knows her, yet she shows up everywhere. If she isn't the murderer, she may know who is. She's hiding something. I'd like to talk to her, personally."

"Oh!" I cried out so loudly that Harvey stuck his head back in the door.

"What happened? Do you need the doctor, Josie?"

"No." I pulled my phone from my pocket. "I just remembered that Kate took the purple hat woman's name and contact information. She expects me to call about a story on her cousin."

"*I* will call her, Josie, *not you*. This woman is intense. It's time to put some distance between you."

I handed the phone to the chief. "Her name is Felipa Garcia. Here's her number."

He read the name and looked at me, a question in his eyes. "Are you sure you want to continue on this case?"

"Like you said, we must be getting close. I can't stop now."

My head pounded—I couldn't tell whether it was from hitting it on the ground, or from the effort to piece together this murder puzzle. The nurse returned with instructions for my sprained ankle.

"The X-rays don't show a fracture, so you should be able to walk again in a week or so. Meanwhile, *rest* is your friend. Keep your ankle elevated, and avoid activities that cause pain, swelling, or discomfort. Use an ice pack on that ankle for about twenty minutes. Repeat the ice treatment every two to three hours while you're awake. The compression bandage will help. Use it until your swelling stops."

"You mean I can't put any weight on my foot?"

The nurse smiled at me. "Most likely, that will cause you pain. Don't do it.

We can get you crutches if you need them."

Harvey waved his hand at me. "Nellie has a pair. She will bring them to you tonight. And Kate has one of those knee scooters you can borrow. We've got you covered on transportation."

Two hours after the attack at the skating rink, Harvey helped me through the door of the cottage. Nellie arrived with her crutches, a huge blooming Christmas cactus, and a cheesy spaghetti casserole.

"What are you doing, Nellie?"

"I'm bringing you holiday joy. The casserole is comfort food; the cactus will boost your spirits."

"It's too much. I didn't have major surgery; I sprained my ankle."

"This is the third time someone has threatened you." Nellie shook her finger in my face. "Just let me take care of you."

I saw the worried look in her eyes and reached out to take her hand. "Thank you, Nellie."

It was late, but my friends stayed to get me settled. Nellie wrapped my ankle in a plastic bag, helped me into a hot shower, and washed my hair. By the time she dressed me in my pajamas, my pain pills had kicked in.

I couldn't believe I was home, in pj's; my sprained ankle propped on an ottoman and packed in ice. Nellie sat next to me on the couch while Harvey made popcorn. We gathered on my couch in front of the television.

"Are you sure you feel up to this?" Harvey studied my face as he asked the question.

"We can't allow that woman to stop our investigation," I said. I still couldn't believe she had plowed me down like a sack of potatoes.

Nellie nodded her agreement, then inserted the thumb drive of the video footage, TV remote in hand. "Let's find a murderer."

Chapter Nineteen

Moe sat close by my side with his head on my lap. He sniffed my ankle and looked at me with sad eyes. I shared my popcorn with him while Nellie fiddled with the TV settings until I suspected she might be stalling.

I understood her reluctance. As much as I wanted to solve this case, I dreaded what we might see. The chief knew he was asking us to witness the murder of Nellie's aunt. Normally, he would avoid sharing crime-scene photos. *This* was a video of the actual crime taking place.

Finally, Nellie looked over at me. "Ready?"

I took a deep breath and stared into her eyes. "This wasn't what we planned for a movie night," I answered. "I don't want to watch it."

Nellie held the remote control in her hand. "Neither do I, but it can't wait. Chief Marshall is counting on us, and so is my Aunt Pearl."

"Go ahead then." I steeled myself for what was to come.

She clicked "play," and the crowded Christmas Market appeared on the screen. The footage was shaky, with gaps and jerks between scenes. It was obvious the videographers were amateurs—still, I was thankful for the access to their cell phone documentation.

We watched all the way to the end, without speaking. I jotted numbers from the timestamp posted in the corner of the screen. The lab had assembled forty minutes of video, intermingling the shots from several

131

different witnesses. They pieced the footage together in chronological order, beginning with crowd scenes five minutes before Opal's fall and concluding three minutes after. The first half of the video played in real-time; the last half repeated the same sequence in slow motion.

When the video ended, no one spoke. I looked at Nellie. "Well?"

She hedged my question. "You watched it, too. What did *you* see?"

"Harvey?" I implored him to tell us what we wanted to hear.

He shook his head. "We can watch it again, but the critical seconds are missing."

I sighed. "But we know she did it."

Nellie patted my arm. "At the very least, the crazy purple hat woman stole Opal's bag."

We watched again, pausing the footage at several points. This time, we scrutinized the crowd for suspicious characters. The scene began with a slow panorama of the plaza. It was a lovely, smooth shot—the lights twinkled, and shoppers strolled through the booths, bundled in heavy coats and scarves.

"There!" Nellie pointed to a man in a dark coat with a cape. "Is that Sean Connery?"

I squinted at the screen. The man stood near the carolers, a pipe in his hand. The lighted tree behind him gave a silhouette effect. The video wobbled—perhaps someone jostled the videographer's arm—as it moved past his shadowed face. "It's possible. The shot is too blurry to be sure."

The scene cut to a different point of view, from another camera. This one focused on the carolers performing. If I looked behind the carolers, and slightly to the left of the screen, I could see Pearl and Opal among the revelers seated at the wishing well. They were in the background, but near a lantern; their faces were clear. Hot tears pricked my eyes as I watched the twins, their heads together, enjoying the concert.

Seconds later, a flash of the red and purple darted across the plaza. Just as the blur neared the wishing well, something—an arm or a shoulder—crossed in front of the camera. It was only for a moment. When the view was clear again, Opal no longer sat beside Pearl. Instead, people screamed as they bent over the edge to peer into the well.

Nellie said it first: "There is no way to tell who pushed her."

We watched twice more, making a list of the spectators we recognized. There were no surprises. Millie Wilkinson was there. I saw the Amish girl, with her brother. Ruth Stewart, the sweet-faced lady who reported a gunshot, hovered behind the carolers. The banker, Michael Fuller, stood with a cup of coffee in his hand. After Opal's fall, the crowd rushed toward her—like an ocean current drawn to the shore—before withdrawing again, into the sea of people.

Most notable were the faces we didn't see: the mysterious Sean Connery or the elusive Mr. Phillips. I knew the Connery look-alike had been on the scene earlier. Phillips claimed to have arrived a day after the event, but I had hoped to catch him in a lie. I searched every face for the bearded gentleman or the bald, limping old man. Neither was captured in the videos.

It was nearly midnight when my friends left the cottage. I was comfortably ensconced in my recliner, with my ankle elevated. Nellie promised to return in the morning. I shooed them out the door and tried to close my eyes. Images of Opal, disappearing from the ledge of the well, hovered in my mind. My pain pills eased the ache in my ankle, but I could not sleep.

Surrendering to my insomnia, I dragged my tote bag onto my lap. I flipped through my note cards, searching for answers. Initially, I was convinced Mr. Phillips was the murderer. He certainly had a penchant for violence hidden beneath his country-boy façade. But how could he have killed Opal if he wasn't shown in the videos? I was the only one who had identified him as a potential suspect.

The purple hat woman—Felipa Garcia—baffled me. She was everywhere—sometimes at three places in one day. Like today, when she appeared at my church in the morning, spoke to Sharon in Tulsa midafternoon, and decked me on the ice this evening. Logistically, it was possible to do. But, why would she put herself at risk of discovery? And how did she manage to disappear so quickly? I made another notecard: Hiding in Plain Sight.

I wondered about Millie Wilkerson. She was present the night Opal died. Perhaps her rivalry with Pearl was more intense than she indicated. Envy sometimes turned sinister. Millie was nearby when Felipa snatched the tote bag. Might she have taken the opportunity to shove Pearl into the well, but mistakenly pushed Opal, instead?

If I considered only people with direct connections to Opal, the list narrowed dramatically. There was the screenwriter—who might lose money with Opal dead. And, there was Mr. Gower—who might be my Sean Connery look-alike. Between the two, Mr. Gower seemed most likely to be the murderer. He had warned Opal she was in danger. Could his phone message have been a ruse to establish his own alibi? Would Opal have pretended she didn't know the British man, when he tried to gain access to Pearl's doll collection? And, why didn't we see him in the videos from that evening?

As these random thoughts swirled through my head, I shuffled the note cards. Stacking them face down, I dealt the first three cards onto my lap. Three names stared up at me: Sean Connery. Edward Gower. Felipa Garcia.

Opening my laptop, I typed: Felipa Garcia. Google delivered 459,000 results, but no exact match. Instead, my trusty resource suggested I check alternate spellings. So, I did. I looked at Phillipa Garcia. I searched under Felipa Howard, and Felipa Howard-Garcia. When Google failed me, I turned to social media—again without success. The woman was not even listed as a member of the UFDC.

We still had two ways to find her: through Kate's information from the doll show, or through the address from the car rental company. I hoped one of those would yield results. The woman was a bully and a thief—and possibly a killer.

If the purple hat woman was an enigma, Edward Gower, Esq. was an open book. My Google search for his name produced hundreds of photographs and articles. Mr. Gower owned an antique shop on Church Street, in London. He had published a number of authoritative articles on collectibles, including several about dolls. He gave money to charities and hobnobbed with socialites. He even had his own page on Wikipedia.

I studied the photographs closely. While he did have a mustache and beard, he looked nothing like Sean Connery. His hair was darker, and he appeared much shorter than the British man pursuing Pearl. His bio told the story of a third-generation antique dealer. He married a woman of comparable heritage, then lost her to cancer after ten years of marriage. He never remarried but was frequently seen escorting wealthy widowed women to high society events.

I browsed through dozens of newspaper clippings, fascinated by the man's connections. He authored an article that appeared in *Antique Doll Collector Magazine*, a London publication. The story described dolls as an art style as old as humanity itself. Mr. Gower compared them to paintings, sculptures, and great works of literature.

Noting that "dolls have existed for as long as we have," the article suggested ever-changing styles were indicative of the gradual shifts in the definition of beauty. Gower wrote: "Dolls have been in existence from the time of the very first humans and are likely to continue to be created for years to come." He predicted doll collection values would continue to rise.

Everything about this man looked authentic. From his Oxford education to his family pedigree, Mr. Gower was impressive. Of all our suspects, he stood out as the least likely to be a murderer.

My ankle began to ache again. I should sleep, but I was fascinated by the wealth of information about Edward Gower. Perhaps he wasn't what he appeared to be? My mind raced with the possibilities. He could secretly be a smuggler or a spy. With access to the rich and famous, he might specialize in counterfeit antiques.

Studying Mr. Gower's social life was like reading a fairy tale. He attended premier nights at The Globe Theatre, and charity balls at the Landmark Hotel. Remembering that Opal loved the theater, I wondered whether she and Edward ever attended the plays together.

One of the most striking photos on the internet showed Edward Gower, Esq., at the London Fashion Doll Festival. The theme for the event was "ROYALS," with attendees being "encouraged to dress themselves and their dolls in their regal best to celebrate all things royal-related." The event took place near Kensington Palace and included an auction and raffle to raise money for children with cancer. There, from the society page of *The Guardian*, he smiled at me.

But it wasn't his smile that attracted my attention. It wasn't his perfectly tailored tuxedo. It wasn't even the beautiful gown Opal wore, standing by his side. What I noticed most in the photo was the doll: he held Pearl's antique doll in his hands.

Chapter Twenty

Monday Morning

My nose awakened before my eyes: I smelled bacon, sizzling on the griddle. Nellie grinned at me over the kitchen island. She had taken my spare key the night before, but it surprised me to see her so early. I squinted to read the kitchen clock, but it was too far away to see.

"What time is it? And, how did you get in without waking me?"

"Good morning to you, too. For your information, you slept till nine-thirty, and Moe greeted me at the door an hour ago."

I rubbed my eyes and squirmed uncomfortably in the recliner. "Ouch."

"Need some help?" Nellie wrapped an arm around my waist, and I limped to the couch. She propped my ankle on the ottoman, covered it with an ice pack, and handed me a mug of coffee. "This will make you feel better."

When Moe nudged my arm and whined, Nellie laughed. "That spoiled dog has already been outside. And, he had two slices of bacon crumbled on his dog food this morning."

I wrapped my arm around his neck, and Moe looked at me with sad eyes. "Is that true, boy? You've already had breakfast?" He laid his heavy head on my knee and whined again.

"Nellie, I think he has forgotten whatever treats you gave him!"

"Moe has a short memory, Josie. He's not getting more. I'll give him a toy to keep him occupied."

The coffee worked its magic, clearing the cobwebs from my aching head. After breakfast, Nellie handed me the crutches, and I hobbled into the bedroom. When I returned, dressed in black sweatpants and a holiday-themed T-shirt, Nellie applauded. "That's the spirit."

I gave her a grateful nod. "Thanks. The ice-skating snowman on this T-shirt seemed appropriate. Plus, it was the first one I pulled out of my drawer."

She handed me my cell phone. "Chief Marshall called. He wanted to remind you that Mr. Gower will be at the station again this afternoon. He wonders whether you and Pearl still plan to identify him."

"If he looks like the guy in a photo I found last night, he isn't Sean Connery," I said.

"The chief will be disappointed."

I shrugged. "Mr. Gower could still be helpful. He can explain the warning he left on Opal's phone. And, he can tell us more about Pearl's doll. Opal purchased it from his shop."

"How do you know all this?" Nellie stared at me, hands on her hips.

"Let's just say I didn't sleep well last night. I spent hours on the internet, instead."

Nellie frowned. "No wonder you slept so late. I thought the pain pills were responsible. Why don't you let me bring Pearl here for lunch? Then, I can take you to the station. You can't drive with that ankle."

I made the call to Pearl. She answered on the first ring. Providing no details, I invited her to join me for lunch at the cottage. "Nellie is cooking. She will pick you up. The chief wants us to meet him at the station afterward. I thought we could ride together."

Pearl readily agreed. "Lunch sounds good, but I don't need a ride to your cottage. We're driving my son Matt to the airport right now. Paige can drop me off on the way back."

I could tell that her son's brief visit had lifted Pearl's spirits. She walked in my door wearing a canary yellow suit and a bright smile. Until she saw my swollen ankle propped on the ottoman. "My goodness. What happened?"

"I had an accident at the ice rink."

Nellie frowned at me and rolled her eyes. She shook her head and looked at Pearl. "She was tackled on the ice." I listened as Nellie told the story of the purple hat lady racing across the pond to send me sprawling into the snow.

When she described my ride in the ambulance and the doctor's report, I shook my head. "It wasn't as bad as it sounds, Pearl."

Pearl's eyes watered. "This is because of me, isn't it? First, someone kills my sister; now they attack my friends."

Nellie ushered her to a seat. "No. This wasn't your fault!"

I hurried to agree. "It's *my* fault. I asked too many questions. The chief says I made the killer uncomfortable."

"Isn't that what we want?" Pearl had a satisfied smirk on her face.

"He thinks we are close to solving the case." I grinned at her. "That's good news. It's worth a twisted ankle if we can arrest Opal's murderer."

The kitchen timer rang, and Nellie pulled freshly baked bread out of the oven. "Lunchtime. No more murder discussions until we go to the police station." She set steaming bowls of soup on the table, and I hopped over to join them.

Pearl waved toward my crutches. "Those sticks won't help your bowling score."

Nellie snickered. Pearl had conjured up an image of me, hopping down the bowling lane with crutches. The sight was enough to keep the two of them going until I regained control of the conversation.

I gave Pearl a stern frown. "I can't believe you said that!"

She looked at me with wide-eyed innocence. "Who, me?"

Her fake smile reminded me of our lunch with Opal, when each insisted the other sister was the troublemaker. For the rest of the meal, Pearl told us about her son's visit. They planned a memorial service, to celebrate her sister's life—scheduling it for late spring, in London. She spoke calmly, with only a tinge of sadness in her eyes.

"Opal loved the springtime. We want to host a garden party for her friends. It will be a celebration of all the things she enjoyed most—with food and entertainment." Pearl described the music and flowers she envisioned at the event; I could easily imagine the lively crowd sharing their memories of her sister.

I placed my hand over hers on the table. "It's a perfect idea."

Pearl squeezed my hand. "Thank you, dear. I hope you will consider joining us."

While Nellie cleared the dishes, Pearl pulled an envelope from her handbag. She set it on the table between us. "I wanted you to see the note Opal tucked under my doll, that day at the inn. I couldn't bear to read it until this morning. Handwritten notes are such a personal thing. It's silly, I know."

Seeing the pain on her face, I squeezed her hand again. "Not at all."

She opened the note and handed it to me.

As I read the words, I understood why Pearl wanted me to see them. She watched my face for a reaction. When I finished, I looked up at her.

"It's important, isn't it? This is why he killed her." Pearl sat on the edge of her seat.

"It might be." I didn't want to give her false hope. But I agreed the note could be helpful. "Let's take it to Chief Marshall."

Pearl sighed. "I'm sorry I didn't read it earlier. It might have led the investigation in a different direction."

I shook my head. "No. Your timing is perfect. The chief is meeting with the antique dealer this afternoon."

Pearl's phone rang, and she scrambled to retrieve it from her purse. She shot me an apologetic look. "It's Paige."

Even listening to only one side of the call, I knew something terrible had happened. Pearl's eyes were wide, and she shot off a series of questions: "Oh my! Are you hurt? When did this happen? Who was it? Did you recognize his van?"

Nellie and I hovered closer. We could hear the panic in the young girl's voice, but not her words. Pearl nodded as she listened, signaling us to stay calm. "Is Chief Marshall there now?"

After a longer pause, she spoke kindly into the phone. "No, dear. This is not your fault. Do as the chief says, and I will call you later this evening. You are safe, and that is all that matters." Pearl ended the call and turned to

Nellie and me, a quivering frown on her lovely face.

"What is it? What happened?" Nellie practically shouted the words.

"After Paige drove me here, she returned to my home. She planned to tidy up the room my son had used. Then, the doorbell rang. She looked out to see a delivery van in the driveway. A man stood on the porch, carrying an enormous bouquet. Paige couldn't see his face, for all the blooms."

"She opened the door." I made the statement with apprehension.

Pearl nodded, sadly. "Yes. The delivery man pushed past her to get inside. He grabbed her and placed a wet cloth over her nose and mouth. That was the last thing she remembered until she woke in the hall closet *a full twenty minutes later.* He covered her head with a pillowcase and locked her inside.

Nellie sighed. "Poor girl. How did she get out?"

"Luckily, she had tucked her cell phone in the back pocket of her jeans. You know these college kids; they are never without their phones! She dialed 911, like the smart young lady she is. Chief Marshall is there now. He's sending an officer to follow her home."

I grasped Pearl's hand. "What about you? Did he wreck your home? Will you be safe?"

Her eyes sent green sparks my way. "I will not let a stranger keep me from my home! The investigators have declared it a crime scene, but nothing appears out of place. We're to meet with the chief, as scheduled. Then, I will go home and take an inventory of anything missing."

Although I admired Pearl's spunk, she clearly underestimated the situation. Today's intruder might be the man who murdered her sister. He pushed his way inside. Why? Was he looking for Pearl or one of her possessions?

"Would you prefer to postpone our meeting with the chief? I'm certain he would understand."

"No! We can't delay the investigation any further. Look at what's happened in the last few days—an explosion, an attack on the ice, and now an intruder in my home!"

"We can't be positive they are related," I said.

Pearl scowled at me. "Seriously? I have no doubt about that."

"Did Paige give you any description? Or, a clue that connects them?"

"No. I'm relying on my own common sense. Paige said it happened too fast. I could hear that sweet girl shaking over the phone. Chief Marshall told her to get some rest. If she remembers any details, she will call him."

I gathered my notes, and Nellie bundled us into her car for the short drive to the police station. "I have a few errands to run," she said. "You two can break the news to the chief that we saw nothing on the video footage."

She dropped us at the door and promised to return in an hour. I took Pearl's hand, and we stepped inside. We were ready to identify Opal's murderer.

Chapter Twenty-One

Monday Afternoon

The smell of scorched coffee permeated the conference room. Chief Marshall pulled a chair out for each of us. I leaned my crutches against the wall and set the thumb drive and three file folders on the old metal table before gingerly lowering myself onto the seat.

The chief drank from a mug of dark brew. He waved toward the glass pot that simmered on a burner in the corner.

"Would you care for a cup?"

I wrinkled my nose, and Pearl nudged me with her elbow. She responded. "No, thank you, Chief Marshall. We just finished a delicious lunch."

"Good decision." The chief nodded his approval. "It took me three years to get used to the distinctive flavor of this blend. Most people find it too strong for their taste buds."

I pushed the thumb drive across the table toward the chief. "I'm afraid we weren't able to identify the killer," I told him. "The most important seconds of the video were blurred."

"Our team came to the same conclusion," Chief Marshall said. "We'll have to find our murderer another way."

"What can you tell us about Paige?" I asked. "Was she able to describe the delivery man who brought the flowers?"

"Only that he spoke with a British accent. She was shaken by the experience. It could be several hours before she recalls details."

Pearl clasped her hands together on the table. "That poor child. We have to stop this man, Chief Marshall."

I remembered the reason for our summons to the station. "What about Mr. Gower? Is he here?"

The chief rested his forearms on the table and turned his gaze to Pearl. "I think it's time we introduced you to Edward Gower, Esq., Ms. Merriweather. He's the British gentleman waiting for us in the holding cell. Normally, I would have you view him through a one-way window for the identification. But in this case, I would prefer that you hear his story firsthand, so you can discern whether it rings true to you."

I laid the photo I had printed from the internet onto the table in front of the chief. "Is this Mr. Gower?"

Chief Marshall studied the picture before answering. "His hair's a little longer now. But, yes, this is the man we have identified as a person of interest."

"I thought he came in voluntarily?" I was confused by the chief's description.

"Mr. Gower arrived here on his own, but we ran into a problem."

I wondered whether the chief intended to get to the point anytime soon. "Did he try to run?"

"No. But when he walked through our security gate, the alarm sounded."

"He had a *gun?*" My shrill voice sounded like it came from someone else.

"Yes."

"Was it a .22 caliber?"

"Yep. Tucked into his coat pocket, plain as could be. Mr. Gower claims he never saw the gun before. Our team will track the ownership and registration. We have already sent the weapon to the Wichita crime lab to check for prints. Then it goes to ballistics. We put a rush on it, so I'll have reports by tomorrow. If we have fingerprints and the bullet is a match, we will make an arrest."

I shook my head. "Something is off, Chief. It doesn't make sense that a killer would walk into the police station with the murder weapon in his coat pocket."

Pearl squared her shoulders. "Is there anything else we should know?"

Chief Marshall nodded. "Mr. Gower didn't arrive at the station until after lunch. It's conceivable he is the intruder who forced his way into your home this morning. We can't be sure."

The blood drained from Pearl's face, and I thought she might faint. I clasped my hands on the worn table and attempted to conceal my doubts by speaking in a level voice. "Chief, are you sure Pearl should be in the same room with him?"

The chief shoved his chair from the table to stand. "Trust me on this decision, ladies. I need to see his reaction when he is confronted with Opal's identical twin. I promise that neither of you will be in danger."

I pointed again to Gower's photo. "This man is not our Sean Connery look-alike. I believe he sold Pearl's doll to Opal. He might know something about her murder. But, if my research is accurate, he is a respected antique dealer."

The chief pointed out the obvious: "Let's hope Mr. Gower is exactly what he appears to be. Unfortunately, someone who appears respectable might also be a murderer."

Pearl's frail hand flew to her heart. "Oh my. If this is the man who sold the antique doll to Opal, he would certainly know its value. Chief, before we see him, I'd like you to read a note my sister wrote me. It's about the doll."

I pushed the second file folder across the table toward the chief. He opened it and removed the note. Opal's bold handwriting practically jumped off the page.

Dear Sissy,

I hope you will fall in love with this beautiful doll, as I did. Please treasure her and protect her always. She is coveted by many. Some would go to great lengths to take her from you. It is only through good fortune and circumstances that I was able to obtain her. I can't wait to tell you that story! Perhaps I will introduce you to the man who made it possible.

Love,

Opal (#2)

The chief raised one eyebrow as he read the last line. "Number two?"

Pearl smiled. "That was our private joke. I was born four minutes before Opal. When we were children, I loved claiming my rightful place as the elder sister. I could be a bit bossy, I suppose. Opal referred to herself as the second twin. As we grew into adulthood, she enjoyed reminding me that she would always be my younger sister."

"The antique doll Opal gave Pearl was highly valued," I said, handing the chief a copy of the article I had printed from the internet. "It belonged to Queen Elisabeth of Romania and has been missing since 1899—more than a century! Edward Gower located it and sold the doll to Opal."

Pearl's voice quavered as she pointed to the doll in the photograph. "As you can see, this rare doll may have attracted someone willing to commit murder, to claim her as his own. The person who shoved Opal must have assumed the doll was still inside the quilted bag I carried at our tea."

"Where is the doll now, Pearl?" The chief asked.

"Safe and sound, in her glass case at my home."

The chief nodded. "Unfortunately, an item this valuable is certain to be noticed. The fact that the doll has been hidden in a private collection for over one hundred years adds to the mystery."

"And mysteries increase the value." As I said the words, I wondered just how much the doll was worth and what Opal had paid for it...then paid with her life.

Pearl and I waited in the conference room while Chief Marshall arranged for an officer to escort Edward Gower down the hall to join us. Pearl fidgeted with her ring, twisting the flashy diamonds around her finger. I made notes of the questions I wanted to ask the antique dealer. Lost in our own thoughts, neither of us spoke.

I don't know what we expected, but when Edward Gower, Esq., arrived, he transformed the room. Like a true nobleman, he knocked gently before tilting his head through the threshold. "Good afternoon, ladies. May I join you?"

Suddenly, the officer who escorted him faded into the background. He became as insignificant as a casual onlooker—a mere bystander in the scene that transformed Mr. Gower into a gracious host with a charming accent and a genteel manner. Pearl shot me a look, and I knew she wished for a silver tea set and crumpets to materialize so we could all enjoy a proper midday treat.

Gower was taller than I anticipated. Although, I should have realized he would be, because the internet photograph showed him standing nearly a head taller than Opal, and she was not a short woman. As he walked through the door, he immediately extended his hand toward Pearl. She placed her hand in his, and, quite naturally, he raised it to his lips.

Tears sparkled in the corners of his eyes. "I am so pleased to meet you," he said. "You are nearly identical to Opal, so I am not surprised by your beauty."

Pearl smiled up at him. "You see the difference?"

"Naturally. You have a lovely beauty mark on your right cheek. Opal did not."

Under different circumstances, I would have stood to greet him. I might even have curtsied. Fortunately, my sprained ankle prevented me from embarrassing myself. Within seconds, Edward Gower, Esq., won our confidence. We sat together, chatting like old friends. He took no offense at my questions. In fact, he seemed as eager to answer them as I was to ask them.

Gower emphatically claimed no knowledge of the gun discovered in his coat. "Why would I walk into a police station with a gun in my pocket? I would have to be a bit of a dolt, wouldn't I?"

He had a simple explanation for the message on Opal's phone at the Philbrook Inn. "I received several calls from a man who wanted to purchase the Queen Elisabeth doll. When he learned it was no longer available, he insisted he would purchase it from Opal. I believed he would be persistent in his endeavor."

"How did he know she owned the doll?"

"Opal was so excited about her purchase that she shared the information

147

with several close friends. Word travels fast in the small circle of doll collectors. I'm afraid she would have been quite easy to find."

Pearl wanted to know more about Mr. Gower's dealings with her sister.

Quite willingly, he told us the story of his friendship with Opal. They met at a theater event where they struck up a conversation that lasted into the wee hours of the morning. He described her wit, her laughter, and her compassion for others. His tale was so engaging and authentic that Pearl begged him to continue.

"As luck would have it, a good portion of the original doll collection suddenly resurfaced amidst the belongings of a recently deceased Earl," Mr. Gower said. "One of rather dodgy character, I might add."

"And *you conveniently* obtained them?" A flicker of doubt flashed into my mind at the timing of the doll collection's recovery. It quickly disappeared when I heard his answer.

"No, but the royal family of Romania did. Then, a mutual acquaintance contacted me on their behalf," he said. "He arranged a meeting. When they authorized me to sell the long-lost Carmen Sylva doll collection, I thought immediately of Opal."

Mr. Gower turned again toward Pearl. "We had become good friends. We attended a few film events and a charity gala together. Your sister had searched for an exquisite doll from the moment I met her. She wanted to give you a treasure—and I knew the Coronation Doll from Queen Elisabeth was the perfect gift."

I interrupted his story to ask, "What is the doll worth?"

"Sold as a stand-alone item, she would sell for at least $250,000 American dollars. At an auction, the doll might fetch twice that amount. Fortunately, the Coronation Doll was one the royal family entrusted me to sell. They allowed me to lower the price if I located a particularly deserving buyer. I was able to offer it to Opal for a fraction of the auction price."

After Mr. Gower returned to the holding cell, Chief Marshall stepped into the conference room to share another important detail. "Paige called. She still can't recall her attacker's face, but she remembered something equally significant. The man wore a large ruby ring. It was all she could see when he shoved the bouquet in her face."

Pearl turned to me, excitement raising her voice. "It's him! The man Josie calls 'Sean Connery.' I remember his ring from the day he confronted me in the restaurant at The Philbrook."

Chief Marshall grabbed his notebook and stared intently at Pearl. "I don't recall you mentioning a ring when we took your statement earlier."

"I didn't. It wasn't until afterward, when I talked to Josie, that I remembered the flash of gold and a ruby stone on his finger." Pearl glanced toward me.

I pushed the third file folder toward the chief. "Sorry. The ruby ring is included on this updated list of suspects. I've added to their descriptions, based on conversations with Pearl and some of the mavens. I planned to give it to you today."

Chief Marshall opened the spreadsheet and scanned the notations beside each name. "It's interesting that Mr. Connery reappeared today. No one has reported seeing him since the day Opal fell into the well."

"Actually, there are several mentions of a man with a British accent. We think those refer to our mystery man."

The chief raised one eyebrow. "Couldn't they also point to Edward Gower?"

I rolled my eyes to indicate my doubt. "Anything is possible," I said.

I motioned to the spreadsheet of suspects. "Each of these people might have desired the doll. How can we determine which one killed Opal?"

"Let's review each of them more closely, tomorrow," Chief Marshall said. "I will issue a statement tonight. Maybe it will prompt new leads from the public. Pearl, you are free to return home. Officer Devon will drive you to make certain you arrive safe and sound. Please give us a call if anything seems out of place."

Nellie was waiting for me in her car when I left the station. Thick snowflakes fell steadily as she drove me back to my cottage. I hummed along with the Christmas carols that blasted merrily from her radio. I felt hopeful that we would solve the murder soon.

How could I have known the case would get even more complicated before nightfall?

Chapter Twenty-Two

Monday Evening

I settled into my recliner while Harvey chopped carrots at the kitchen counter. He and Nellie had organized a tag team for meal preparation after my fall. Although I protested, we all knew arguing was futile. With the two of them in charge—and a generous casserole supply from the mavens—I was covered for meals the next several days.

I had just swallowed a pain pill and turned on the television set when Sharon stopped by with a homemade pumpkin pie and two packs of colorful winter napkins. The messages made me smile. One packet featured a pair of ice skates over the phrase *Keep Calm and Skate On.* The other showed a question mark etched in ice with a two-word message: *Go Figure.*

"Ha-ha," I said. "I'm not likely to be figure-skating anytime soon."

"Good girl," Sharon said. "Keep your foot up and get some rest."

"She's not going anywhere," Harvey assured my friend. "Josie's investigating days are *over.*"

I was too tired to argue with a man who had just baked a chicken pot pie, *and* tossed a fresh salad, for my dinner. Moe hovered at his feet, hoping for a scrap to fall within reach. Harvey served the pot pie with a flourish. The comfort food was perfect for a snowy night. After dinner, I relaxed into my chair again to elevate my aching ankle.

I closed my eyes to doze through the weather report before the main news began. As the news anchor appeared on the screen, I woke to see bold red

150

letters race across the screen: *Breaking News.* I pumped up the volume and called Harvey. "Here comes Chief Marshall's statement."

The cameraman captured a close-up of the chief behind a podium I had never seen before. Standing tall in his starched blue uniform and gold badge, Chief Earl Marshall was a commanding presence. He looked directly into the camera and spoke with authority.

"Tonight, we ask for your assistance in locating a person of interest. Please be on the lookout for a tall man, approximately six-two and fifty to fifty-five years of age. He is white, with a neatly trimmed graying mustache and beard. He speaks with a British accent."

I laughed when the camera cut to a police artist's sketch of an old Sean Connery photo. "I think that pose is from a James Bond movie."

Harvey stood beside my chair to watch the interview. "Chief Marshall looks great on camera."

"Yes."

We admired the chief's flawless appeal to the public. He rarely sought the limelight, preferring to keep a low profile in our little town. The television news team had ventured here to feature our picturesque holiday festival. The murder case was a bonus story. We watched as the reporter narrated clips from the Christmas Market, zeroing in on the wishing well where Opal had fallen.

"Those reporters are like vultures," Harvey said. "Do you think the newscast will help find Sean Connery?"

"I hope so. With the whole town looking for him, the man can't hide forever."

The chief concluded with a word of caution. "If you see anyone matching this description, do not confront him. Call the number at the bottom of this screen. We appreciate your support."

As I turned off the TV, my cell phone rang. Harvey groaned at the timing. "There you go. The public is already responding."

I rolled my eyes at him and showed him the caller ID: Pearl Merriweather. "Hello, Pearl. Did you make it home okay?"

"Yes, dear. And you will be happy to know the Coronation Doll is still in her glass case, and nothing is missing."

"All of your dolls are where they should be?"

"Oddly, no."

"What are you saying?"

"My girls have been moved into different places, but they are all here."

"How can you be certain?"

"I keep a current inventory list in a small jewelry safe, inside my closet. I've gone through the entire list and checked off each of the dolls. To be honest, it was a bit like a scavenger hunt. The intruder had moved many of the dolls—in their glass cases—to different rooms. But I was able to find all of them."

"How many dolls do you have?"

"The list shows 243. My new Coronation Doll makes 244. I added her to my insurance policy the day after Opal died, but I haven't updated the printed inventory."

"Two hundred and forty-four!"

Pearl was quick to respond to my shock. "I know it seems like a lot, but most have only a sentimental value."

"The Coronation Doll is *truly* safe?" I wanted her to reconfirm her answer to this important question.

"Yes. She had not been moved. Every other doll was rearranged, but the most valuable doll was still in her glass case on my dresser."

"Are all the dolls in glass cases?"

"Only half of them. The others are on stands protected by plastic cases."

"And you're *sure* nothing was taken?"

"I believe you already asked that," Pearl's voice held an edge of irritation before she reassured me one final time. "Don't worry, Paige will be here in the morning to help me count them again. We will let you know if anything is amiss."

I sighed as I ended the call. Harvey raised an eyebrow. "Something wrong?"

"It makes no sense for a man to force his way into Pearl's home, rearrange all of her dolls—except one—and leave again."

"Nothing is missing?"

"Not that Pearl can see."

Harvey frowned. "I agree with you. No one works that hard to gain entry, only to leave empty-handed."

"Paige will double-check Pearl's inventory tomorrow. Maybe they will uncover a discrepancy."

"I'm sure the chief will handle it from here," Harvey said. "Let it go, Josie."

I shoved my disturbing thoughts to the back of my mind as Harvey started a fire and cleared the dishes. From my vantage point near the fireplace, I could see the streetlights along Persimmon Lane blink on—turning the lazy snowflakes into silver sparkles. The snow was heavier now, and twilight quickly turned to dusk. As I watched, a dark vehicle turned into my driveway. Bright headlights flooded the living room. For two long minutes the car idled in the drive while its piercing high beams drilled into the cottage.

"Are you expecting someone?" Harvey peered out the window.

I squinted against the light but could discern nothing beyond the glare and the falling snow. "No."

"Turn off the lamp." Harvey's voice quivered with urgency. My heart raced as he moved efficiently through the cottage, flipping light switches and closing the window coverings. He slid the deadbolt into place and turned on the porchlight.

Seconds later, both doors of the vehicle slammed shut, and two hooded figures rushed up the sidewalk. I saw one sling something across his shoulder. The second person carried a package; he ran with a blanket over his head. I lowered the recliner and prepared to throw myself to the floor. Harvey stepped to the side of the door, where he could observe the unexpected visitors.

They stood, apparently arguing with each other, on the front step. Harvey shrugged his shoulders but motioned me to stay seated. When the doorbell rang, I jumped. Harvey leaned his head into the glass pane. Then he turned back toward me.

"I believe it's the paparazzi." He rolled his eyes.

"Who?"

"One of them is carrying a large camera. The other has an easel slung over his shoulder."

Now, it was my turn to roll my eyes. "I thought it was a gun."

"Shall I send them away?"

"Yes, please!"

Harvey opened the door far enough to stick his head outside. I could hear the voices, but not their words. He allowed them several minutes to make their pitch; then, he firmly sent them on their way. He handed me a business card with a grimace. "Looks like you've got a fan club."

I glanced at the card and recognized the name of the reporter who had interviewed Chief Marshall on the evening news. "Why would they want to see me?"

"They wanted details about the murder case, and someone suggested you could help."

I shook my head. "The last thing I need is my face plastered over the late news."

"Don't be surprised if the reporters try again," Harvey said. "They are determined to interview you."

"That's not going to happen," I said. "When *we* solve this case, I will write the crime story for *The Village Gazette*. They can read it like everyone else."

"Don't you mean, when *Chief Marshall* solves the case?" Harvey's eyes had returned to steely blue, again.

Before I could reply, my cell phone rang. I didn't recognize the caller ID, so I answered with a question. "This is Josie Posey. Why are you calling me?"

Ava hesitated, her soft Jamaican accent soothing in my ear. "It's me, Josie. Breathe easy. It's all good, girl."

I heard the thunder of the bowling lanes in the background. "I'm sorry, Ava. I thought you might be a news reporter. How are you?"

"I'm okay, ya know? One of my employees saw Chief Marshall on the news tonight. She said he described a customer who stopped here last night. She came to tell me about him. He's gone now. Should we still call the chief?"

"Is your employee reliable?"

"She's an old woman. In Jamaica, we say, 'de olda de moon, de brighter it shines.'"

I laughed at her description. "She's smart."

"Yes, ma'am. She's a smart cookie. If she says the man was here, he was."

"Is he a regular? Do you know his name?"

"He only came in one time. But I can tell you about him. Like the chief said—he was a charmer with a British accent. Not some ragamuffin street guy."

"What else did you notice?"

"He rented shoes and a ball, but he didn't stay long enough to wait for a lane. He left his belongings in the locker."

"Wait. You mean his things are still there?"

"Are ya listening, girl? That's what I'm sayin'. He walked out. We still have his driver's license and whatever he stored in the locker. We always keep the license until our customer returns the locker key."

"Eva, I'll call Chief Marshall. Stay where you are. Act natural."

"Natural?"

"Do what you would normally do. If the man returns, call the chief. I'll give you his direct number. Don't try to stop the guy. If he wants to check out, let him."

"Got it. I'll wait to hear from you."

Harvey stood with his arms crossed and glared at me as I dialed the chief's number. His body language told me everything I needed to know, but I placed the call anyway.

Chief Marshall's deep voice was rich and warm. "This is Police Chief Earl Marshall. If you have an emergency, please hang up and dial 911. If you need assistance with a traffic ticket or another pending legal matter, please call the station during regular office hours. If you need to speak with me personally, please leave your name and number, and I will return the call."

I was surprised to hear the recording. The chief had always answered my calls. I left a message and waited.

While I scribbled notes onto my ever-present cards, Harvey took the opportunity to reason with me. "You've done all you can, Josie. It's time to let the chief do his job."

"Chief Marshall needs my help," I said. "I can't stop now."

"Yes, you can," Harvey insisted. "No one expects you to hobble on crutches in pursuit of a killer."

"You don't understand, Harvey. This is important."

"More important than your own safety?"

"I'm not worried about that."

"*I am!*" Harvey shouted. "And I want you to stop all of this."

I swallowed hard and fixed my eyes on Harvey's red face. "What, exactly, do you want me to stop?"

"All of it. The research. The investigative reporting. Everything."

As I stared up at him, my phone rang again, and I broke eye contact to check the caller ID. "It's the chief," I said and swiped to accept the call.

Harvey threw his hands in the air and stomped into the kitchen.

Chief Marshall apologized for not picking up my earlier call. "Sorry, Josie. We're getting leads from all across the county. Dozens of people claim to have seen Sean Connery. Judging from the locations and times, some of those sightings were actually of Edward Gower. The two men are quite similar when you consider their physical attributes alone. Do you have something new?"

I explained the call from Ava, including the details, as concisely as I could. The chief listened. He asked questions. Then, he made a decision, and it was my turn to listen. His calm voice was reassuring. "Okay, Josie. Here's the plan."

Chapter Twenty-Three

Late Monday

After the chief's call, I convinced Harvey to pack up some gear and take me to the bowling alley to meet Chief Marshall. It wasn't an easy sell. Harvey was still angry that I refused to drop the case, but he knew if he didn't drive me, I would find another way to get there.

I also suspected that he couldn't resist the opportunity to show off his bowling skills. His only requirement was that we stop at his place to pick up his bowling bag. "It will look more authentic if I'm bowling with my own shoes and ball."

I agreed. "The suspect may not show up. But, if he does, we need to blend into the crowd."

Harvey stared pointedly at my bright blue ankle wrap and crutches. "Not likely, with that foot of yours," he said.

I lifted my chin and glared at him. "I'll camouflage it with my coat while I watch you bowl."

"If you were smart, you'd stay home," Harvey muttered.

Orchard Lanes bustled with people when we arrived at 8 p.m. It was League Night; rowdy teams wore matching shirts and carried personalized bowling balls to their assigned lanes. When Ava met us at the check-in counter, she lowered her voice to explain that she had quietly shuffled two of the competitive teams to vacate lanes for our sting operation.

She offered to retrieve the suspect's driver's license from her safe, but the chief asked her to hold onto it until he could arrange to secure it in a plastic evidence bag. "We'll take care of it after we catch this guy tonight," he said. "I want to preserve it properly so we can document our receipt of the license in our official chain of evidence. The fewer fingerprints we have on the license, the better."

Chief Marshall positioned his team in the upstairs office. The tinted window allowed them an expansive view of the entire building. Ava provided extra bowling shirts to four of the chief's officers so they could blend into the league teams. I recognized Patrolman Devon, in a bright orange shirt with LARRY embroidered over the pocket, and "KINGPINS" on the back.

The plan was a simple one: position ourselves throughout the bowling facility, spot the mystery man if he showed up to empty his locker, and detain him for questioning. The timing for this sting was critical. Chief Marshall hoped to catch the suspect after he opened his locker, but before he removed his belongings from the building. Otherwise, he could claim the items were not in his possession.

We huddled briefly in the employee break room behind the racks of rental shoes. Chief Marshall, the four officers wearing bowling shirts, Harvey, Ava, and me. The chief summarized our assignment. "In the past twenty-four hours, our Sean Connery look-alike has stored items in the bowling alley locker room, forced his way into Pearl's home, and rearranged her doll collection. The man is likely to disappear again, once he removes any evidence from the locker."

Ava was the first to comment. "I know we want to catch a *queffa*, but can it be on the down low? I have customers to keep."

I was accustomed to Ava's lyrical accent, but she occasionally lapsed into words I didn't understand. "A *queffa*?"

The chief answered without hesitation: "A killer."

"Oh."

He smiled at Ava and turned to address the rest of us. "Listen to the lady. We want to catch the suspect without creating a brouhaha in the bowling alley. The best place to do that is in the locker room, after he opens it to remove his belongings."

Everyone nodded as he gave final instructions. "If you see our guy enter the building, alert the team. Each of you will be wearing an earpiece. All you have to do is give the suspect's location. The nearest officers will respond. We will approach the locker room and block the exits. I will direct the response from that point. Remember: we have no evidence this man is a killer. We simply want to talk to him, based on his behavior and his interactions with Pearl."

Harvey and I tried on our earpieces and practiced transmittals with Patrolman Devon. We walked out of the break room and stood near the registration desk. I leaned against my crutches to scan the crowd. Ava directed us to the lane nearest the entrance. Pearl and Paige waited for us there.

I saw the excitement in Pearl's eyes. "Tell us everything!"

"Our job is an easy one. We keep our eyes open and enjoy the evening. If we see our Sean Connery mystery man walk through the door, we alert the chief."

"That's it?"

I shrugged. "No tackling allowed."

Pearl sighed. "If you insist. But I do hope he shows up."

"Me, too."

Harvey set his powder blue bag on the floor and shoved the retractable handle into place. The case looked like an overnight luggage bag, complete with wheels. He unzipped the side pocket and removed his shoes. Then he gave Pearl a lopsided grin. "I heard you took advantage of a beginner the last time you played."

"Pshaw! That was no game. It was a teaching session." The old woman's green eyes flashed. "I took it easy on them."

He laughed. "You might want to go easy on me, too. I haven't bowled for years."

Pearl arched one eyebrow. "You have a ball with your name on it," she said.

"That's just window dressing."

Pearl gazed at him, shrewdly. "And I'm an old woman."

If the two had been on the set of a Western movie, they would be circling each other with ivory-handled pistols holstered and at the ready. Paige grinned at me from behind Pearl's shoulder.

I interrupted the sparring. "Why don't the two of you play? Paige can keep score, and I'll watch the door to see if our mystery man appears."

Paige handed me a bright yellow pillow. "This is to brace your ankle. You have a perfect excuse to position yourself on the bench, facing the entrance."

Soon, we fell into the rhythm of the bowling alley. The noisy league bowlers welcomed the undercover officers as "fans" wearing jerseys that matched their team colors. Otherwise, the boisterous activities mirrored other league nights. Waitresses delivered a steady stream of pizza and beer to the lanes. Music blared over the speaker system, mostly drowned out by the sound of bowling balls and tumbling pins. I kept my eyes glued to the front door to study every person who entered.

Pearl and Harvey bantered as they vied for bragging rights on the lanes. She clearly had the edge when it came to longevity at the game. After years of practice and competitive play, Pearl's style was consistent and productive. Harvey was taller and stronger. He launched his ball like a missile, driving it powerfully down the lane toward the targeted pins. In their first game, Pearl won by a narrow margin. She promptly stepped into the lane to take an exaggerated bow and shake Harvey's hand.

All the while, I kept a watchful eye on the door and one ear tuned to the police earpiece. Harvey's battery had died, so he could no longer listen to the police chatter. No one reported a Sean Connery look-alike at either of the other entrances. I began to wonder whether the man would return. The busy league night seemed a perfect distraction, if our person of interest wanted to slip into the locker room, unnoticed. Still, I saw no sign of him.

Ava stopped by the table in our lane. She flashed a bright smile as she delivered cups of hot coffee and a platter of chocolate brownies. *"This be brain food,"* she said in her Jamaican accent.

Harvey took a bite of the decadent treat. "The coffee might keep us clearheaded, but chocolate is purely an energy boost—which is exactly what I need, to beat Pearl's bowling score."

I shared a knowing look with Paige. "So far, he's trailing by thirty points in game two," I said.

Pearl patted Ava's hand. "Thank you for the treats, my friend. I will save mine for later; I'm coaching Harvey now." She raised her ball, gracefully trotted down the lane, and released it to roll smoothly down the center for a solid strike.

Harvey threw his hands in the air, and Pearl pranced back to his side. "Did you see that one?"

Under the surface of their laughter, I heard the chief's low voice in my earpiece. "Josie, someone has entered the door closest to you. My angle from this overhead office isn't good, and there's a bit of a crowd exiting the same door. I believe the man in the dark coat is walking with a familiar limp. Do you see him?"

I strained to separate a limping man from the rowdy league bowlers gathered near the exit. "Yes! There he is. That's not Sean Connery. It's the detective—Howard Phillips. What is *he* doing here?"

The chief's calm voice provided precise guidance: "Officer Devon, break away from your league bowlers and walk toward the men's locker room. You are to observe an older gentleman, wearing a black duster coat. He has a red bowling bag on a wheeled cart. Do not reveal your identity."

I ducked my head to avoid eye contact with the detective. Unaware of his entrance, Harvey and Pearl continued to bowl. The man walked behind our lane, just twenty feet from where I slid lower in my seat. The chief noticed my efforts. "Nice job, Josie. Stay where you are, until we apprehend Mr. Phillips. I don't believe he is here to bowl with his buddies."

The next several minutes were a whirlwind. I saw Officer Devon saunter behind the detective and tail him into the locker room. Chief Marshall hustled down the stairs from the loft office and reached the lobby seconds after the other two disappeared behind the swinging doors. Another pair of officers blocked the rear exit. They looked like regular bowlers engaged in a raucous argument over whose team would win the championship trophy.

Were it not for my earpiece providing a play-by-play, I would never have suspected there was an altercation taking place in the men's locker room.

161

When I pressed my hands over my ears to block out the exterior noises, Harvey and Pearl raced to my side. Harvey knelt beside me. "What is it, Josie? Is he here?"

I shook my head. "This wasn't the plan. We have to clear the building. Now."

The words had barely escaped my lips when I spotted the remainder of the sting team, rounding up bowling patrons and directing them to an exit at the far end of the building. Ava turned off the party music and handed a microphone to Officer Devon.

"In the interest of public safety, we need everyone to walk quickly to the West exit. This is not a drill. Please gather in the parking lot and wait for further instructions. Do not leave the area. We will get you back inside as soon as we can."

I grabbed my coat and handbag. Paige helped Pearl with her cape, and Harvey handed me my crutches. For a crowd hovering around three hundred people, the evacuation went smoothly. I hobbled the distance of the lobby, trying to listen to my earpiece as we made our way outside. Ava was behind us, chattering in her native language—something about a headache. Despite the chief's best intentions, her best customers were forced into the cold. With any luck, they would tell the story of this night to their grandchildren for years to come.

The snow fell in huge flakes as we stepped outside the glass doors. The chief's microphone must have disconnected in the locker room scuffle. I could hear only muffled conversations. Someone shouted.

Harvey suddenly realized I was still connected to the police communication system. "Where's the chief?"

I groaned. "Everyone is in the locker room. But it wasn't Sean Connery who walked in the door—it was Howard Phillips."

"The bomber?"

"Yes! And he was dragging a red bowling bag behind him."

Chapter Twenty-Four

Late Monday Night

Everyone from the bowling alley clustered into groups to stay warm in the snowy parking lot. The crowd milled around the open area nearest the exit doors, clearly confused by the unexpected evacuation. For the most part, they gathered in clumps to speculate about what might have prompted the police to shoo them so quickly into the cold. No one panicked, though a few began to complain loudly about the inconvenience.

We made our way down a sloping sidewalk to a concrete bench, where Pearl and I claimed a seat. Surveying the crowd, I could see that most people had carried their drinks outside with them. Paige had the presence of mind to bring our tray of coffee cups, and Harvey had stuffed the brownies into his coat pocket. We sipped hot coffee and devoured the treats while we waited for news.

My earpiece was useless at this range. I worried about what might have happened inside the locker room, but I figured we would know soon enough. We spent twenty minutes shivering in the frigid parking lot before the officers directed everyone to return to the building. Ava offered free coffee to her customers; the music blared again, and the bowling resumed as though nothing had interrupted the evening.

I hobbled back to our seats, searching the lobby for a glimpse of Chief Marshall or the elusive Mr. Phillips. I didn't have long to wait. They emerged from the back hall and hurried in our direction. The shady detective was in handcuffs; Officer Devon escorted him discreetly to the exit, where a police car waited, lights flashing. The chief followed, wheeling the red bowling bag at his side. He stopped at our lane and nodded to Pearl and Harvey before he spoke to me.

"Thanks for your help tonight, Josie. We didn't capture Sean Connery, but Mr. Phillips may be able to enlighten us to his whereabouts."

"You're sure there's no bomb?" I motioned toward the red bag.

"Positive."

"Just a harmless bowling bag?"

The chief grinned at my persistence. "The bag is ordinary, but its contents will surprise you."

"Can I look inside?"

"I suppose you will need the information for your big scoop in the *Village Gazette*," the chief said.

Now, my curiosity soared to new heights. "Could I see it tonight?" I dared to ask even though I saw a scowl darken Harvey's face as he sat on the bench a few feet away from me.

Chief Marshall's eyes darted to the bench before he answered. "You should go home and rest," he suggested, with a slight tilt of his head toward Harvey.

"That's impossible," I insisted. "I'll just lie awake all night."

Finally giving in to my pleas, Chief Marshall shrugged his shoulders. "You have a point," he conceded.

Then, the weary chief approached the bench, where Harvey remained with his jaw clenched. "Sorry, Harvey, but she's right. Please bring Josie by the station on your way home. I'd like her opinion."

Harvey and Pearl halted their game and declared a tie. I suspected that Pearl orchestrated the results, hoping for a rematch. The evening had taken a toll on her energy; she was content to go home to a warm bed. "Call me tomorrow, dear. I know the chief will have news you can share."

We drove to the police station through the snow without speaking. Harvey was focused on the road and I was lost in my thoughts, trying to guess why Mr. Phillips showed up at the bowling alley instead of Sean Connery. The chief had appealed to the public to locate our British mystery man, and Ava responded. How would Phillips know anything about the locker?

Like most mysteries, the answer would be in the details. My mind raced with possibilities. Did the detective know Mr. Connery from another case? Could they have met casually at the Philbrook Inn during the Christmas Market? Were they old college roommates?

And what was he hiding in the red bowling bag?

As we turned into the parking lot, Harvey finally spoke. "Josie, you know I don't approve of this encounter. I'm asking you again to back away from the case. The chief has his man now."

"You can't be serious." I stared at Harvey for so long that he finally broke eye contact.

He raised his hands in a small gesture of surrender. "Okay. I give up. Go inside…but please be careful around this guy. Don't forget that he tried to leave a bomb in your living room."

"Aren't you going with me?"

"I'll walk you into the building and wait for you in the lobby. The chief wants your opinion, not mine."

"Oh, Harvey…" I started to argue with him, but he shook his head to silence me.

"You know it's true," he said. "If the chief offers you an exclusive interview with Phillips, he's likely to speak more freely one-on-one. I don't care to listen to the guy's explanations. He's a crazy man."

"Surely he wouldn't attack me in the police station," I said.

Harvey's face pinched tight with an emotion I didn't recognize. I wondered whether it was fear or anger. "The guy is a cowboy, Josie. Who knows what he will do? Just be cautious."

"Please come with me to see what the chief found in the bowling bag," I said. "You don't have to stay if I interview Mr. Phillips."

Harvey paused for a second, then ducked his head and shrugged without looking at me.

A blast of warm air greeted us when we entered the lobby. I saw the chief near the conference room door. He motioned for us to join him; my heart beat a little faster as we walked down the narrow hall. I heard Harvey's footsteps on the tile behind me. As we turned the corner into the room, my eyes searched for the old man who had frightened me twice before—once in his car and once on my doorstep. He wasn't there. Instead, I saw only the bright red bowling bag positioned in the center of the conference table. A box of disposable latex gloves rested beside it.

I sighed with relief and turned to the chief. "I thought Phillips would be here."

Chief Marshall laughed. "He's in the holding cell. I figured it would be good for us to talk before you confront him."

"Has he confessed?"

"That would be too easy. He did apologize, though."

"For what?"

"For the mini bomb in your gift basket. He feels terrible about it and has offered to pay any damages. He still doesn't know it went off in Harvey's truck, instead of your living room."

"What excuse did he have for delivering it?"

"Mr. Phillips admits to being a hothead. He was angry that I allowed *you* to help with Opal's murder investigation, and not him. He thought the mini-bomb would scare you away from the case."

"I guess he didn't know it would only make me more determined to solve it."

"We have arrested him for manufacturing an explosive with intent to intimidate or cause alarm to another person; distributing an explosive without a Bureau of Alcohol, Tobacco, Firearms and Explosives (ATF) license or permit; and transporting explosive materials without a license or permit."

"Are those felony charges?"

"The DA will decide. The device exploded outside, and no one was injured. They may reduce it to a misdemeanor."

My eyes darted to the red bag again. Chief Marshall slid it toward me, along with the box of gloves. "We photographed the contents and dusted for fingerprints. You can open the bag; just handle it with care."

I looked up at him. "Is it dangerous?"

The chief shook his head. "There's no booby trap, Josie. See for yourself."

After I pulled on a pair of gloves, I unzipped the front pocket. Inside, I found a metal ring about the size of a silver dollar. Over a dozen miniature keys dangled from the hoop, jingling merrily as I set it on the table. At Harvey's hardware store, the staff often made duplicates when a homeowner provided the master key. But the keys on this ring were much smaller. One key was slightly larger and marked with the number 55. "Interesting...*this one* must fit the locker at the bowling alley."

"Good guess, Josie." The chief nodded his approval. Then he handed Harvey a pair of gloves and gestured for me to pass him the keyring.

Harvey studied them, as I had. "They aren't house keys," he said.

"Could they be padlock keys?"

"Possibly. They would also fit a specialty lock. I've seen keys this size for file cabinets or jewelry displays.

"Or *doll cases!*" I exclaimed.

Chief Marshall crossed his arms and gave me another approving nod. He watched without comment as we set the keys aside to retrieve the next item. I reached into the same side pocket and removed a folded paper. It was a standard sheet of bond paper, with a brief set of instructions. The list was typed; it contained no names or addresses.

1. 8 p.m. Monday: Park vehicle in rear Philbrook Inn lot, with trunk open. (Enter the restaurant and order coffee to go.)
2. Return to vehicle. Trunk will be closed.
3. Drive to Orchard Lanes. Remove bag from trunk and proceed to Men's Locker Room.
4. Use Key #55 to open the Locker #55.
5. Remove the package from the locker, place it, unopened, in the bag.
6. Leave Key #55 in the locker.
7. Return the bag to the trunk of the vehicle and drive back to the Philbrook parking lot.
8. 8 a.m. Tuesday: Unlock trunk of vehicle and enter the hotel lobby. (Sit by the fire and read the newspaper. Wait 15 minutes.)

9. Return to vehicle. Your job is completed.

I looked at the chief. "What is this?"

"Mr. Phillips claims he knew nothing about when, or how, the package was placed in the locker. Says he was hired by an anonymous client to pick up a package and return it to its owner." The chief gestured at the paper in my hand. *"Those* were the instructions he received."

"But you stopped him before he could complete the job."

Chief Marshall tapped the face of his watch. "We still have nine hours before the vehicle is supposed to park in the lot, trunk opened. I plan to be there to apprehend his anonymous client—*Mr. Connery*, we hope."

"What if he doesn't show? Someone may have alerted him to the bowling alley sting."

"Let's hope not. We believe he will try to retrieve his bag for the contents inside."

I turned back to the bag and unzipped the larger pocket designed to hold a bowling ball. Inside, someone had stuffed tissue paper into a nest. Within the nest was a package wrapped in brown kraft paper and tied with string. "FRAGILE" was written in a wide black marker along one side. Carefully, I lifted the box out of its cocoon and set it on the table.

The top of the box was sliced around all four sides. I removed it and reached inside, only to discover another container. This one was made of glass; I recognized it immediately. "It's a doll case!"

The chief nodded. He watched as I gently tugged the glass out of the box. I set the display case beside the red bowling bag and studied it. A tiny locking mechanism secured the glass to the wooden base—with a keyhole the size of the miniature keys on the ring. Finally, I scrutinized the doll inside. "This is Pearl's new Coronation Doll!"

"Not a bomb, but a bombshell, nevertheless." Chief Marshall agreed. "I had never seen the doll. I suspected this might be the one we've heard so much about, but I appreciate your verification. Mr. Phillips claims he had no knowledge of the contents."

"I don't understand how the doll can be here; Pearl told me it was on her dresser, where it belonged. In fact, she said it was the only doll from her collection that wasn't touched when the British intruder delivered flowers and locked Paige into the closet. She's *certain* he pranked her by shuffling the dolls into different rooms, without removing any of her treasurers. The Coronation Doll had not been moved."

Harvey frowned. "Could there be two of them?"

Chief Marshall raised his eyebrows and gave me a look I couldn't decipher. "Josie? What do you think?"

"Twin Coronation Dolls? One for Pearl and another for Opal? I saw nothing in my research to indicate that two dolls were made...but I suppose it's *possible*."

I pulled the doll closer to study her face. "She looks authentic."

Suddenly, I knew how to solve this piece of the puzzle. "We should ask Mr. Gower to look at her! As an appraiser, he can tell us whether one is real and the other is counterfeit."

The chief sighed. "He is still in the holding cell, voluntarily, until we can find our other British suspect."

I raised my eyebrows at the chief. "Isn't that even more convenient? We could show it to him *right now*."

Chief Marshall uncharacteristically evaded my question, and I felt a tingle of irritation. *Why wouldn't he accept my suggestion?* "It's late. I will talk to him in the morning. First, we need to prepare Mr. Phillips to complete his delivery. I have my own decoy package to put into the bowling bag."

"What should I do?"

"Go home, Josie. Elevate your ankle. Sleep. If you promise to stay in the car, I'll let you ride along with Officer Devon to watch the action in the Philbrook Inn parking lot tomorrow morning."

"Count me in," I said, not realizing that everything I did in the next several hours would be a total waste of time.

Chapter Twenty-Five

Tuesday Morning

After Harvey dropped me off at home, I managed a hot shower and tried to follow the chief's advice, but it was impossible to sleep when I was so filled with adrenalin over the long-anticipated arrest.

Instead, I spent two hours scouring the internet. First, I searched for information on the Coronation Doll, hoping to learn more about the designer who created her. Instead, I followed a rabbit hole into doll making. During the 1890s, the expensive models were likely to be made of unglazed bisqueware, with a lifelike pink coloring. Coiffures precisely followed contemporary fashions. Wigs and glass eyes were common, and a few designers created dolls that could close their eyes. I hadn't noticed whether Pearl's doll had eyes that closed, but her hair matched photos of Queen Elisabeth of Romania.

I read that doll appraisals were influenced by the type, make, age, and condition. Original clothing and accessories added to the value. Collectors and museums considered the doll's provenance as well as its authenticity—without restorations or replacements of various parts. They preferred dolls with their original eyes, arms, legs, and fingers intact.

I learned that a doll collector was called a "plangonologist," and that the best of them were registered with national and international organizations. Unfortunately, my search for little known facts about the Coronation Doll produced no results.

Frustrated at my failed search for Carmen Sylva information, I spent another hour digging into the detective, Howard Phillips. As in my earlier search, the man was a phantom—with one exception. This time, one reference popped up: the photo from his purchase at the Christmas Market. His name was attached, but the clickable link led nowhere. If Howard Phillips had a social presence, I could not find it.

I peered more closely at the picture. The detective stood next to the same vehicle I remembered chasing me to the police station. The Amish boy beside him held the huge basket that exploded in Harvey's truck that same night. The detective bent his head toward the basket, obscuring part of his face in the photo.

Running out of leads, I thought again about the Sean Connery look-alike who continually slipped from our grasp. We still didn't have his real name. I sat for several minutes staring at my laptop in the wee hours of the morning. In a last-ditch effort, I logged into a favorite research site from my days as a crime reporter, *The Journalist's Toolbox*. The site requested my User ID. Suddenly, the word "ID" jumped off the screen, ringing a tiny bell in my head. Ava still had Sean Connery's ID at the bowling alley! We could track the man through whatever name he used on his driver's license! I texted the chief to remind him that I needed Sean Connery's real name.

Overall, my midnight googling had been nothing more than an energy drain. Exhausted, I let Moe outside to run crazy circles in the snowy backyard before we both fell heavily into sleep around two a.m.

When I finally closed my eyes, I saw Coronation Dolls dancing in their glass cases. There were dozens of them, spinning around my head until I grew dizzy watching them. I grasped at the air, trying to catch a tiny golden key that would unlock the one case that held the true Carmen Sylva collectible.

No wonder my eyes were dry and itchy when the officer knocked on my door at six. I climbed into his unmarked car and rode with him to the Philbrook Inn. Then, after my sleepless night, I wasted three more hours of precious time sitting beside Officer Devon in a frigid parking lot, waiting for a guy who never showed.

Our big sting was a bust.

The chief called it off at nine a.m. and sent us home, where I crawled back into bed and promptly fell asleep.

When Nellie arrived at ten, she balanced a breakfast casserole under one arm and opened my front door with the other. I was relieved that *she* had meal duty today, not Harvey. I wasn't ready for another heated discussion about my role in the murder investigation.

Nellie entered with an energetic "Hellooo." She set the casserole on my kitchen island and called out merrily, "Wake up, wake up! It's going to be a beautiful sunny day."

I rolled my eyes at her cheery greeting. "I see the sunshine, but what is the temperature?"

She laughed. "I think we might reach thirty-two degrees this afternoon. What do you expect? It's December in Kansas. Just be thankful it isn't snowing again."

We talked late into the morning. I described the showdown at the bowling alley, my failed internet research, and the unsuccessful morning sting. "We waited *forever*, but no one came for the bowling bag. We think someone must have tipped him off."

The only thing I omitted from my report to Nellie was the simmering argument between Harvey and me. Some stories were too painful to share.

After I'd finished, Nellie peppered me with questions. "Did you just say that the chief has two men in custody, and neither of them is the murderer?"

"Technically, he has Howard Phillips and Edward Gower in custody, but Chief Marshall hasn't charged either of them with the murder."

"And one of them had a gun?"

I stirred my coffee and tried, again, to explain. "Yes, Mr. Gower had a gun in his pocket, but we don't yet know whether it was the murder weapon.... Meanwhile, Mr. Phillips had a doll hidden in the bowling bag. It resembles Pearl's, but we don't have proof that it belongs to her, or that he stole it."

Nellie threw her hands into the air. "This is getting too complicated. People are getting hurt. My Aunt Opal is dead, you were injured, and

CHAPTER TWENTY-FIVE

Harvey's truck exploded. Someone should be arrested!"

"Mr. Phillips has been charged for the mini-bomb that damaged Harvey's truck," I offered, helpfully.

Nellie huffed. "That's a good start. What about the woman who tackled you?"

"We haven't seen her again."

"And Sean Connery?" She asked.

"The chief should be calling me any minute now, with a name from the driver's license Ava kept at the bowling alley."

The words were barely out of my mouth when my cell phone rang. I glanced at the caller ID and punched the speaker button.

Chief Marshall's familiar voice filled the room. "We have the mystery man's driver's license," he said. "It's from the United Kingdom, so it may take longer than normal to trace it. The man's name is *Phillip Howard*."

"What??" My voice came out in an incredulous shriek. "That can't be a *real* name, Chief. Not when the mysterious detective's name is *Howard Phillips*, and the purple hat lady is named *Felipa*!"

"Er, yeah, that does sound suspicious..." Chief Marshall's voice trailed to a halt as we both pondered the nearly identical names of our persons of interest.

After several seconds of silence, we heard a heavy sigh from the chief. "Look, something is obviously wrong with this picture," he said, "but I'd still like you and Pearl to look at the photo ID to see whether this is the man you saw at the inn. Can you do that?"

"Of course. We'll be happy to look at it."

"Perfect," the chief said. "Once you confirm his identity, our investigation will move forward. We'll apprehend Mr. Connery—or Mr. Howard— whatever his name is, and get to the bottom of this case."

We ended the call, and I turned to shrug my shoulders at Nellie. "I don't know how Howard Phillips and Phillip Howard are connected, but the similarity in their names can't be a coincidence."

The next few hours, Nellie made a grocery list and ran errands to restock my pantry and refrigerator. I busied myself with the morning crossword puzzle and dozed in the recliner with my throbbing ankle elevated, just as the doctor had ordered. I woke again when Nellie entered the front door, bags of groceries in her arms.

We worked side-by-side in the kitchen. She unloaded the bags and I sat on a bar stool and directed her where to store each item. In truth, my friend had spent nearly as much time in my kitchen as I had. She could easily have distributed the food to the appropriate shelves, without assistance.

When Nellie slid the final item into the refrigerator, my cell rang. I waved the caller ID in Nellie's face.

"Again?" She raised an eyebrow. "Let's see what's new."

I swiped to put the phone on speaker mode. "We traced the registration on the gun from Edward Gower's coat pocket," Chief Marshall said.

"And?"

"It belonged to *Opal*. She must have checked it with her luggage at Heathrow."

"Opal *carried a gun*? I wonder if Pearl knew about it?"

"Let's add that question to the list for this afternoon, when you look at the ID together."

"What happened to the detective—Howard Phillips?"

"He's temporarily a guest in one of our holding cells while Officer Devon drives to Tulsa to pick up his cousin Felipa. We want to ask her a few questions about the car rental and her whereabouts over the past few days."

"Do you think they were *both* involved in Opal's death?"

The chief sighed heavily. "I don't know what to think. But Phillips has popped up randomly, ever since we got involved in this case. He arrived one day after the murder and offered to help solve it. Then he attempted to frighten you off of the case. And, finally, he walked into our sting operation at the bowling alley."

"Too many coincidences?"

"Too many connections, but no solid evidence."

I understood the chief's frustration. Howard Phillips knew more than he had shared. As did Edward Gower. And neither man was in town the day of the murder. We desperately needed to investigate Phillip Howard (aka Sean Connery).

And just when I thought we would never find him, it happened. Our mystery man contacted the banker, and the banker contacted us. After I talked to Chief Marshall, I set my cell phone on the kitchen island and noticed a missed voice message. It was Michael Fuller, alerting us to another encounter with the British doll collector.

"Ms. Posey, this is Michael Fuller, from the bank. I heard from your 'Sean Connery.' He stopped into my office without an appointment, insisting that I value an antique doll on the spot. Please call when you receive this message."

Nellie and I debated whether to involve the chief, ultimately deciding to return the call ourselves. Her reasoning seemed logical. "Chief Marshall has his hands full with the other two suspects—plus cousin Felipa, who arrives this afternoon. The banker phoned you, Josie. It would be rude not to return the call yourself."

I pictured the round Mr. Fuller in his vested banker suit, his owl eyes peering from behind large spectacles. "You're right, Nel. I should gather the facts before we concern the chief."

The banker-doll-appraiser answered on the first ring. "Thank goodness! I've been waiting for your call. The man you described was here! He brought an antique doll and a photograph for my review."

"When?"

"Less than an hour ago. I called you the moment he walked out of my office."

"He resembled Sean Connery?"

Mr. Fuller chuckled. "My father would say he was the spittin' image of the actor. And with that accent. Of course, the *real* Connery is Scottish, but in all of those James Bond movies, he really sounds British."

"He showed up out of thin air and wanted you to appraise a doll?" I wondered what doll the man had taken to the banker. Pearl's doll was still in her home, and another was at the police station with Chief Marshall.

"Yes. Johnny-on-the-spot. No dillydallying, so to speak."

"Did you provide the appraisal?"

"Absolutely not. I promised to have it ready this evening. No self-respecting appraiser would certify a value without careful examination. I explained that my tools were at my home workshop."

I shook my head, trying to make sense of this latest development. "Mr. Fuller, are you saying that you have the doll in your possession?"

The banker spoke slowly, emphasizing each word, as though he doubted my comprehension skills. "Yes, Ms. Posey. It is normal procedure for an appraiser to possess the item he is valuing. I have the doll and a photo. Would you like to see them?"

And that is why Nellie loaded my borrowed crutches into her car and drove me immediately to the bank in Lindsborg, where Mr. Fuller waited with an antique doll.

Chapter Twenty-Six

Tuesday Afternoon

Farmers National Bank of Lindsborg was a half-hour drive from my cottage. We put away the remains of lunch and climbed into Nellie's car. Next to English Village, Lindsborg was my favorite Kansas town in what I referred to as the "Old Country Corridor." I was fascinated that our Kansas ancestors created a string of communities along the I-70 highway– each one celebrating a different country.

Within a four-hour span, a tourist could easily visit the UK, Sweden, Czechoslovakia, and Germany. These small towns across four counties were nationally recognized for their architectural style and their themed festival attractions. The tiny German town of Schoenchen, population 207, was as famous for its ornate St. Anthony's Catholic Church as it was for its annual Oktoberfest.

From an earlier trip to Lindsborg with the mavens, I knew there were pony-sized colorful, Swedish Dala horses scattered around the community for tourists to discover. The town boasted a private college and a lovely art museum featuring work by internationally known artist Birger Sandzen. Swedish flags of sky blue and yellow adorned the local shops, and a Svensk Hyllningsfest attracted crowds every October. It took me several tries to correctly pronounce the name of this Swedish Festival.

It was impossible to drive through Lindsborg without seeing the influence of their heritage, even on a day like this one, when I was focused on a murder investigation. We located the bank in the two hundred-block of South Main; the two-story building occupied a corner lot in what the locals affectionately called "City Center." It was made of red brick, and the entrance consisted of a simple wooden door with a transom window above it—fitting for the year it was built, in 1887.

A large Dala horse stood in front of the building, proclaiming the bank's Swedish pride. We stopped to read the plaque before we entered the lobby: *"Kronor the Dollar Horse is named for the Swedish money unit, but it has the green-tinged features of a one-dollar bill. Thanks to artist Shirley Malm, a horse never looked so rich."* Nellie groaned at the pun, but I loved it.

Inside, the bank lobby was both opulent and cheerful. Brass-framed teller windows and mahogany wall paneling were a testament to the historic nature of the building. Sunlight poured through large windows, and fresh flowers adorned the scattered desks and counters. Typical of a small-town bank, the staff welcomed us with smiles and greetings as we entered. Michael Fuller sat in a glass office with his name etched in gold on the door. He noticed our arrival and waved for us to join him. I introduced Nellie, pleased that she could witness our conversation. She sat tall in the leather chair, with hands folded on her lap. I held a notepad and pen, poised for information.

The banker was comfortably in control behind his antique desk. The last time I had seen him—the night of Opal's death, at the Philbrook—he was visibly shaken. Here, he was confident and in command. I understood why Kate was impressed with his knowledge and his professionalism.

"Thank you for driving here so quickly. I have only a few hours to study the doll and write an appraisal. Your Sean Connery will be in touch by seven this evening." He lifted a cardboard box from the credenza behind his desk and set it in front of us. "Here is the doll he delivered to me this morning."

The banker pulled thin white jeweler's gloves from his drawer and slid them onto his hands before he removed a glass case from the box. The doll inside was breathtaking. He removed a miniature key from an envelope on his desk, unlocked the case, and lifted the antique doll from her resting place. To my inexperienced eyes, she was an exact replica of the Coronation Doll we had seen at the police station. She wore the same white gown, and her delicate hands and face were made of rosy pink bisque. I clasped my hands to keep from touching her.

"Is she authentic?" Nell whispered.

Mr. Fuller turned the antique full circle, so we could observe the tiny buttons on the back of her dress. "It is rare to see this quality and condition in a doll from this era. To the naked eye, she is a perfect representation of the Carmen Sylva Coronation Doll. Her face and hair are exquisite. She has no damage that would mar her value. At auction, I believe this doll would bring $300,000 or more."

I gasped. "She's real?"

The banker smiled. "I would stake my reputation on it."

Nellie raised an eyebrow. "Don't you need to study it with a microscope or test the materials in some way?"

He nodded. "I'm afraid I wasn't totally honest with Mr. Connery. I always carry an extra set of appraisal tools with me. While I waited for you to arrive, I conducted an assessment. Would you like to see how I verified her authenticity?"

We leaned closer as Michael Fuller lifted the hair from the nape of the doll's neck. He held a lighted magnifying glass so we could read the date. "Here is a tiny marking that indicates the year she was created, the country, and the initials of the maker."

I read the lines he indicated: "1897 *Roumania LS.*"

Nellie studied them next. "Like an artist's signature on a painting!"

"Yes. Although we don't know the full name of this artist, the date is accurate. The coronation of Queen Elisabeth—who was also known as Carmen Sylva—took place on May 10, 1881. Her famous doll collection toured the country from August to January of 1898. The doll was created specifically for that tour. The spelling of the country is consistent with that era, too."

While the marking appeared to be genuine, I wondered how the appraiser could be certain it was original to the doll. "Couldn't someone have added the engraving later?"

"Ah, a skeptic!" Mr. Fuller was delighted by my question. "Allow me to provide additional proof." He turned the doll face up and focused the magnifying glass on her face. "See the grains of dust in the bisque? They are an indication of her age; they cannot be faked. Likewise, the fine cracks in her head; they do not detract from her beauty, but they confirm her years. Any antique doll would have similar cracks. Her eyes, cheeks, and lips are also slightly dulled with age. Additionally, her wig is made from mohair and is glued to her head. Both are typical of the year she was made."

I watched as he again turned the doll to point out two small holes near her shoulders. "The head, neck, and shoulders of antique porcelain and bisque dolls are made using one mold. These holes show where the head was attached to the rest of the body."

He indicated the tightly stuffed limbs of the doll. Her arms and legs were made of packed horsehair. "Antique dolls are never loosely filled," Mr. Fuller said.

"Was there anything suspicious about her?"

Mr. Fuller stared at me through his round spectacles. "At first, I was puzzled by her eyes. Antique dolls made before 1870 had eyes painted onto their faces. From 1870 to the early 1900s, the dolls had inset glass eyes which didn't move. This doll has eyes that close when she is tilted onto her back."

"But that wasn't done back then?"

"It wasn't done *in most dolls*. However, I found an article about the Carmen Sylva collection that indicates an exception. The Coronation Doll was one of the first to have eyes with lids that closed when she was placed on her back."

Nellie admired the doll's white gown. "She looks like a queen."

The appraiser nodded. "Her gown has faded with time, but it was made of a quality fabric—quite possibly from the actual cloth used to make the original queen's gown."

I desperately wanted to touch the fabric, but resisted the impulse. "No wonder this doll is valuable," I said.

Mr. Fuller set the doll aside and referenced the notes he had written on an appraisal pad. "My only concern is her provenance," he said. "There is no paperwork to track the ownership of the doll. Without that, it is impossible to provide a proper Certificate of Authenticity."

"What about the photograph he provided?" I motioned to the unopened white envelope that remained on his desk.

"Ahh, yes. *This* is a treasure." The banker removed a photograph from the envelope and slid it across the desk toward me.

The picture was one I remembered from my research on Carmen Sylva. It was from an article in *The Strand* magazine. The photographer had captured the Queen seated in her study, surrounded by many of her favorite things. She posed in a leather chair, her elaborate gown spilled gracefully into a pool at her feet. She held a book in her left hand, while she reached for a pen with her right. There were many items in the picture—framed artwork, easels, lamps, and books. I had seen it at least a dozen times and never noticed the doll positioned on the top shelf of a bookcase to the right of the photo. Now I saw her clearly, and my heart beat a little faster; she was undoubtedly the Coronation Doll.

I pulled my camera from my handbag and scrolled through my recent photos to find the ones I wanted to share with Mr. Fuller. "Could you examine these pictures, please?"

As Mr. Fuller bent over the camera, I explained. "The first photo is one of Pearl and her doll. She has the paperwork you described, and the doll is at her home."

Fuller raised his eyes to mine. "This looks identical."

"The next photo is a third doll—currently in the possession of the police department."

Mr. Fuller became agitated as he studied the two photos. "Long ago, there were rumors that a second doll was created for the queen's private collection. One doll for the tour, the other for the queen to keep. Those rumors were never verified. But a third doll? Impossible!"

"What should we do?" I asked.

The banker stood and paced the floor of his office. "I need to appraise the three dolls side by side. The fraudulent doll—or dolls—must be identified and removed. We should notify the authorities immediately."

Returning to his desk, he gently lifted the doll again and said with certainty,

"I guarantee you, *this doll is authentic.*"

I photographed the doll Fuller held in his gloved hands and forwarded it to Chief Marshall. Then we dialed his number from the banker's office. He didn't ask what Nellie and I were doing in Lindsborg; he reserved his questions for Mr. Fuller.

"Thank you for the photo, Mr. Fuller." The chief's voice boomed over the speakerphone. "I assume you heard from our 'Sean Connery'?"

"Yes. I didn't see identification—he said he had lost his driver's license—but he introduced himself as Phillip Howard, a British doll collector. I explained we would require a passport or another official ID card, to prepare a certificate naming him as the doll's owner."

I nodded when I heard the name. This definitely matched with the man who left his driver's license at the bowling alley. Chief Marshall didn't skip a beat.

"And the doll is genuine?"

"Yes, sir."

"When will our suspect return?"

"I'm to call him at seven. I don't know the meeting place."

Chief Marshall's deep voice filled the banker's office. "We need to intercept him before he retrieves the doll. Are you prepared to assist?"

"Yes, sir."

For the second time in two days, the chief outlined a plan to capture the elusive Mr. Howard. While the banker prepared his written appraisal, Nellie drove us back to English Village.

We had just four hours to set everything in motion.

Chapter Twenty-Seven

We stopped at Pearl's home on the way to the police station. Nellie waited in the drive with the motor running.

Paige opened the door and invited me inside. "Mrs. Merriweather is upstairs. She wants you to see the Coronation Doll—to verify for yourself that she is here. I can show you to the elevator."

I stared at her. "There's an elevator?"

"Yes, ma'am."

Paige led the way around a corner to open a door I had never before noticed. I hobbled into the tiny elevator on my crutches and gratefully rode to the second floor. Then, I made my way to the master bedroom and rapped on the door. "Pearl?"

"Come in, dear. I want you to see her with your own eyes."

Sunlight poured through the windows, silhouetting the old woman where she stood near her bed. I approached her, smiling. "I trust your eyesight, my friend. If you say the doll is here, I believe you."

She motioned to the locked glass case on her dresser. "As you can see, she is exactly where I placed her. I still have her original paperwork in my closet safe. I've made a copy of the Certificate of Authenticity, as you requested."

I stared at the doll. Her case was an exact match for the others I'd seen at the police station and the bank. When I walked closer, the doll's bright blue glass eyes captured my attention. "Tell me, Pearl: do her eyes close, when you lay her on the bed?"

"Yes, dear. It is one of the features I love most."

Having just come from the banker's office, I had hoped to see a difference between the dolls. If this one was a counterfeit, only an expert would know. I kept my suspicions to myself. Pearl would learn of the other dolls soon enough.

Instead of broaching that subject, I pulled a sheet of notepaper from my purse and handed it to Pearl. "The chief has another plan to capture the man who killed Opal. Here's what he is asking of us."

Pearl's green eyes sparkled with tears as she read. Then she returned the list to me. "I'm ready. Let's catch this murderer."

"Nellie is waiting in the car," I said.

If Pearl was afraid, she hid it well. She put on her coat, draped her purse over her shoulder, and picked up a soft leather bag with the Coronation Doll inside it. Her hands trembled as she slid the strap over her shoulder. "Let's go identify Sean Connery. This is for Opal."

"I'll be right beside you."

Riding down in the elevator, Pearl glanced at me and giggled like a schoolgirl. "If only he were the real Sean Connery! I had quite the crush on the actor for many years. I always hoped Opal would use her movie connections to make his acquaintance. Once, I sent her a telegram suggesting that she arrange an invitation to his red-carpet premiere of a James Bond film."

"Did she respond?"

"Oh, yes. With her own telegram. She turned me down—using words that aren't acceptable in polite society." We were still chuckling when we said goodbye to Paige and climbed into the warm car; Nellie insisted that Pearl tell the story again.

Ten minutes later, we arrived at the police station, and no one was laughing. Officer Devon directed us past Chief Marshall's office on the way to the conference room. I glanced inside to see the chief behind his battered wooden desk, the surface stacked high with papers. He leaned back in his chair and repeatedly clicked his pen with one hand while he barked orders into his phone.

We took our seats around the familiar old metal table in the room that always smelled of stale coffee. Pearl gazed around the bare walls and raised her eyebrows. "This place could use a woman's touch."

Nellie nodded. "I agree, but it's not going to happen. He likes it this way."

I laughed at Pearl's sour expression. "The chief wants to make visitors uncomfortable," I told her.

She surveyed the room again and bobbed her head. "Ah. This should do the trick."

When Chief Marshall joined us, he came directly to the point. "Good afternoon, ladies. I need your assistance in identifying our suspect."

All three of us nodded, without speaking.

He handed out three enlarged photocopies of the driver's license he had retrieved from Ava's bowling alley. "Each of you will answer separately. Do you recognize this man?"

One by one, we studied the photo before looking up at the chief.

"Josie?"

"Yes. This is the man I call Sean Connery. I saw him at the Philbrook the day Opal died."

"Pearl?"

"Yes, sir. He was at the inn; he tried to give me his business card. The man claimed to be a doll collector, interested in seeing my collection."

"Nellie?"

"No. I have never seen him before. But I do think he looks a bit like Sean Connery."

The chief pointed to the name on the license. "Does the name Phillip Howard mean anything to you?"

Nellie and I glanced at each other before we raised our hands. She nodded toward me to answer.

"Not until today, Chief. The banker, Michael Fuller, mentioned this name. He told us Phillip Howard was a doll collector in need of an appraisal. This is the man he described, and he is the one we phoned you about this afternoon."

Pearl hesitated. "That name is familiar to me, too. I can't place him, though."

Chief Marshall nodded at Pearl. "Let me know if you remember where you heard it. Meanwhile, did you bring what I requested?"

"Everything is in my bag." She handed him the leather satchel.

"Thank you." The chief's dark eyes rested on the old woman's face. "Michael Fuller will be here soon, to give me his formal statement. Meanwhile, Mr. Gower is in the back room. He has something to tell you about Opal, and the gun."

Pearl reached out for my hand and took a deep breath. "Can Josie go with me?"

"Yes. Follow Officer Devon to the holding cell. While you meet with Gower, I will prepare the banker for tonight's encounter with our suspect."

Nellie stayed with the chief while Pearl and I made our way to the back of the police station. Edward Gower rose from his chair when we stepped into his cell. He held a white envelope in his hand and greeted us with a cheery grin. "Welcome to my temporary quarters."

I took the chair he had vacated; Pearl perched on the narrow cot, and Gower sat beside her.

Taking my notepad and pen out of my bag, I began the interview. "Thank you for meeting with us."

He smiled and nodded. "Someday, I would like both of you to visit me at my home in London. We will have a proper tea." He described a table set for high tea in an English garden, rambling on about flowers and tea cakes.

His voice transported me to a faraway land, where castles and kings were an everyday occurrence, and Mr. Gower would be perfectly at home. Suddenly, I realized the room was silent. I shook the daydreams out of my head and looked up from my notepad. Pearl still sat on the edge of the cot beside Edward Gower, her hands clasped primly on her knees. He stared at her, then stood abruptly and stepped across the room to lean against the wall.

"My apologies, Mrs. Merriweather. I cannot stop looking at you."

Pearl raised one eyebrow. "What do you see?"

"The beauty of an angel, with the spirit of a Phoenix."

I gasped at the scene that played out before me. The two flirted as elegantly as characters in a Shakespearean play.

"You are an audacious man," she lashed out at him.

"Faint heart never won fair lady," he retorted.

"Ahem." I cleared my throat, to remind them they were not alone in the room.

Pearl laughed and clapped her hands. "Mr. Gower, that was delightful. We must do it again sometime."

The gentleman smiled and walked toward her. I watched, speechless, as he gave a slight nod of his head and took her hand in his. "So we shall, Mrs. Merriweather. So we shall."

I rolled my eyes at their performance. "Could we talk about the gun now?"

Gower grinned at me. "Always the detective, Ms. Posey? You must learn to follow your heart on occasion."

He handed me the white envelope and returned to his seat beside Pearl. "Inside, you will find a photo and a copy of the gun registration," he said.

I read the paper and passed it to Pearl. She gasped when she saw her sister's signature. "This is her handwriting. She wrote with such a flourish that the O and L were nearly the same size."

"Was she experienced with firearms?" I asked.

Pearl's eyes filled with tears when she answered. "Yes. My sister believed in being prepared for anything. Long ago, when we were in college, she insisted that we learn to shoot. On summer break, we joined a firing range and practiced every week. Opal bought a gun. She loved it. I never understood her fascination with the weapon."

I pointed to the stamp on the bottom of the paper. "It's a current registration for a rather old Derringer pistol. The purchase date says 1967. Is that possible?"

"Oh!" Pearl's voice trembled. "I was there when she bought that little gun. The steel barrel had a blued finish, and the handle grips looked like ivory. Opal always said it fit her hand perfectly. She has kept it all these years for protection."

Gower bowed his head. "I fear that I am responsible for this," he said.

"You! How is that possible?" Opal focused her bright green eyes on the antique dealer.

"I am the one who suggested she should carry it again, to protect herself and her property."

Pearl sighed. "Opal had a mind of her own, sir. She must have tucked it into her bag that night."

I studied the photo of the weapon. It was a tiny thing, only five inches long and three inches high, and thin enough for a woman to grasp easily. "Opal may have reached into her bag to fire the weapon at her attacker. When the thief tried to snatch the doll, the gun misfired and struck Opal, instead."

Edward nodded. "The weapon's safety latch must not have been set properly. Even the thief wouldn't have realized the bag held a gun."

Pearl wiped a tear from her cheek. "The robber had nothing to show for his efforts but a quilted bag with odds and ends of a woman's life–a tube of lipstick, a linen hanky, a billfold, and a pocket pistol."

"It's possible there were two individuals determined to take advantage of an elderly woman," Mr. Gower suggested. "One person might have pushed her while another opportunist attempted to snatch the bag containing the valuable doll."

My brain raced to process his suggestion. "Yes. That would make sense, if the two were working together," I said. An image of the obnoxious Phillip Howard and his purple hat cousin Felipa filled my head, and I was eager to share the thought with Chief Marshall, when I could talk with him privately.

Pearl took the photo and studied it. "Opal chose the Derringer because she thought it was safer. She would never have imagined being shot by her own gun."

I turned to Mr. Gower. "How did the gun end up in your pocket?"

He shrugged. "My coat was on the rack in the Philbrook lobby when I had breakfast. Anyone could have put it there. I didn't notice it until I arrived at the station and tried to go through the security gate. The weapon only weighs six ounces."

I closed my eyes and tried to replay that moment in my mind: the scene in the video where the action blurred, leaving only a glimpse of a powder blue bag, followed by a crowd descending to the spot where Opal had fallen into the well. It had all happened in seconds, but we would remember it for a lifetime.

Pearl interrupted my somber thoughts with another question for Edward Gower. "Could you explain how you were connected to the queen? Why did her heirs choose you to sell the doll?"

A faraway look filled his eyes. "Ah, yes. That's an interesting story. Allow me to share it with you."

Chapter Twenty-Eight

Tuesday Night

Pearl and I stayed with Mr. Gower for another half hour, hanging on every word of his doll story.

"My grandmother Lillie and the future queen were childhood playmates. The princess was named Pauline Elisabeth, but she preferred to be called Lizzie. Imagine! Two little girls called Lillie and Lizzie, running about the castle like sisters."

As he described them, I thought of two other little girls who played together as children—Opal and Pearl.

Lillie was the daughter of a lady-in-waiting; Lizzie, the daughter of royalty. Both were entranced by fashion and by dolls. They were inseparable. I imagined the young girls in the castles of Austria, as they dressed their dolls in the lush gardens and enjoyed tea parties on the terrace.

As young Lillie learned to sew at her mother's knee, she began to make doll clothes. Lizzie was willful and precocious; she designed the dolls' dresses and secured scraps of cloth from her mother.

Mr. Gower told of an idyllic life, where the young Elisabeth formed early ideas that favored a republican form of government over a monarchy. Many years later, parts of her diary were published, and her opinions were controversial. Gower stood and recited in his best imitation of Princess Elisabeth: *"I must sympathize with the Social Democrats, especially in view of the inaction and corruption of the nobles. These 'little people,' after all, want only what nature confers: equality."*

We laughed at his falsetto interpretation, but his description was powerful.

"By the age of sixteen, Lillie was in demand as a seamstress for all the ladies of the court. She ruined her eyesight, one tiny stitch at a time. In fact, she was nearly blind before she turned forty. I'm proud to say that Lillie created Queen Elisabeth's coronation gown. The two women spent many hours together, fitting and refitting, all while they laughed over memories of their shared childhood."

Pearl sighed. "What a lovely story!"

Edward Gower smiled at her. "Lillie saved scraps of fabric from the gown and created a miniature version for the Coronation doll to wear. She made two of them, to assure the doll would have a spare. It wasn't until much later she heard rumors that the Queen had commissioned a second doll—keeping one with her at all times, while the other was on tour."

I recalled reading about the queen when I researched her doll collection. "I never saw any mention of a second doll. By that time, Queen Elisabeth was famously known as Carmen Sylva—a writer, an artist, and a performer. She spoke several languages. It must have been rare for someone of her stature to remain friends with a commoner."

Gower nodded. "Yes. Queen Elisabeth was determined to maintain their friendship. She and my grandmother remained close their entire lives; the two families were intertwined. The queen had many jewels and treasures over the years, but none she loved more than the Coronation doll made in her own likeness and dressed in the gown Lillie created. No one ever reported seeing a second doll, and the rumors dissipated."

Pearl was entranced by the story. "Is your family history the reason you were selected to sell the doll?"

"Yes. The queen's heirs decided to sell the collection and donate the proceeds to charity. They contacted me to represent them. The money was important, but they also wanted the doll to go to someone who would treasure it, as the queen had. After I met Opal, I knew she would be the perfect buyer."

Pearl and I left the antique dealer in his holding cell, all the happier for having heard his story. We were still at the police station when the banker called. He had heard from the doll man. The delivery was set for 7:30. Mr. Fuller was on his way to the meeting point—a tiny Swedish coffee bar on the edge of the Lindsborg city limits.

Exhausted after the interview with Mr. Gower, Pearl went home to rest. Nellie thanked me for the day's adventure and made me promise to call later with any news. She was off to have dinner with her husband.

The chief signed me in as a ride-along for the evening, and I climbed into his patrol car, crutches and all.

"I appreciate you joining me," he said, "particularly since Harvey called to tell me you had decided to drop the investigation."

"Harvey phoned you?"

Chief Marshall kept his eyes on the road. "Yes."

"I see," I said. My voice sounded calm to my own ears, but inside, I was seething with anger.

"He didn't mention it?"

"Not yet. We haven't talked since yesterday."

We rode the rest of the way in silence. I was so distracted with my thoughts of Harvey that I forgot to tell Chief Marshall my theory of the two cousins as dual murder suspects. The chief pulled his patrol car into the coffee bar parking lot and found a space between a gray pickup truck and a shiny new black Lexus. I figured the Lexus belonged to the banker.

The place smelled delicious: the aroma was a rich blend of coffee and chocolate, with hints of butter and cinnamon. I hoped the chief noticed the difference between the scent of these roasted beans and the burnt brew at the police station. From where we stood in the vestibule, we could see a dozen tables filled with guests, engaged in lively conversations over coffee and desserts.

I strained to see Sean Connery but couldn't locate him. In the corner of the restaurant, I caught a glimpse of the rotund Mr. Fuller, still in the pinstriped suit he had worn earlier. A woman sat across from him. She was rather tall, and she wore a wide-brimmed purple hat with feathers. My eyes nearly popped out of my head when I saw her.

Chief Marshall reacted with a gruff comment. "This could get interesting."

As customers at the table next to Mr. Fuller stood to exit the restaurant, they blocked our view, and I attempted to maneuver my crutches sideways. That purple hat woman had a way of disappearing into thin air, and I didn't want to lose sight of her. I focused on the feathers that bounced slightly above the crowd.

A waitress waved to us on her way to bus a table. "I'll be with you in a second, hon." She pocketed her tip and then cleared a cluster of coffee cups and balled napkins before she returned to seat us.

"We will join the couple at that table," Chief Marshall said, motioning toward the banker. As we approached, Mr. Fuller stood to greet us. The chief helped me into a chair, then circled the table to sit across from me. I stared at the blond woman to my left, but she hid behind her menu and avoided eye contact. There was something unsettling about her appearance. Was it her hat or her hair? I wished I had seen my ice rink attacker more clearly.

Mr. Fuller rushed to provide details. "Chief, this woman has come to retrieve Mr. Howard's doll and my appraisal. The man phoned as I arrived at the café. He apologized that he would be unable to attend our meeting, and he requested that I give the doll and the paperwork to a woman wearing a purple hat." He motioned again toward the silent woman who sat across from him. "She arrived only a few minutes ahead of you."

"And does she have a name?" The chief directed his comment toward Mr. Fuller.

"Not that she has shared with me," the banker said. "She prefers not to say."

The chief set a small spiral notepad on the table and turned to glare at the woman. "We hoped to have a conversation with the doll's owner. Can you tell us anything about him?"

She shifted toward the chief to respond and managed to tilt her head in such a way that her wide-brimmed hat cast a shadow over her face. I could not see her clearly. "The man called me for the first time this afternoon," the woman said. "The United Federation of Doll Clubs gave him my name as someone interested in expanding my collection. He had a valuable doll to sell and wanted me to have the first opportunity to purchase her."

Chief Marshall scribbled onto his pad. "You agreed to buy it sight unseen?"

"No. I agreed to pick up the doll and the appraisal."

"He trusted you with this valuable antique?"

The woman's voice dripped with outrage. "The UFDC recommended me!"

As I observed their conversation, something in her demeanor struck me as familiar.

The chief continued. "What did you agree to do with the doll?"

"The man wants a decision tonight. I have to buy the doll before midnight, or return it."

"Didn't the deadline raise a red flag for you?"

The woman lowered her eyes. "Yes. But I was intrigued to see the doll, and he promised a low price for the quick sale."

As I watched her, I suddenly realized her identity. This wasn't the purple hat woman who had plowed into me on the ice rink. It was the jealous doll collector, Mildred Wilkerson. I interrupted the chief's interview. "Millie, is that you? And why are you wearing that purple hat?"

She ducked her head again and mumbled her reply. "Yes, it's me," she admitted. "I'm sorry. The disguise was one of his requirements. I thought it was silly. The guy felt it was best that I not be recognized. He left the wig and hat with the café owner. I arrived early and put them on in the restroom before Mr. Fuller arrived."

The chief shrugged his shoulders. "Okay. I have no reason to stop the transaction. Thank you both for your time tonight. Ms. Wilkerson, you are free to go."

I stared at the chief with my mouth open. "What? You're letting her take the doll?"

"Yes, Josie. This is a private transaction between a buyer and a seller."

Spinning on my heel, I propped the crutches under my arms and stomped out the door.

A light snow fell on our drive from Lindsborg back to English Village. I texted Harvey and asked him to meet me at the police station. I needed a ride to the Philbrook Inn. He responded with a simple "OK."

The rest of the way, the chief whistled under his breath, while I fumed in silence. Two blocks from the station, he spoke.

"Josie, do you trust me?"

I was startled by the question. The chief and I were friends. We worked together regularly; he had accepted me as a team member even though my only qualifications were those of a news reporter. It wasn't until he pulled the squad car into his parking spot that I whispered an answer.

"Yes."

"Then, you should know I wouldn't jeopardize this case by allowing our suspect to escape."

I stared at him with my mouth hanging open. "What did you do?"

Chief Marshall's voice was a low grumble. "I don't owe you any explanation."

"I know."

"But, since you asked, I installed a GPS tracker on the doll case. Wherever that doll goes, we will follow. Officer Devon is in an unmarked vehicle right now, tailing Millie Wilkerson."

"Chief! That's brilliant."

He rolled his eyes. "I have your full confidence?"

"Always." I smiled back at him.

Harvey waited in his pickup truck in front of the police station, motor running; I moved from one warm vehicle to the other. As I had requested, he drove to the Philbrook Inn, where this case began less than a week earlier. So much had happened since then, yet nothing had changed in our little town. The Christmas Market was still packed with visitors; carolers sang on the plaza; the boy at the Amish basket booth snapped photos of happy customers. If anyone remembered the crowded evening when Opal fell into the well, they showed no sign of it.

We ordered dinner in the restaurant. Harvey carried the conversation while I tried to figure out what I wanted to say. My mind was a jumble. I hoped we could resolve the rift between us, and also that returning to the scene of the crime might inspire a breakthrough in the case.

Finally, I excused myself to hobble to the ladies' room, where I splashed my face with cold water. When I returned to the table, I decided it was time to clear the air. "I know you aren't happy with my decision to continue working on the investigation," I said. "But I can't believe you called Chief Marshall to tell him I had dropped the case. Is it true?"

Harvey didn't blink. "I only did what you should have done on your own," he said. "I was trying to protect you."

I felt a hot rush of color flood my face, and it was all I could do to keep my voice level. "You had no right to speak for me, Harvey. I'm an adult. I make my own decisions. And in this case, I was the only person, other than Pearl, who could identify the man who approached her at the tea. Chief Marshall needed my help."

Harvey raised his hands in surrender. "Alright, already. I apologize for stepping out of bounds."

He looked contrite, but I knew the issue still loomed between us.

"Please," he said. "Let's eat dinner. We can talk again tomorrow, when you've had more time to think about it."

Like a coward, I shrugged my shoulders and let the comment pass.

The beef stroganoff was creamy and tender in my mouth. My mind drifted, but I savored each morsel while Harvey told stories of his day. An older gentleman had stopped at the hardware store for glow-in-the-dark duct tape to put on his grandson's bike. A harried mom rushed in for superglue for her daughter's school project. And a teenager asked for information on Phillips screwdrivers.

"What did you say?" I had caught only the last of his conversation

"Which part?" Harvey gave me a lopsided grin.

"The last part. Tell me who came into the store, again."

When he repeated the story of the Phillips screwdrivers, something clicked in my brain. "That's it!"

"What?"

"The name: Phillips. That's what I've had on my mind to discuss with the chief. There are too many Phillips involved in this murder case. We have *not* just *two*, but *three* of them: Howard Phillips, the private detective; Phillip Howard, the Sean Connery look-alike; and Felipa Garcia, the detective's cousin."

Harvey nodded. "Coincidence?"

"No. This is far more than a coincidence. It's a thread that links all three of these suspects together...I just need to figure out how they are related."

Pearl called my cell phone as Harvey drove me home after dinner. "Josie, I found a letter from the screenwriter—the one who wanted more money from Opal. It was tucked into a corner pocket of her luggage."

"What does it say?" I turned my phone on speaker so Harvey could listen as Pearl read the note.

"Dear Mrs. Crawford—The pittance you agreed to pay me for my television royalties is not enough. I saw you at the antique shop. I know you can afford to pay what I deserve. If you don't, I will tell the world that Sonny cheated me out of my rightful pay. His reputation will be tarnished forever."

"That's extortion! Is there a signature?"

"Yes. The letter is signed by P. Howard."

I ignored the stony look on Harvey's face and dialed Chief Marshall to tell him about the screenwriter's letter and those of our other suspects. "Pearl believes P. Howard is the Phillip Howard who called the banker."

"That's another confirmation that they are all connected somehow, Josie. We will have it sorted out soon. All three of these *Phillips* characters should be in the station by nine tomorrow morning. Officer Devon is on his way back from Tulsa with Felipa Garcia now. Her cousin Howard Phillips is waiting in one holding cell, and Edward Gower is in the other. The elusive Mr. Phillip Howard, aka Sean Connery, will meet Millie Wilkerson before midnight, where she will either pay him or return the doll—whichever she has decided to do. We'll be there to escort him to the station on potential charges of theft, fraud, or more—"

"Shall I bring Pearl in the morning?"

"Why not? We may as well get everyone into the same room."

Harvey spoke only once on the drive to my cottage. "You won't ever let it go, will you?"

I clasped my hands tightly on my lap and remained silent. Maybe Harvey knew me better than I realized.

Chapter Twenty-Nine

Wednesday Morning

We assembled around the conference room table: Pearl Merriweather, Nellie Nester, Edward Gower, Michael Fuller, Harvey, and me. I brought pastries and coffee from the Cozy Cups Café. It was an awkward gathering. There were bursts of nervous chatter followed by uncomfortable periods of silence. I studied the faces around the table.

Pearl sat with her hands clasped on the worn metal surface of the table, her sparkling green eyes the only color on her pale face. She was dressed in all white: white wool pants, white cashmere sweater, a strand of pearls around her neck, and pearls hanging from her earlobes. She looked like a snow queen, poised and still. Edward Gower hovered to Pearl's right, dapper as always, after the chief had allowed him to retrieve his luggage from the Philbrook Inn. He wore gray pleated pants and a black turtleneck—I supposed it was casual attire, for an antiques dealer. Gower certainly didn't look like a man who had spent the night in a jail cell. He fiddled with a ballpoint pen and glanced often toward Pearl, as though to determine whether she was still there.

I balanced on the edge of my seat to Pearl's left, my wrapped ankle heavy at the end of my extended leg beneath the table. Harvey sat beside me but refused to acknowledge my presence. If Edward and Pearl were dressed like aristocrats, Harvey and I were the commoners. We might have been plucked from a ski lodge and dropped into the room, in jeans and winter sweaters.

Nellie Nester always dressed a step above the occasion. She was casual but smart, in stylish black and white checked pants, a crisply starched black shirt, and a quilted red vest. Her graying hair fell in a flawless bob, and she tucked it behind one ear as she reached for her coffee. The banker to her right was the most surprising sight. The rotund little man wore a brown tweed jacket over a soft brown turtleneck. His wide eyes peered from behind the round tortoiseshell spectacles, and he looked more like an owl than ever. I seriously hoped he didn't ask "Who?" during the meeting, which would send me into a giggling fit that I would not like to explain.

Our group sat together like strangers at a cocktail party—anxious but eager—waiting for the chief to get the action started. I wished we had music to fill the gaps in our conversation.

We waited on pins and needles to see Phillip Howard, our Sean Connery lookalike, and hear his story. I wanted details for the *Village Gazette*; Pearl planned to give the man a tongue-lashing on thievery and murder. I already knew that both of us were in for a major disappointment. Chief Marshall had phoned me the night before, to let me know the exchange between Mildred and Mr. Howard had not taken place, after all. Although Mildred showed up at the meeting point near the Eisenhower National Airport, in Wichita—with a check for $100,000 in her hand—the slippery Phillip Howard was nowhere to be seen. I'd promised the chief I would keep the news to myself. Now, I fidgeted in my seat. *What was taking him so long?*

The bald Mr. Phillips and his purple hatted cousin Felipa were set to appear soon. I had dozens of questions for the two of them, and I knew the chief did, too. The interfering detective already faced charges for the mini-bombs; his cousin would likely be arrested for assault, as a result of the attack at the ice skating rink.

Pearl's hands shook as she lifted her coffee, splashing a pool of liquid over the scarred tabletop. Edward Gower immediately mopped the spill with a napkin. It had been less than fifteen minutes, but the wait seemed interminable. Mr. Gower looked at me but spoke to the group in general.

"Before we meet Mr. Howard, I'd like to tell you more about my experience with him."

I was the only one who replied. "If you think it will be helpful, I'm happy to listen."

The British gentleman spread his hands wide and took a deep breath. "The man showed up at my antique shop the morning Opal planned to pick up her doll and the official paperwork. Mr. Howard wore a tweed jacket and spoke with a British accent that seemed genuine—at least, it fooled me, and I was born in Wales."

Pearl interrupted him. "You couldn't have known to be suspicious!"

"I should have suspected something when he asked specifically about the Carmen Sylva doll. He said he had seen it in a magazine and wanted a closer look. I explained the new owner had purchased the doll as a gift for her sister in America and planned to leave the country that evening."

Gower rubbed his eyes before he continued. We waited, spellbound.

"Mr. Howard pleaded for a peek at the treasure, and I obliged. Like a fool, I even allowed the man to photograph the doll inside her protective glass case."

"What happened next?" Nellie prompted him to continue.

"I left his side to welcome another customer while Mr. Howard browsed through the showroom. He selected an inexpensive antique doll the same size as Opal's, but of no historic value."

Harvey pulled his chair closer to the table. "I don't see your point," he said. "It seems like a logical purchase, if the man was originally interested in a doll."

Gower shook his head. "It would have been, but he seemed a bit dodgy after that."

"Dodgy?" Harvey raised an eyebrow.

"Yes. One minute, he was a posh gentleman. Everything was hunky-dory. The next, he hurried to choose an inferior doll and rushed out of the shop."

I understood Mr. Gower's concern. "He might have been late for an appointment? Or in a hurry to get away?"

"Precisely my thought, at the time."

"What changed your mind?" I stared intently at the antiques dealer, somehow dreading his reply.

"When I looked out my shop window, I saw the man I knew as Phillip Howard in the shadows of a doorway across the street. He held a newspaper to his face, but he never turned a page."

Edward Gower looked at Pearl with grief-stricken eyes. "Opal arrived shortly afterward. I had created a special red carry-on case for her trip. We packed the case, and she was off. When I looked across the street again, the man had gone. I couldn't shake the feeling that he had followed her."

Pearl placed her hand over his. "You mustn't blame yourself."

"When I wasn't able to reach Opal by phone, I decided to come to America. I closed my shop and booked a trip to Kansas. Opal had told me about the lovely Philbrook Inn where she planned to stay."

"You followed her here." Pearl looked up at him.

"Yes. To protect her—and the dolls. I was the only one who knew she had acquired two of them. *Twin dolls, for twin sisters.*"

Pearl's eyes widened at the news. "The rumors were true? There was a second doll?"

"Chief Marshall will explain more." Gower nodded to the chief, who had stepped through the doorway as he completed his story.

The chief stood near the head of the table and scanned the room with serious, dark eyes. "I'd like to start at the beginning, if I may," he said.

Everyone at the table nodded.

"We've learned that Mr. Phillip Howard was a screenwriter who knew Opal's husband, Sonny Crawford, from his time in Hollywood," the chief said. "When Mr. Howard saw Sonny's obituary in the *Los Angeles Times*, he seized the opportunity to extort money from Crawford's widow. First, he contacted Opal using his Screenwriters Guild of America name. He phoned to complain that her late husband failed to credit Mr. Howard as the screenwriter on the paperwork for a hit television series."

Pearl slapped her hand on the table. "Yes! That's what Opal told me."

The chief poured a cup of coffee from the scorched glass pot and dropped two sugar cubes into the thick black brew. "The man told a convincing story. He shared his SGA card and all the details of the show. He told Opal the production company sold the syndication rights and cut him out of half a million dollars. She believed him, and agreed to pay him a share of every royalty check she received."

I glanced at Pearl. "You and Opal disagreed on that decision."

Pearl nodded. "We did. As always, Opal won the argument. Rather than tarnish Sonny's name, she met Phillip Howard's demands."

Since I already knew Phillip Howard had escaped into the wind, I was astonished when the chief set his coffee cup on the table and said: "Ladies and gentlemen, some stories are too complex to convey in mere words. Let's see what Mr. Howard, aka *Sean Connery*, has to say for himself."

Then he opened the conference room door and motioned to the officer waiting in the hallway.

The patrolman entered the room, dragging with him a handcuffed Phillip Howard. Seeing him, I wondered why we had ever imagined him as Sean Connery. The man was scruffy, with a poorly groomed mustache and beard. His eyes were rimmed in red, and his clothes were rumpled.

Pearl stood and walked toward Mr. Howard; her eyes flashed like green daggers. She pointed a finger at his face. "How could you take advantage of my sister?"

The man glared back at her. "Her husband, Sonny, stole from me. I only wanted what I deserved."

I heard no trace of the British accent from our earlier encounter. "But Opal had agreed to your demands," I said. "Why did you attempt to steal the doll, as well?"

He scoffed at the question. "Royalties are paid over many years. It would have taken far too long to accumulate the money I wanted. Why should I wait, when I could sell the doll for immediate cash?"

Out of the corner of my eye, I saw Edward Gower rise and edge closer to the man to stare intently at his face. When he stood within a foot of the suspect, his hand shot forward. He grabbed the corner of his Sean Connery mustache and ripped it from Mr. Howard's face.

"Ow!" the screenwriter yelped in pain.

"I *knew* it was a fake," Gower said.

Chief Marshall separated the two, and Mr. Gower returned to his seat at the table. The chief glared at the screenwriter. "You also disguised yourself as the floral delivery man to gain entrance to Pearl's home. Please explain why you did that."

Mr. Howard rolled his eyes. "To steal the second doll, of course. When the newscasts only told of Opal's death without mentioning the doll I had stolen from her room at the inn, I realized no one knew a doll was missing. That meant the rumors about the two dolls were true. I guessed the second doll had to be at Pearl's home. Why steal only one, if I could have two?"

Pearl pointed her finger at him, again. "But you didn't touch my Coronation Doll. She never moved from her case on my dresser!"

The con man shook his head. "You are a gullible old fool, just like your sister. I replaced your doll with a counterfeit, made to look exactly like the original."

It was my turn to interrupt the suspect with a question. "You dressed the doll you purchased from Edward's antique store to match the Coronation Doll? That couldn't have been easy to do."

"I'm an actor," the man puffed with pride. "*A master of disguises.* It wasn't difficult to accomplish. I took the cheaper doll and a photograph of the Coronation Doll to the Doll Cradle in Kansas City. They were happy to provide a fresh wig and gown as a special gift for my precious fictitious daughter."

He turned to face the chief. "Then, I drove to Pearl's home disguised as a florist. I shoved my way in, dosed her young assistant with a sedative, and locked her in a closet." He beamed with satisfaction.

"While she was incapacitated. I moved many of the dolls from Pearl's collection into new locations—leaving the *imitation* Coronation Doll in place on the bedroom dresser," he continued.

The cagy man pointed at Pearl and laughed. "I knew *you would never suspect that I had substituted a fake doll for the real one.* Afterward, all I needed to do was convince an appraiser to provide a certificate of authenticity to verify the value of the doll. All because *you* had inconveniently stored the paperwork in your safe."

Chief Marshall frowned. "So you stored one doll in the bowling alley locker while you verified the authenticity of the other," he confirmed.

"Yes. It was the one I stole from Opal's room at the Philbrook Inn. I had to stash it somewhere while I verified the authenticity of the doll I had taken from Pearl's home. I needed proof that both dolls were genuine, and I only had the paperwork for the one—the doll Opal had kept as her own, in the red carry-on case."

The chief marched the handcuffed suspect man toward the door. "We can all agree that you were quite clever, Mr. Howard. Would you care to share the rest of your story with our guests?"

It wasn't until that moment that I knew the chief had already solved the case.

Mr. Howard turned to look directly at me, and I felt a tingle of fear ripple up the back of my neck. "You still haven't figured it out, have you?"

At the man's threatening cackle, Chief Marshall grabbed him by his elbow. Mr. Howard laughed louder. Finally, he erupted into a hearty farmer-style belly laugh. And I knew.

"It's him," I shouted. "Phillip Howard is also Howard Phillips!"

The suspect tugged at his own beard and peeled it from his face. Next, he removed a wig from his head, and the bald detective leered at me from across the table. "Well, hello, little lady. Remember me? I tried to scare you away from the investigation, but you were too stubborn to let it go."

I glared at him across the table. "You also disguised yourself as *your own cousin*, the woman in the purple hat. No wonder we never saw the three suspects in the same room."

A collective gasp filled the room.

"As you say," the suspect admitted, "I did, in fact, borrow my cousin Felipa's identity for a few cameo appearances. *However,* the Sean Connery doll collector and the Phillip Howard private investigator were *entirely* my own creations. As you now know, I am but a humble screenwriter who was cheated out of my rightful payments."

I stared at him, trying to find the words to respond to his preposterous claim.

The actor bowed from his waist. "Bravo, Ms. Posey. You win the prize."

"She does, indeed," Chief Marshall said. "We suspected you had close ties to the shady detective and his so-called cousin Felipa Garcia, but it wasn't until Josie told me about your reputation as a master of disguises that I realized you had transformed yourself into each of these characters by wearing elaborate costumes."

Howard's face turned bright red as he struggled to release the chief's grip from his elbow. "Humph. You would never have caught me if that nosy reporter hadn't asked so many questions. *She's* the one who ruined my foolproof plan."

The chief shoved the fuming murderer toward the door, where another officer waited to escort him to a cell. "You've just admitted to being a murderer and a thief, Mr. Howard. Who's the fool now?"

I was pretty sure all the drama had ended, but Chief Marshall had one more surprise up his sleeve. As soon as the suspect exited, the chief motioned for Officer Devon to wheel a rolling display table into the conference room. On top of the table, *all three* Coronation Dolls stood side by side in raised glass cases—identical, except for the evidence tags hanging from them. A rush of excitement filled the room as we admired the beautiful collection from our seats.

Doll Number One was marked as the one Millie had carried from the coffee shop to the airport.

Doll Number Two was tagged as the one belonging to Pearl—retrieved from the safe in Opal's room and carefully stored at Pearl's home until she had delivered it to the chief for inspection.

Doll Number Three was described as the one belonging to Opal, stolen in its red case from her room shortly after the commotion on the plaza and not retrieved again until after the sting at the bowling alley.

I hoped no one would remove the tags and shuffle the cases because it would be impossible to discern which was which. Sometimes, evidence lingered in a locked cabinet for months before making its way back to its rightful owners. With any luck, these dolls would be returned far more quickly.

Chief Marshall cleared his throat, and the room grew silent. "I want to thank both our doll experts, Mr. Gower and Mr. Fuller, for their assistance in identifying these dolls," he said.

"At various points in this investigation, all three of these dolls were in the possession of our murder suspect. Fortunately, our banker friend, Mr. Fuller, confirmed that Pearl's doll had been replaced with a fake one. We were able to switch the two dolls prior to his meeting with Mildred at the coffee shop. This allowed us to protect the two authentic dolls in our evidence room, leaving only the counterfeit doll to be returned to its rightful owner—the thief."

After a silent drive home, Harvey again walked me to my front door. He cleared his throat and repeated the question that had wedged itself between us. "If that man had a gun this morning, he would have shot you. Is this the end of it, Josie? Will you give up your reporting job? Stop all of these dangerous investigations?"

I lifted my chin and looked into his kind eyes. "It isn't that simple," I said.

"Why not?"

"Don't you see, Harvey?" I searched for the words to explain my decision. "Asking questions. Finding answers. They aren't just *what I do*. They are a part of *who I am*. You want me to change that."

Harvey squared his shoulders and clenched his jaw. "I can't stand by and watch you put yourself in danger anymore. That's not *who I am*."

"I respect that. Stay true to yourself, Harvey." I swallowed the lump that formed in my throat and tried to keep my voice steady. "That's also what I plan to do."

We stood on my porch a little longer, but neither of us had anything more to say. Finally, I turned on my crutches, entered the cottage, and closed the door gently behind me. What this meant for the future of our friendship was impossible to determine...at least, for now.

Chapter Thirty

Wednesday Noon

After all the commotion, Nellie called the mavens to invite them for a wrap-up lunch at my house. We were set to play mahjong, but I knew no one would focus on the game until we had put the murder case to rest.

Nellie and I were eager to report that the chief had dropped the explosives complaint against Howard Phillips and replaced it with new charges—for the bomb, the theft of two dolls, and the second-degree murder of Opal Crawford.

It didn't take long for everyone to arrive. Nellie brought sliced deli meats and buns, along with a platter of pickles, cheeses, and condiments. Kate hurried through the door with a salad and a celebratory bouquet for the table. Sharon waltzed in, carrying a cranberry-apple pie and a basketful of plates, napkins, and plasticware. "No sense making a mess!"

I peeked inside the basket to see what special napkins Sharon had tucked inside. They featured a pipe-smoking Sherlock Holmes with the phrase "I don't have a clue!" When I smiled across the basket at my friend, she winked. "I found these in the billiard room, where Colonel Mustard hid them."

In addition to the mavens, Nellie invited Pearl Merriweather, Edward Gower, Harvey, Chief Marshall, and Lorene. It seemed only fair to include them in the wrap-up party. Nellie also suggested that Michael Fuller join us, but the banker graciously declined; he had customers waiting for him in

Lindsborg.

For the second time in one day, I studied the faces around a table. This time, the table was in my own dining room, and everyone was smiling, except Harvey. The conversation was lively. Snippets of the information about the murder case spilled over each other as we all talked at once. I sat at the head of the table, and the chief was at the foot. Kate and Nellie prepared the sandwiches to order—calling out to each guest as they arrived. "Turkey and Swiss, Lorene? Coming right up!"

Accustomed to supervising a kitchen crew, Lorene smiled as she watched Kate and Nellie hustle. "Careful, ladies, I may try to recruit you to work at Cozy Cups." She sat next to her husband, tiny beside the chief's imposing bulk.

I propped my ankle on a footstool beside me and tried to stay out of the way. Nellie hurried about, placing the loaded plates on the table, until—finally—everyone was served. The chief raised his hands to get our attention, and the room fell silent. We sat, his rapt audience, while he made an emotional statement—a combination of gratitude and blessing.

"Friends, I thank you from the bottom of my heart, for your diligence in solving this case. Our police officers worked hard, but your efforts made our job easier."

He tilted his head toward me. "Josie, your insights were remarkable. I appreciate you."

A flush of heat flooded my face, and I kept my eyes focused on the chief. Looking around the table, he paused to make eye contact with every person, reciting their names as he went. "Harvey. Kate. Nellie. Sharon. Lorene. Edward. Pearl. Each of you helped crack the case, and I am grateful."

He took the hands of Lorene and Nellie and motioned for us to continue the circle. When we all held hands around the table, the chief bowed his head. "Let us take a moment of silence to remember Opal Crawford, a beautiful woman who is lost to us, but will never be forgotten."

My heart swelled with love for these friends around my table. They turned to me with eager eyes. Kate was the first to speak. "Tell us the story. Which of the suspects killed Opal, and why?"

I nodded to Chief Marshall to begin. "It turns out Phillip Howard wasn't a British doll collector; he was an American hustler. The guy was a screenwriter—which is how he met Opal's husband, Sonny. But he spent most of his career as a low-budget actor and part-time stuntman. He co-wrote scripts used in three episodes of a popular TV show, but he never made it to the big leagues."

Pearl shook her head, sadly. "After Opal's husband Sonny died, the screenwriter called my sister with false claims of misappropriated funds and unpaid royalties. He wanted money. She paid him."

Edward Gower glanced at Pearl. "Mr. Howard saw a photograph of Opal and me with the Coronation Doll taken at the charity ball in London. He became convinced she could afford to pay him more. First, he tried to extort a bigger share of the royalties, then he set his sights on taking the doll away from Opal to sell it for quick cash."

My brain reeled with the complexity of the heist. "Mr. Howard—disguised as Felipa Garcia in the purple hat—shoved Opal into the well as he attempted to snatch the quilted bag he believed held the doll. He didn't intend to murder her," I said. "Unfortunately, Opal had removed the priceless doll from the bag and replaced it with a small handgun she carried for protection. When the would-be thief grabbed the bag, the gun discharged. The bullet struck Opal in her lung."

"I suspected the purple hat woman was a man!" Sharon interrupted.

"As soon as our suspect realized he had stolen an empty bag, he broke into Opal's room to retrieve the red carry-on case he had seen Opal roll out of the antique shop in London," I continued. "He was thrilled to have successfully claimed the doll, complete with the authenticity paperwork still inside the case."

The chief nodded. "However, when there was no announcement about a missing doll, our suspect wondered why. He decided to search for more answers. The man dressed in various disguises to get closer to the murder investigation. First, he appeared as Detective Howard Phillips. He asked enough questions around the village to learn that Pearl's valuable doll was safely at her home."

I recalled how persistent the man had been in his effort to view Pearl's collection. "That convinced him there were *two* matching dolls," I explained. "He possessed one; he needed a plan to steal the other. He had already prepared a surrogate to use as a decoy for the original."

Sharon jumped ahead of me in the story. "With help from the unsuspecting proprietors of the doll shop in Kansas City!"

"Yes. He drove to the Doll Cradle in Kansas City and handed them two items: the doll he had purchased from Mr. Gower's shop and a photo of the Carmen Sylva doll. The shop obliged him with a new wig and gown for the cheaper doll. Her glass eyes were the same brilliant blue as the authentic dolls. There was only one problem: the eyes did not close."

Pearl clapped her hands. "*That's* why you asked me if my doll's eyes closed!"

"Yes," I said. "He gambled that no one would notice that detail."

Chief Marshall continued the tale. "He shoved his way into Pearl's house, locked Paige in the closet, and shuffled the dolls into different places. He placed the decoy Coronation Doll in the same spot where Pearl had displayed the real one, so she would not suspect the switch. Then he stored the original doll in a locker at the bowling alley."

Kate looked puzzled; I could see her logical mind at work. "I don't understand what that accomplished. Why leave a genuine doll in the bowling alley locker?"

The chief shrugged. "He needed to keep the dolls separated. With the fake doll at Pearl's home, he now had two matching dolls. He believed both were authentic, but he wanted an appraiser to confirm it. He needed a place to hide one while he verified the value of the other. The lockers at the bowling alley were convenient."

Nellie took over the story. "Then he contacted Michael Fuller, our trustworthy small-town banker who would handle the matter with discretion. The thief had no idea we had already alerted Mr. Fuller to a potential scam involving the dolls."

Chief Marshall spread his arms wide. "When he returned to retrieve the doll at the bowling alley, he wore his third disguise: as the bumbling private detective. We were on the lookout for the Sean Connery character. When the detective walked in, we assumed he had disrupted our sting operation. If we had realized he was the same guy earlier—preferably when he sat in our jail cell dressed as Howard Phillips—we could have saved a lot of time."

I rolled my eyes. "The names of his personas should have been a big clue. Phillip Howard, the screenwriter/actor who dressed as Sean Connery, was on our suspect list as *three people*. He was also known as Howard Phillips, the cowboy investigator, and as Felipa Garcia, the detective's female cousin in the purple hat. One man, playing three roles. And juggling three dolls."

Sharon raised her hand. "I still don't understand how Opal obtained two dolls, instead of one."

I glanced at Edward to provide the explanation. "When Opal arrived to pick up the doll she had purchased for Pearl, I gave her the red carry-on case. It held Pearl's doll in the main pouch. A twin doll, in a matching glass case, was in a second compartment of the same bag. The dolls were lightweight. Opal easily rolled the cart onto the plane and traveled to America with both dolls."

Reflecting back to the day I'd first met Opal at the Philbrook Inn, I completed the story. "When she arrived, Opal tucked Pearl's doll into a blue quilted tote bag and gave it to her during our tea. Before the two ladies went outside to see the carolers, Pearl locked her doll and its authenticity paperwork into the safe in Opal's room. Opal carried the nearly empty tote bag to the market with her."

I clasped my hands on the table in front of me to continue. "What we didn't know was that Opal had secured her own twin Coronation Doll in the carry-on case in the closet of her room at the Philbrook. She intended to surprise Pearl by showing her the matching doll later that evening. Before she could do that, she was, um, killed." My voice choked up, and I couldn't continue.

Chief Marshall finished the story. "The thief—Phillip Howard dressed as Felipa—assumed the original doll was still in the quilted bag at the Christmas Market. He knocked into Opal and snatched the bag, causing her gun to discharge. When he realized the bag was empty, he ducked into the inn, switched his disguise, and broke into Opal's room to steal the doll and its carry-on case while the crowds gathered around the wishing well outside. At the time, he had no idea there was a second doll—Pearl's—in the safe of Opal's room. Only Opal and Mr. Gower knew that two dolls existed...a fact he shared with me, on his arrival to English Village."

Edward Gower wrapped his arm around Pearl. "I arrived one day too late. When I heard about Opal's death, I knew a valuable doll was likely missing. I thought the police had their best chance of capturing Opal's killer—and reuniting the doll with her rightful owner—if no one else knew of the second doll. I explained all of these things to the chief the first time we talked. He asked me to stay out of sight, lest the culprit recognize me. We feared he would attempt to escape with one doll, making it more difficult for us to apprehend him and reunite both dolls."

Lorene rubbed her temples and stared at her husband. "You knew there were two dolls from the beginning?"

Chief Marshall nodded. "Yes. But no one was aware of the third, counterfeit doll. I was baffled when we ended up with two dolls at the station and a third at Pearl's home."

I shook my finger at the chief. "When you allowed Millie to take Pearl's doll to the con man, I was furious!"

The chief's smile was so wide it nearly split his face in two. "I told you to trust me, Josie. While Edward Gower intentionally delayed you and Pearl in his cell, Mr. Fuller clarified which dolls were real and which one was not. He carried the fake doll to his meeting with Millie Wilkerson. The valuable twin dolls were safe and sound, right here at the station."

"Chief! You could have told me!"

"I could have. But then I might have missed seeing you stomp away on your crutches, when I told Millie she was free to go."

Pearl was the first to giggle. Then, Nellie, I think. After that, the whole room erupted in laughter, even Harvey. I did the only thing I could: I joined them, laughing until my cheeks hurt. At last, Chief Marshall stood and held his hands up, waiting for the commotion to stop. Sharon hiccupped, which sent us into one last round, before the chief gained control again. He glanced at his wristwatch and tapped its face with one finger.

"Friends, I believe this case is closed. It's time for me to go back to work."

I smiled to see Edward Gower help Pearl with her coat. Harvey followed them out, headed to his hardware store for an afternoon shift. He gave me a slight nod before he left, which I took as a sign that he might consider remaining my friend—though from a safe distance—in the future.

And the rest of us? We set up the mahjong table.

We always play on Wednesdays.

Nellie's Breakfast Casserole

INGREDIENTS

- 6 eggs, beaten
- 1 C half & half cream
- 3 green onions, chopped
- 6 slices Texas toast
- 1 lb mild Italian sausage, browned and drained
- 1 C grated cheddar cheese
- 1 tsp pepper

DIRECTIONS

1. Blend eggs, milk and onions together with pepper.
2. Spray casserole dish with PAM.
3. Line dish with Texas toast.
4. Sprinkle sausage and cheese over bread.
5. Pour egg mixture over entire pan.
6. Cover and refrigerate overnight.

BAKE

1. Preheat oven to 350 degrees F.
2. Let casserole warm to room temperature, about 30 minutes, before putting in oven.
3. Bake covered for 30 minutes or until egg mixture is set.

Grandma Molly's Sugar Cookies

INGREDIENTS

- 2 ¼ C all-purpose flour
- ½ tsp baking powder
- ¼ tsp salt
- ¾ C butter, softened to room temperature
- ¾ C granulated sugar
- 1 large egg
- 2 tsp pure vanilla extract
- ½ tsp almond extract

DIRECTIONS

1. Combine flour, baking powder and salt in medium bowl.
2. In large bowl, use mixer to blend butter and sugar together on high speed until smooth and creamy (about 2 minutes).
3. Add egg, vanilla and almond extract to butter and sugar combination, mix for about 1 minute until smooth. Scrape sides and mix again.
4. Add dry ingredients from the medium bowl into the large bowl and mix on low until combined. Dough will be soft. If too sticky to roll, add 1 T of flour.
5. Divide dough into two parts. Place each portion onto lightly floured parchment paper and use a lightly floured rolling pin to roll the dough onto the paper.
6. When dough is about ¼" thick, dust the top with flour.
7. Place a sheet of parchment on top to separate the two layers of dough.

Place the second rolled-out dough on the top of the parchment paper.

8. Cover with plastic wrap and refrigerate to chill. (Leave in the refrigerator 1-2 hours, or up to 3 days.

BAKE

1. Preheat oven to 350 degrees F.
2. Line 2-3 large baking sheets with parchment paper.
3. Remove the top dough layer from the refrigerator. Cut the dough into shapes using holiday cookie cutters.
4. Reroll remaining dough and repeat cutting until all the dough is used.
5. Place cookies on the baking sheet 3" apart.
6. Bake for 11-12 minutes or until lightly browned around the edges.
7. Allow cookies to cool for 5 minutes on baking sheet. Transfer to another sheet of parchment or a wire rack to cool completely before decorating.

DECORATE

1. Smooth your favorite icing onto cookies.
2. Adorn with sprinkles or use decorator icing to add final details.
3. Arrange on a platter or baking sheet.
4. Chill in the refrigerator for 20 minutes to set icing.

Peppermint Pinwheel Dog Cookies

INGREDIENTS

- 1 overripe banana
- 2 large eggs
- 3 Tbs honey
- 3 Tbs unrefined extra virgin coconut oil, liquefied
- ½ tsp natural peppermint flavoring
- ½ tsp baking powder
- 1 ½ + ¼ cups of oat flour
- ¼ cup carob powder

DIRECTIONS

1. Mash the banana.
2. Add the eggs, coconut oil, honey, and baking powder
3. Mix until well combined.
4. Stir in 1 ½ cups of oat flour until a dough is formed
5. Divide dough into two batches.
6. Add ¼ cup carob powder to one portion and the ¼ cup oat flour and peppermint flavoring to the other portion. (Both batches should form a stiff, non-sticky dough).
7. Roll out each batch of dough to about 3/8 inch thick (roll it as rectangular as possible).
8. Stack the 2 rolled out batches on top of each other.
9. Roll up tightly, jellyroll style.
10. Wrap rolled up dough in plastic wrap and refrigerate overnight.

BAKE

1. Preheat oven to 350 degrees F.
2. Line baking sheets with parchment paper.
3. Remove plastic wrap and cut up roll into ¼" slices.
4. Place cookies on the baking sheet 1" apart.
5. Bake for 13-17 minutes (Oven times may vary)
6. Allow to cool before serving to your pups.

A Note from the Author

I am often asked what prompts my choice of subjects for the Josie Posey mystery series. Generally, I select a topic I find interesting, because I will spend many hours researching the details—whether it be ballet, timekeeping, or doll collecting. I enjoy including bits of history within each story.

Although *Dolled Up for Murder* is a work of fiction, many of the details and locations were inspired by true events. The real Elisabeth, Queen of Roumania, did share her expansive doll collection with the public to raise money for an orphanage for deaf children under the care of the Dowager Princess of Wied (Elisabeth's mother). The Queen, who wrote literature under the pen name of Carmen Sylva, was a progressive woman who devoted many hours to charities.

When Her Majesty sent word that she desired dolls to show at a Fancy Fair in Neuwied, citizens from across the land responded: dolls arrived by the vanloads. Carmen Sylva's doll collection attracted crowds wherever it appeared on display. The dolls filled four train cars when they were shipped to their destination.

The photo that inspired *Dolled Up for Murder* can be seen here: (Can you spot the doll on the top shelf of her office bookcase?)

https://www.victorianvoices.net/ARTICLES/STRAND/1898B/S1898B-Dolls.pdf

The Kansas communities mentioned in the Josie Posey mystery series are (mostly) real towns, or based on actual places. For example, Lindsborg does have a town square filled with Swedish flags and decorative "life sized" Dala horses—including the one described in this story. My hometown of Haysville features a historic park with a gazebo and a working blacksmith shop that inspired the park in the book's English Village.

The Doll Cradle exists as a wonderful resource for doll collectors in Kansas City, with the real Connie Harrell as its owner. Otherwise, the people and events in this story are (mostly) fictional, although some individual character names have been used with permission from their families. Occasionally, readers familiar with small-town events may recognize an incident that actually occurred—like the Grinch sighting at a small-town Christmas tree lighting.

I include these references to enhance the authenticity of the story and to illustrate the charm and character found within the small towns of Kansas. I hope you will enjoy them, and forgive the times when I alter the details.

Weaponry is not my specialty, so I spend a great deal of time studying poisons, head injuries, handguns, and the particulars around how they work. Although my goal is to represent law enforcement agencies and their procedures accurately, I often make exceptions to the rules in order to provide my amateur sleuth greater access to the case. Thankfully, cozy readers allow some leeway in the storytelling.

Please connect with me on social media, or sign up for my newsletter. I would love to hear from you.

Anna

Facebook:
https://www.facebook.com/cozyauthor/

Website:
https://www.anna-stjohn.com/

Acknowledgements

As always, I am grateful to the readers who have discovered *the Josie Posey Mystery Series.* Your time and feedback are generous gifts. I hope you enjoyed reading this story and solving the mystery alongside Josie and her meddling Mahjong Mavens. I would love to hear from you, so please feel free to reach out through my website or social media.

It is impossible to mention everyone who has supported this book, but I would like to try.

First, to the writing community who gave professional guidance, suggestions, editing, and encouragement: thank you. This includes my wonderful agent, Cindy Bullard, of Birch Literary Agency; the brilliant editor, Patrick Price, at Ask a Book Editor; and my talented editor, publisher, and friend, Shawn Reilly Simmons, at Level Best Books. This book would not have happened without you.

Many thanks, also, to Verena Rose, Deb Well and the rest of the Level Best Books team. And to all the LBB "Besties" and Birch Literary authors who willingly shared their time and their wisdom when asked.

I am also indebted to other authors across the country, most of whom I have met through Pitch to Published, Pitch Perfect, Sisters in Crime, or Mystery Writers of America. The list has grown too large to include without me forgetting someone's name. You know who you are, and I appreciate each of you.

My thanks, again, to my photographer friend Steve Rasmussen, for the "mysterious author" photo. To artist Lyndsey Mbwauike, for her wonderful book cover art. And to illustrator Kamilla Sims who created the map of English Village.

To the real Mahjong Mavens who inspire and support me every week, and who may see themselves in some of this story: Diane, Susan, Karen, June, Carolyn, Jane, and Cheri. Thank you for believing in me.

My gratitude also goes out to all the people who contributed to the content of this story by sharing their expertise, allowing me to use their name, or providing a recipe. To Dr. Lorene Hemphill Stone, for her insights into the world of doll collecting. To the family of Les Anderson, who approved my tribute to his memory through a female character bearing his name. To Barbara Chamberlin, for the use of her name. To Karen Townsley and Susan Neff for the recipes.

Several close friends have shared this writing journey from the beginning. I'm lucky to have them by my side for the adventure. Hugs to Sharon, Janet, Jane and Karen.

Special thanks to my sister Teresa, who always provides encouragement when I need it most. To the rest of the family: sisters Jan and Ann, aunts and cousins, nieces and nephews. Each of you has inspired me in some way. (Yes, this includes you: Martha, Winona, Jeneva, Andi, and Abby.)

I can't forget Oliver, our sweet and silly Old English Sheepdog who patrols our property to protect us from birds and squirrels, and who prompts me to head for the gym every morning and the park each afternoon.

Most of all, I want to mention those closest to my heart: Son Matthew and Tatiya, and granddaughters Madeline and Matilda. Son Zachary and Sarha, and grandchildren Zander and Magnolia. We treasure our time with you.

And, always, I am thankful to be spending my life with my husband Bruce, who helped to name this book, and who makes me believe all things are possible.

About the Author

Anna St. John writes cozy mysteries featuring a mature yet feisty former crime reporter, Josie Posey, as the amateur sleuth. Her debut novel, *Doomed by Blooms*, was released by Level Best Books in February 2023, followed by *Clocked Out* in 2024. *Dolled Up for Murder* is the third book in the Josie Posey Mystery Series. Anna is a former journalist, award-winning advertising copywriter, and ad agency owner. She is a member of Mystery Writers of America, Sisters in Crime, and the Kansas Authors Club. Anna is represented by Cindy Bullard of Birch Literary Agency.

AUTHOR WEBSITE:
www.anna-stjohn.com

SOCIAL MEDIA HANDLES:
https://www.facebook.com/cozyauthor/
https://twitter.com/AuthorStJohn

Also by Anna St. John

Doomed by Blooms, A Josie Posey Mystery

Clocked Out, A Josie Posey Mystery